DIRTY TRUST

SPECIAL WEAPONS & TACTICS 6

PEYTON BANKS

"Feelings that come back are feelings that
never went away.

UNKNOWN

"You think they will miss a Cinnabon?" Iker whispered into his comm. The aroma of the sweet-smelling cinnamon goodness floated through the air, teasing Iker's senses. His gaze landed on the Cinnabon kiosk located two hundred feet from him. His stomach chose that moment to rumble.

He cursed.

He should have eaten something today, but he hadn't had the chance.

"Seriously, you're thinking of food now?" Jordan's sharp response came though his ear.

Iker leaned against the fake stone wall and peered through his scope. He scanned the area and didn't see any motion in the food court of the mall.

"Stay focused," Mac's low growl vibrated in his ear.

Iker rolled his eyes. Marcas MacArthur was the serious sergeant, as always. Iker didn't have to look at the man to know he'd have his infamous scowl on his face.

Iker exhaled, sweeping the area with his gaze.

Shit, how was he supposed to focus with that scent distracting him?

"See anything?" Zain came to stand next to him. The mall was quiet, having been evacuated of consumers over thirty minutes ago.

A call had come through about a shooter in the local shopping mall. SWAT was dispatched to handle the situation.

"No," Iker murmured. He held his weapon steady while waiting for the shooter to make himself known. A calmness settled inside Iker. Situations such as these weren't always as easy.

He loved what he did. He thrived off the adrenaline of a good gunfight and kicking some ass.

A disgruntled man who discovered his woman was having an affair could go downhill quickly. From the reports Mac gave, the guy was hyped up on some drugs. Jeffrey Brown, a known meth head, apparently didn't appreciate his ex-girlfriend moving on.

He'd stormed the mall, took Kim Ogler and her coworker hostage, and marched them through at gunpoint.

Guns and drugs didn't go well.

Currently, the three people were housed inside a small gift shop located near the exit doors. The local boys in blue were waiting on the outside of the doors, trapping Jeff inside.

The air was tense as they waited for the right opening.

This was what Iker and his men did best. They trained hard and were one of the top SWAT teams in the state.

If you asked Iker, he'd say the entire damn country.

He and his men—team—were all about business when it came to rescuing hostages. No matter how the situation played out, no one deserved to die.

That was where they came in. Their top objective was to remove the hostages safely while disarming the target and securing him.

Iker glanced around, his gaze landing on other members of his team. They had spread out around the food court, waiting for the negotiator to talk the target down.

Myles and Ash were located behind another

faux stone wall nearest the gift shop, while Jordan and Brodie were stationed across the food court, behind a free-standing kiosk. Mac and Dec were posted in a cellphone accessory store next door to the shooter and hostages.

"He's no longer answering his cellphone," Mac reported. Their external hostage negotiator who was posted with the rest of the crew waiting outside must have updated Mac.

No communication was dangerous.

There was no telling how far Jeff had escalated. Meth in his system would make him unpredictable.

"Get the fuck out of here!" The man fitting the description of Jeffrey appeared in the doorway of the gift shop.

Iker stiffened at the sight of the man dragging a small woman in front of him. His eyes were wild, his hair was disheveled, and his clothes were unkempt. He waved the gun around while curses spewed from his lips.

Son of a bitch was using her as a shield.

Iker bit back a growl. His finger rested on the trigger, itching to shoot. Jeffrey was lower than slime.

At the moment, the woman's safety was their primary objective.

"Jeffrey, let's talk about this," Ash's level voice echoed through the air.

"There's nothing to talk about!" Jeffrey spat. He pointed his gun in Ash's direction. "I just want to leave. This is between me and Kim."

"We can't let you go," Ash responded.

"This is none of your damn business!" Jeffrey yanked Kim back to him. He kept his body lowered as if not wanting to give them a good shot.

"It became our business when you started waving a gun around in a crowded mall." Ash stood from his perch with his hands facing Jeffrey. His weapon was in the holster.

Ash had plenty of experience with negotiating. At the moment, he was attempting to gain the target's trust.

"I wasn't going to shoot anyone," Jeffrey shouted.

Kim whimpered. Her wide-eyed gaze scanned the area, taking in the weapons aimed in their direction.

"Jeff, we could have talked about this," Kim cried out. Tears streamed down her face. "We were broken up. You left me. I've moved on."

"You weren't taking my calls," he snarled. He brought the gun to the side of her head, caressing her cheek with the weapon. "I just had a lot on my mind and I needed to get some shit off my chest."

"We are here now," Ash interjected, distracting the couple. Ash was damn good at what he did. He couldn't allow them to argue and escalate the situation ever further. "Where is the other hostage?"

Iker didn't see any movement in the store behind them. There was a sinking feeling in the pit of his stomach. He felt Zain shift next to him as they held their position.

"He's tied up on the floor." Jeffrey brought his gun back up and waved it around. "Let me and Kim go. You can get him once we leave."

"No can do." Ash shook his head and took a few steps toward the gift shop.

"Stay right there!" Jeffrey cried out. He leveled his gun on Ash. "I know what you are doing. I've watched enough cop shows."

Iker held back rolling his eyes. Television shows were exaggerated reality. He couldn't believe the amount of people who thought those shows were lifelike.

"I'm not trying anything funny," Ash lied. He took another step forward. "I just want to make sure I hear you. We can speak man to man. Tell me what you want."

Jeffrey paused, his frantic gaze sweeping the area. He was too focused on the police he could see; he didn't see Dec and Mac creeping to the opening of the store front near him. Both of their guns were put away as they waited for the cue.

"I want me and Kim to walk out that door right there. No one bother us. My car is right out there. We're all going to forget about the incident."

"And no harm has come to the other hostage?" Ash questioned.

Jeffrey shook his head. "Tell everyone to stand down so we can leave."

Jeffrey made the mistake of stepping out of the store.

Ash made a slight motion with his finger.

Mac and Dec sprang into action.

They rushed from their hidden area, surprising Jeffrey.

Mac easily blocked Jeffrey's arm that swung in his direction with the weapon drawn. Dec grabbed Kim and swung her out of the way while Mac had Jeffrey on the floor in two easy take-him-down moves.

"Clear," Mac growled, kicking the gun away from them. He kept his knee in Jeffrey's back while he whipped out handcuffs.

With the target secured, the team moved in, converging on them. Iker held his gun steady as he reached the gift shop with Zain right on his six. They swept into the small store. His feet carried him over behind the register.

He exhaled, finding Kim's coworker lying on the floor, hog-tied with a bandana muffling his mouth.

"Cleared," Iker called out over his shoulder.

"Thank goodness," Zain muttered. He sheathed his weapon and bent down to untie the guy.

Zain must have been thinking the same as Iker. Not seeing or hearing from a hostage wasn't good. They'd had plenty of situations where the outcome had been fatal.

They exited the mall with Jeffrey in handcuffs. Declan escorted Kim to the waiting ambulance while her coworker insisted he was fine.

Today was a day to celebrate.

⚬⚬

"GOOD JOB, MEN," Captain Spook's voice belted out. He came to stand at the edge of the lockers.

Iker pulled a clean CPD t-shirt over his head.

"Thank you, sir," Iker said.

"That was fine police work, and no one was

injured. The mayor is extremely pleased with the way you handled that situation. It was on the local news." Spook folded his arms in front of him.

"It was easy. We didn't really do anything," Myles commented. "Mac, Dec, and Ash did most of the work."

"We work as a team," Mac commented. "You had our backs just in case shit didn't go the way we had planned."

Mac slammed the door to his locker and hefted his duffle bag onto his shoulder.

Iker grinned. Mac never wanted to take credit for anything. That was why he was such a good leader for their group. He always stressed everything that they did, it was as a team. No matter what.

Police work or getting in trouble after hours.

They always did it together.

Iker loved his brothers and sister of SWAT as if they were blood-related. There wasn't anything he wouldn't do for them. He'd been on SWAT for years now and spent more time with them than his own family. Jordan was the most recent recruit, and they had all taken her under their wing. She was like the little sister neither of them had. He loved pulling her chain, and Jordan may be smaller than them all, but she scrapped harder than any of them.

"Either way, good job. I appreciate that none of you shot anyone." Spook gave a dry chuckle.

Iker inclined his head. The fucker Jeffrey had it coming. If there was one thing Iker couldn't stand it was men taking advantage of women. Hell, if Jeffrey was the one who'd broken it off with the woman, then why—

Iker paused.

The situation at the mall was getting a little close to home.

The only difference was that Iker wasn't crazy enough to run into her job with guns blazing, demanding she speak with him.

Blowing out a deep breath, he turned back to the conversation at hand. Right now was not the time to think of her.

"See you tomorrow, sir," Ash said.

Iker blinked and found the captain headed toward the door. Once he disappeared through it, the locker room was buzzing with different conversations.

"You good?" Zain walked over and leaned against the wall.

"Yeah, why?" Iker asked. He pulled his boots out and dropped them on the floor. He stepped into them and turned, lifting his foot to rest it on the bench behind him so he could tie them.

"You look a little off right now." Zain never missed anything.

"Just a headache," he lied. He wasn't in the mood for the fifty questions from his friend. Zain knew him better than anyone else on the squad.

"You sure?" Zain raised an eyebrow at him. "Let's go out for a drink. I'm sure that will help."

"Not tonight. I'm heading home. Nothing a little Tylenol, dinner, and sleep won't cure." He dropped his foot back to the floor and grabbed his bag from the bottom of his locker. Sliding the strap on his shoulder, he shut the door and offered a grin to his friend. "Tonight will be one night I am sad to say will be spent alone."

"Wait, did I just hear what I think I heard?" Declan chuckled.

"Iker does not want to go out for drinks?" Myles scoffed.

"What?" Iker looked around at everyone. "I don't go out every night."

"Sure you don't," Ash snickered.

"Leave him alone," Mac said. He moved toward the door. "He's probably only on his first penicillin shot."

The room exploded with laughter.

Everybody wants to be a comedian.

"Fuck all y'all." Iker shook his head. He couldn't help the grin that spread on his face. "I'm clean, just so you know. Not that it is any of your businesses. I'm going home." He stepped around Zain who was leaning back against the lockers with tears streaming down his face.

"Ah, shit. That was a good one." Ash cackled.

Iker flipped them all off and headed out of the locker room. He walked down the hallway that led to the back exit of the precinct.

"Where you off to?" Jordan's voice appeared behind him.

Iker looked over his shoulder to see her coming out of the women's locker room.

"Home," he replied.

She fell in step with him, eyeing him.

He glanced down at her. "What?"

"No hot dates? Or going out to those sleazy bars you like to frequent?" Jordan chortled.

"Nope. Not tonight."

Did everyone assume he went out drinking and partying every night?

He pushed open the door to the parking lot and held it for Jordan.

He followed behind her, shutting the door once he was out.

"Well, I'll see you tomorrow. Goodnight." Jordan waved to him and headed off toward her car.

"Yup." He gave her a salute and strode toward his truck. He paused by his door to make sure she got in her vehicle safely. It was dark, and one could never be too careful.

Even in the parking lot of a police department.

Jordan blew her horn and drove out of her spot.

Iker hopped into his oversized pickup truck and hit the 'start' button. He was bone-tired and just wanted to sleep.

Pulling out of his spot, he guided his car onto the road and headed home. The radio was on an 80's rock channel. His fingers tapped on the steering wheel, but he couldn't get into the song.

You broke up with me.

The hostage's words echoed through his head.

His chest grew heavy.

A beautiful brown-skinned vision came to mind.

"Get out of my head," he muttered. As much as he tried to push the memories of her away, he couldn't.

Jessica Horton.

A sophisticated, curvy woman, with a body of a goddess, and eyes of an angel who owned his heart.

But two years ago, he'd walked away from her. She was too good for the likes of him, and he didn't want to bring her down to his level.

She was meant to do great things in life.

He would have been a burden to her. A man on a cop's salary who was never home, always getting called out at all times of day or night, was no way for her to live.

She needed someone who would be there for her, afford the lifestyle she deserved.

Lately, he found himself becoming obsessed with her. Everything had been reminding him of her.

Turning the music up, he was going to drown her out.

"Another one bites the dust," he sang along with the tune flowing through the speakers.

Twenty minutes later, he turned onto his driveway. Killing the engine, he exited the vehicle and went inside his home.

"Shit." Blowing out a deep breath, he dropped his bag on the stairs that led to the second floor. He went into the kitchen to find something to eat. His gaze landed on the counter.

Memories came to mind of Jess sitting there with him between her legs.

"I missed you," she whispered. Her legs crept up his sides, locking him in.

He tilted her chin up and dropped a short kiss on her lips. Her big brown eyes softened as she reached up and entwined her hands at the base of his neck.

"Not as much as I missed you," he murmured.

He had been gone close to twenty-four hours. She had a spare key to the house and had let herself in. When he'd come home, he had found her asleep on his couch waiting for him.

He cupped her cheek, staring down at her. He had memorized every freckle and every mole on her body. The love he had for this woman took his breath away.

Iker blinked, the memory disappearing.

Maybe he should move. It had been two years since they had separated, and still he could see her in his home.

What the hell was he to do?

2

"Move it over another inch," Jessica instructed. She bit her lip watching the art intern adjust the sculpture. It was a magnificent piece of art, and she had a gut feeling it was going to sell.

"How's that?" Chris stepped back and waited for her reply.

"Perfect." She grinned, her gaze scanning the room. The exhibit was set up for public viewing and would be going on sale this weekend. "Now that owl will need to be brought in. Can you handle that?"

"Yes, ma'am. I know where it should go." He gave her a salute. He reached for the cart and pushed it in front of him as he left.

Jessica spun and strolled around the room. Her

heels clicked on the marble floor. Pride filled her as she took in each piece of work.

Jessica Horton had an eye for beauty.

The artist, Zakir Cross, was a local talent whom Jessica had found by accident. The second she had seen his art, she'd known she had to help him get his work in a gallery.

Lucky enough, she was the sales manager and artist liaison for one of the most popular galleries in the city.

Zakir was a genius.

She hadn't seen raw talent like this in years. From his paintings to his sculptures, he knew how to draw an emotional response out of whoever laid their eyes on his art.

Jessica's life work was bringing beauty to the forefront. She'd been an art major in college and double majored in finance.

When she'd approached her boss about Zakir, he'd trusted her, allowing her to book Zakir.

Because he was a local starving artist, the gallery didn't take such a big cut from the proceeds that would be earned during the sale.

"My dear Jessica." Saffiro Ablo, the owner of The Ablo Gallery, strolled into the exhibition room.

"Mr. Ablo." Jessica turned around and watched her employer make his way to her.

His gaze scanned the room. He paused midway and slowly spun around. "You certainly have an eye. This work is stunning."

Saffiro Ablo was an Italian art dealer who'd started his gallery when he'd moved to the United States. He was an older man who took great care of himself. His dark hair was just starting to gray at the edge near his ears. He wore a tailored suit with perfect measurements.

"Isn't it?" She folded her hands together. Pride filled her that her shows were able to deliver on a promise. It made her feel good to be able to spotlight unknown artists. After this weekend's sale, Zakir would be making a name for himself.

"You have never let me down," he admitted. He stalked over to a large painting hanging on the wall. It was that of an elder black man sitting on a bench in a park.

Jessica had gazed at the item for a while. The man stared straight ahead, and it would appear as if he was truly looking her in the eye. The stories she knew were housed in those eyes, captivated her.

If he were a real person, she was sure he would share some interesting tales.

"This has to be one of my favorites." She moved over to stand beside Mr. Ablo. The attention to detail on the painting was breathtaking.

"I can see why," Mr. Ablo murmured. "Mr. Cross is a lucky man that you came across his work. He stands to make a great deal of money this weekend."

"That he does. The guest list is full of your most loyal clients. I'm sure they will be very generous with their purse strings."

When The Ablo Gallery held sales, people came from near and far. They were known to have exquisite works from established artist along with up-and-coming. The last sale they hosted, the artist sold out of all of his pieces.

"I take it everything is set for this weekend?" Mr. Ablo questioned.

They strolled over to another painting hanging on the wall.

"Of course." Jessica nodded.

Jessica took pride in her job. She was one lucky girl to get the position of the sales manager of such an accomplished gallery. Working for Mr. Ablo had given her all the experience she could ever wish for. He was an amazing man who cared for those he employed.

She'd traveled the world for him. She had just recently returned from Italy and already had an artist from Venice booked for their next showing. She was a world-renowned artist, and Jessica had negotiated to get the exhibit to be shown at their gallery.

Jessica would never have thought that a girl from the inner city of Cleveland, Ohio, would grow up to hold such an esteemed position.

She got to combine the two things she was passionate about, art and traveling, and it was her job.

She was living the life.

"A little birdie told me you have some wonderful things lined up for us." Mr. Ablo faced her.

"That I do. I was going to sit down with you next week to go over some of my ideas and things I have lined up."

"I'm sure you already have the meeting set up." He laughed, apparently sensing her excitement.

"You know me well. Tuesday morning."

"Very well. I will be flying out to go to Romania on Wednesday, so I'm sure whatever you have planned will be fine."

"Thank you, sir." Jessica beamed.

His cell phone rang. He reached inside his suit jacket and pulled it out.

"Make sure there is plenty of champagne at the event. We have much to celebrate." He began walking away. "I have to take this. We'll chat later."

Jessica grinned and slowly followed him out. She had a crazy amount of work to accomplish before the event. She was sure Chris would be fine setting up the rest of the pieces. She'd come back later and review the displays.

She entered her office, hearing her phone chirp. Walking over to her desk, she picked up her cell and saw there was a message from her best friend, Darby, asking if they could go grab lunch. Instead of responding, Jessica called her.

"This can't be good if you're calling me." Darby sighed.

"I would love to go, but I have plans with Bradley," she admitted. Sitting in her chair, she kicked her heels off.

"Oh, goodness. Bradley, how could I forget about your boring boyfriend?" She snickered.

Jessica rolled her eyes. She had met Darby when she had moved to Columbia right after college. They had lived in the same apartment building and became friends. They were as close as sisters and had been inseparable since the first time they'd hung out together.

"Be nice," Jessica murmured.

"I just don't get it. Bradley is as interesting as standing in front of a freshly painted wall and watching it dry."

"He's not that bad." Jessica laughed.

"He is. You two are as opposite as can be. There is nothing in common between you," Darby scoffed.

"There are a lot of relationships between people who are opposites, and they work just fine," Jessica argued. She had met Bradley Berry one day while going for coffee at a café located near her job. She'd seen him there a few times, and finally he'd approached her. He was a banker at the bank on the corner. He appeared to be sweet, and Jessica exchanged numbers with him.

"How long have you been dating him?"

"Two months," Jessica replied proudly.

"And you haven't even fucked him yet!" Darby hooted. Her laughter filled Jessica's ear.

"Hey. Sex isn't everything."

Darby grew silent. "Hello, my name is Darby Clarke. Is Jessica Horton there? The sex fiend?"

"Wait a minute. Why do I have to be a sex fiend?" Jessica fell into a fit of laughter with her friend.

"You do know what is in that nightstand of yours, right?" Darby snorted.

Jessica rolled her eyes. Of course, her bestie would bring up her drawer of toys. Hell, Darby had just as much as she did. They usually went into the toy store together for moral support.

"What's in my nightstand is none of your business," Jessica replied haughtily.

"That I would agree, but I will say this." Darby paused, unable to stop giggling.

"What is it?"

"Do you need batteries? I'm sure you do. With no sex with Mr. Banker, I'm sure you are wearing out Mr. Bob." Darby fell into another fit of laughter.

"You are such a bitch," Jessica muttered. She settled back, unable to keep the grin off her lips. "And just so you know, I buy batteries in bulk."

Darby's laughter grew louder.

Her friend was right. Bradley was the complete opposite of her, but that was okay.

Bradley was what she would deem safe and routine.

He was a nice guy who was a true gentleman.

Something completely different for her.

Her eyes fluttered shut as the image of a tall,

muscular, cocky cop with forest-green eyes came to mind.

Iker Baldwin.

He had been the love of her life. Crazy, unpredictable, and sex games that kept her completely satisfied.

He was her everything. She had imagined a future with him, but he'd ripped that dream from her.

He'd broken her heart.

She blinked back the tears that threatened to come. It had been two years now, and she was trying to move on with her life.

She'd dated after Iker left her. Not a lot. Even had sex a couple of times. It had been okay.

Nothing to write home about.

Each time, there was something missing.

But then she'd met Bradley.

"Well, Bradley had called me earlier and said he had somewhere special he wanted to take me," she announced.

"Okay, Mr. Banker. Well, you better call me and spill all the details."

"That I will," Jessica promised. "He's not that bad."

"I'm sure he's not. If he makes you happy, then I'll give him a chance."

"Thanks, bestie." Jessica sighed.

"You know I love you. Now have fun with your beau, and I'll call you later."

Jessica disconnected the call and exhaled. She caught sight of the time on her phone and jumped up.

Brad—Bradley—would be on time. He didn't like the shortened version of his name. He was a very punctual man. She slid her shoes back on and snagged her purse from her drawer. She quickly freshened up her lipstick, then threw everything back in her purse. Remembering the weather report this morning, she grabbed her dress coat and pulled it on.

She made her way through the building and stopped by the front desk.

"Hey, Nat. I'm going out for lunch." Jessica hoisted her purse strap up higher on her shoulder.

"That handsome man of yours is right over there." Natalie jerked her head in his direction.

Jessica found Bradley standing in front of a sculpture.

Jessica tossed her a wink and headed over toward Bradley. As she grew closer, she tiptoed over to him.

"That particular piece of art will be available for sale. I could cut you a deal. I know the sales manager," Jessica teased, coming to stand beside him.

Bradley was of average height. Dark-skinned with short, cropped hair. His suits were always impeccable. He had a nice smile with bright-white teeth which was one of the first things she'd noticed about him when they'd met.

"I'm sure you do, but this is still a little too rich for me." He smiled. He took her hand and drew her closer. He placed a soft kiss on her wrist, entwining their fingers together. "Are you ready to go?"

"I am." She smiled.

"Come. Let me feed you." He guided her toward the entrance. Being the gentleman he was, he opened the door for her.

They stepped out onto the sidewalk and set off down the street. He opted for the outside nearest the curb. She held back a smile. He was one of the sweetest men she had ever met.

"So, what do you have in mind?" She was a little shocked that they were on foot, but then there were a few restaurants within walking distance. She had tried them all. She considered herself to be a foodie and loved trying out different restaurants.

"Well, I'm not sure if you realize it, but today is our two-month anniversary," Bradley announced.

"It is?" She gasped, shocked. Today was actually the two-month mark? She hadn't really paid attention to the day they had started dating. She had guesstimated when she was on the phone with Darby.

Welp, she certainly sucked at being a girlfriend.

How could she not know what today was?

"I know. You probably think I'm corny—"

"No, I don't. It's cute, and now I feel bad that I didn't realize it," she rushed out. She entwined her arm with his, patting his hand. "I swear I'm not a good girlfriend."

"You are perfect, Jessica."

His brown eyes met hers, and she could see he was entirely sincere. It didn't make her feel better at all.

"And to celebrate our two-month anniversary, I figured we'd go have lunch at the café where we met."

They strolled down the street. The air was slightly chilled, but they didn't have far to go. Jessica's gaze landed on a black sports car parked near the curb.

She was sure, but if she didn't know any better,

there was someone in there watching them. She couldn't see inside the vehicle due to the dark tint on the windows.

It wouldn't be...*him?*

No, there's no way he'd be following her. He had broken up with her. Why would he be in a new car, parked near her job?

Shaking her head, she tried to tune back in to what Brad—Bradley was saying.

She thought back to Darby's words.

Maybe she would have to initiate things with her shy boyfriend. He'd only ever attempted second base.

Never further than that.

Jessica was curious how things would be between them. Would the sex be satisfying? Would Bradley shock her and take her on a wild ride? Or would it be as dull and boring as he was?

There was only one way to find out.

She'd invite him back to her place this weekend after the exhibition and she wasn't going to take no for an answer.

Was sex the most important thing in a relationship? No, but it would be nice if it was at least enjoyable.

"Here we are," Bradley announced. His face lit

up as he reached for the door. There was no doubt that he had thought this was a great idea. There was no way she would burst his bubble.

Hell, he was trying and had remembered the day they had started dating. That earned him bonus points.

Jessica forced a smile and went inside.

3

He fisted the steering wheel and had to release it for fear of tearing it off. Iker sat in his newly purchased sport car. He had wanted to take it out for a joyride and somehow found himself in downtown Columbia.

On the same street where Jess worked.

He hadn't realized it until he had pulled over and parked.

There weren't any spots near her art gallery. He had been staring at the building trying to get the nerve to go in and see her.

His heart had all but leaped into his throat at the sight of her exiting the building through the glass doors.

She was just as beautiful as the last time he had

seen her. His gaze had been locked on her the entire time.

She had glanced in his direction. Thanks to the dark tint on the windows, she wouldn't have seen him.

Iker eyed the man she was with.

The boyfriend.

The moment he had heard that she was dating someone, he had done a background check.

Two years ago, Iker had walked away from her, leaving his heart in her possession. The look on her face that day had brought him to his knees, but he had done it to protect her. She would never understand what he went through on a daily basis.

The heat was too hot on him and his fellow SWAT teammates.

Watching Mac go through his turmoil when Sarena was kidnapped made how dangerous his job was a reality.

Mac and his other brothers were better men than he.

Any threat to Jess would end with body bags and his badge being stripped from him.

Instead of taking the risk, he'd decided to walk away to ensure she would never have a target on her back.

Iker blew out a deep breath.

The man she was dating, Bradley Berry, was as clean as one could be. He was a banker and specialized in investments. He was an upstanding citizen of Columbia. Paid his taxes and had used the same dry-cleaning service for the last five years.

Iker could set his watch by Bradley. He was a man of routine.

Since backing away from Jess, Iker had kept tabs on her. She'd dated after him. He had expected it. Hell, he would have thought she'd be married by now.

He hadn't been a saint after her.

Iker had tried to drown her out.

Dull the pain of having his chest ripped open and his heart torn out.

There had been women. Never any committed relationships, only faceless women to scratch an itch.

He continued to watch them make their way to the café on the corner. Once they disappeared inside, his body relaxed.

Leaning back, he closed his eyes.

He shouldn't be here.

He needed to let her go.

The shrill ringing of his cellphone broke the silence.

He picked it up and saw 'Lil Bro' displayed onto screen.

"Yo," he answered. He ran a hand over his face, grimacing. His beard was unruly, and it was time for him to visit his barber and allow him to shape it up.

"What's up, big bro?" Dylan's voice greeted him.

"Nothing much. What's up with you?" he asked.

Iker was extremely close with his brother. Dylan was younger by two years. They were always glued at the hip as his mother would say.

Iker's childhood had been amazing with a great set of parents. His father, Hank Baldwin, a foreman for a construction company, had been very involved in his boys' lives. He had taught them everything they needed to know. Each of the Baldwin boys grew up with a hammer in their hands.

Hank had instilled hard work, love for family and the Carolina Panthers into his boys. Iker had countless memories of watching football with his father and brother growing up.

Damn, he missed his old man.

Hank had died five years ago from pancreatic cancer.

It seemed like yesterday they had got the diagnosis. At the time, Hank was still working and denied feeling sick. He'd boasted he was too strong for pancreatic cancer to take him out.

But Hank had been wrong.

The cancer was aggressive, and Hank was dead six weeks later.

With his death, there was a hole left in all of their hearts. Tess, their mother, was a strong woman, but the death of her husband was a hard blow even for her.

It about killed Iker to watch his mother grieve for their father, but she was resilient. She was able to pull herself together and carry on.

Hank wouldn't have wanted her to mope around for years.

Get your ass in gear, woman.

Those were his father's infamous words when joking around with their mother.

"I was wondering if you had any plans this week?" Dylan asked, breaking through Iker's thoughts.

"What's going on?"

"It's the porch on the back of the house. I promised Mom I would reinforce it and clean it up this weekend. It would go quicker if I had an extra set of hands." Dylan had followed in their father's footsteps and gone into construction. He currently worked as a foreman for a local company.

"I can come through. Just let me know when." Iker would make time. If his mother needed something done, then he'd damn well make sure he was there to help.

"Thanks, bro. With the two of us, it shouldn't take long. How about Saturday morning?"

"That would be fine." He was off this weekend, and it would be perfect. Mentally, he went ahead and cleared the day so he could just stay at his mother's to ensure she didn't need anything else.

"See you then." They disconnected the call. Iker returned his phone back into the cup holder where it had been resting. His gaze landed on the café.

He should leave.

He had no business being there.

But Iker was never one to do things he was supposed to. Grabbing his keys and phone, he exited the vehicle. He jogged across the street and headed toward the café.

Iker entered the establishment and casually walked up to the counter. He stood behind a gentlemen to wait his turn. He studied the menu and decided to just get a large coffee.

He'd picked up overtime and had worked the

graveyard shift last night. He was dead tired. Throwing himself into work helped him sleep. It was either that or go out binge-drinking.

But even drinking couldn't keep dreams of a beautiful curvy art enthusiast away. Alcohol dulled his senses and encouraged behaviors he'd cringe at when he was sober. He would have stumbled home this morning after waking up in some strange woman's bed.

"Hi, can I help you?" the barista asked.

The man before him had moved down to the pickup counter. Iker stepped forward and ordered a large black coffee.

He'd never picked up coffee from this place. Normally he would grab a cup of the tar that was at the precinct before going home.

Today, he had bolted home, needing to get away. The plan had been to hop in his new ride and test its speed, but somehow, he'd found himself here.

After paying, he walked over to where the other customer had been standing. He casually leaned against the counter and allowed his gaze wander around the cozy café.

"Here you go, sir."

Iker turned and found the woman standing

behind the counter holding a large paper traveler filled with a delicious-smelling brew.

"Thanks." He tossed her a wink and took it from her. He stole a quick sip and bit back a groan. This was definitely not the thick darkened water the precinct served them. He spun back around, his gaze landing on Jess and her asshat of a boyfriend.

He should go, but for some strange reason, his feet were already carrying him over to her. Iker had never been one to shy away from confrontations and would not likely start today.

He had to speak with her.

Even if she yelled and screamed at him, he would take it.

He arrived at their table.

"Hello, Jess," he murmured.

Her head jerked up from the menu she was studying. Her big brown eyes widened, her mouth parting open.

"Iker," she breathed. She blinked rapidly and cleared her throat. "What are you doing here?"

"I was in the neighborhood and decided to stop here for coffee." He shrugged nonchalantly.

Jess was staring at him suspiciously. He had forgotten how she could always see past his bullshit.

"Jessica, darling. Who is your friend?" the

banker asked. He nudged her with his elbow. He pasted a fake smile on as he eyed Iker.

"Oh, um. Bradley, this is Iker." She waved to them. "Iker, Bradley."

Bradley stood from his seat, adjusting his jacket. He quickly sized Iker up. Iker already knew they were complete opposites. Hell, he and Jess were as different as night and day. She was sophisticated, always wearing dresses, skirts, and heels, and always looked as if she'd just stepped off the cover of a fancy magazine. Iker, on the other hand, tall, muscular, with a shit ton of tattoos, loved his jeans and t-shirts.

"Nice to meet you," Iker said, holding out his hand.

Bradley took it in a soft shake, barely gripping Iker's hand.

Iker held back a growl, his dislike for Bradley growing even more. A soft handshake equaled weak and no backbone in his book.

Iker was always taught a man should show his strength when shaking hands with another man.

"Likewise. Wow, what a strong grip." Bradley's eyes widened. He stepped back and glanced over at Jess.

Iker focused on her and found he could barely look away from her. She was curvier than he remembered. He had spent many hours worshipping her body. He remembered everything about her. She was no shy woman when it came to the bedroom.

Hard and rough to soft and loving.

Jess never bit her tongue, demanding what and how she wanted it. They were always evenly matched when it came to lovemaking.

Looking back at Bradley, there was no way in hell he could handle a woman like Jess. A woman like her would eat the poor man alive.

She deserved so much better.

"It's been a while, Jess," Iker murmured.

"It has." Her eyes narrowed on him, while her lips pursed together in a firm line.

She was pissed, which she had every right to be. This was the first time he'd actually spoken with her since ending their relationship.

"So how do you two know each other?" Bradly asked. He slid his hands in his pants pockets while flicking his gaze in between the two of them.

Iker took notice that neither of them offered him a seat at their table. That was fine by him. There was no way he could stay any longer. If he did, he couldn't promise he wouldn't toss the banker through the nearest window.

"Iker is an old friend of mine," Jess lied smoothly.

Iker bit back a grin.

Ouch.

He'd been put on the 'old friend' shelf.

Apparently, Jess didn't want to share their real history with her little boyfriend.

"Yes, we go way back." Iker nodded, playing along with her game. He decided to take the game a little further. He loved when she was pissed off. His cock jerked to attention. Jess with her claws out was always a turn-on. After they argued, their make-up sex would be earth-shattering. He had to admit he definitely missed those days. "We should catch up sometime."

"Jessica has a big show this weekend at The Ablo Gallery. She's been the talk of the town with her latest discovery. My girl has one hell of an eye for art."

"I know how special Jess is. I'm not surprised the world is just now finding out how great she is." Iker and the asshat could agree on that. Jess was an amazing woman, and he was always in awe of her.

"Are you free on Friday? The debut of the exhibit is Friday night. You should come." Bradley moved over to stand beside Jess. He rested a hand on her shoulder, smiling at her.

Iker's gaze locked on that hand on her. The urge to rip it off grew inside him.

He blinked.

He'd given up that right.

"It's by invite only, Bradley." She faced Bradley with a false smile on her lips. "Plus, I'm sure Iker has other things to do with his Friday nights," Jessica said.

Iker didn't miss the sarcasm that laced her last few words.

"Actually, I don't have anything planned." Iker grinned, loving the expression on her face. If looks could kill, he would be pushing up daisies.

"Come on, Jessica. I'm sure you can add his name on. It would be nice for you to have friends to support you this weekend."

"Fine. Iker, if you want to come, I can add your name to the guest list. Should I put you down with a plus-one?" Her perfectly sculpted eyebrow rose.

"Nah, I'll come alone." He took a sip of his coffee, attempting to appear innocent.

"Great. We'll see you on Friday," she replied coolly.

Bradley took his seat next to her again, a wide grin on his face.

"That you will." Iker nodded to Bradley. "Nice to meet you."

Iker spun around on his heel and strode out of the café. He didn't know what had made him go over toward her.

Once outside, he inhaled sharply, taking in the fresh air.

He was like an addict needing another hit.

It had been two years, and even though he'd kept his distance from her, he was eventually going to need to cut her out of his life completely.

4

The computer screen stared back at her. Jessica didn't see any of it. Her gaze was unfocused, and she had lost track of how long she had sat there at her desk.

Her hand shook as she reached for the mouse. She clicked out of the program she was working in.

Settling back in her chair, she closed her eyes and exhaled. Pain filled her chest when she tried to drag air back into her lungs.

Why?

Why had he showed up?

After all of these years, seeing Iker had caused so many emotions to swirl around inside her.

First was shock.

It had been a while since he had walked out of her life. She had to give it to him. Time had been kind to him. He appeared a little more filled out. Muscular. The beard gave him a more rugged appearance, and his hair was still as wild as before. Those green eyes of his had bored into her. She'd always felt that Iker could see her soul.

Then there was anger.

How dare he show up as if nothing had gone down between them. Jess had never wanted to do bodily harm to anyone before in her life, but she'd ached to smash her fist into his face. That cocky grin of his was painful to see.

She rested her elbows on her desk and held her head in an attempt to push the image of him from her mind.

His smile would have disappeared had she attacked him.

Iker had taught her how to defend herself, how to carry and shoot a gun. He'd always been obsessed with making sure she could take care of herself.

Today, she wanted to use everything he'd taught her against him.

Once the anger dispersed, numbness infused her body. Seeing him again had taken her back to the dark place she had gone to when he'd left.

She immediately went on autopilot. After he'd left, she'd barely tasted the lunch Bradley had ordered her.

Jess had returned to the gallery. She had put on the mask she had perfected wearing so that no one would detect something was wrong with her. She had become a master of disguising her feelings, built walls to keep everyone away from her.

Even her own parents and brother didn't know the toll their breakup had taken on her. She kept up the front that their separation was a mutual decision and that she was okay.

But it had all been a lie.

The only person who knew the complete truth was Darby.

It had been her best friend who'd helped pick up the pieces of a broken Jessica Horton.

There was no telling where Jessica would be had it not been for Darby.

Lifting her head, Jessica blinked back the tears that teetered on her eyelids. She couldn't stay here. The room seemed as if it were drawing closer to her. The walls were shrinking inward.

Pushing up from her chair, she grabbed her coat and threw it on. She reached for her purse, flipped off the lights in her office, and exited the room, closing the door behind her.

Her heels clicked on the marble floors as she headed toward the back. She took her cell phone out of her purse and sent Natalie a quick message that she was leaving early for the day.

Jessica couldn't face anyone at the moment.

She couldn't.

Arriving at the back door where the employees parked, Jess slipped outside. She hurried over to her car and got in. She hit the button, turning the engine on, and pulled out of her parking spot.

Her hands trembled as she guided the car out onto the street.

There was no way in hell she could go home.

Darby.

Her friend should be home by now. Whenever Jessica had this stifling grief or a sense that she was about to lose her shit, Darby would know what to do.

It always helped to have a best friend who was a counselor.

Jessica pressed her foot down on the pedal, the engine roaring to life. She just prayed she made it before she exploded.

Angrily, she wiped the wetness away.

Gripping the steering wheel with both hands, she bit back a sob.

How dare he stroll up to her and strike up a conversation as if he hadn't taken her heart and stomped it in the ground.

She didn't know what had gone wrong in their relationship. They had been extremely close; he had been her everything.

Jess had struggled with the reality that it wasn't her. She had at first blamed herself. Maybe she hadn't been the best girlfriend. Was she not attentive enough for him? Did she not satisfy him? Was it her weight? Looks?

"Stop!" she cried out. She tightened her hands on the wheel. Tremors snuck through her. She coasted the car to a stop for a red light. "There is nothing wrong with me."

She closed her eyes and repeated the mantra.

It was something Darby had wanted her to say to herself.

The muscles in her body had grown tense until they hurt. She blew out a deep breath through pursed lips then inhaled through her nose.

She opened her eyes and stared at the stop light until it changed to green. Pressing her foot down on the pedal, she sped off.

Her vision blurred again. She blinked, this time allowing the trails of tears to fall. The car ride passed by in a blur. She pulled into Darby's driveway, thankful to see her friend's car parked there.

Killing the engine, Jess sat in silence.

We should catch up sometime.

Iker's words echoed in her head. What would they need to discuss? How his leaving wrecked her? Or did he think they would have a simple conversation as friends do when they haven't seen each other in a while?

"Fuck." She slammed her hand on the steering wheel. She snatched her purse from the seat beside her and exited the car.

She blinked, uncaring the tears were streaming down her face. She took the two stairs and stopped in front of the Darby's door. She rang the doorbell and waited.

Her shoulders slumped, her head falling forward. She drew in a shaky breath while waiting for her bestie to open the door.

"Hold a sec!" Darby called out from somewhere in the house.

Jess bit her lip, holding back the sob that threaten to spill out. The warm wetness on her face continued. Her shoulders shook.

Jess reached up and banged on the door.

Not out here.

Not where Darby's neighbors may hear or see her.

The door swung open. Jess glanced up, unable to see her friend due to the fat tears swelling in her eyes.

"Oh shit. Come in, Jess." Darby reached forward and took her arm, guiding her into the house. She shut the door and towed Jessica behind her.

Jessica's feet moved of their own accord, following Darby inside and over to the couch.

Darby gently pushed Jessica down on it.

"Darby," Jessica hiccupped. Her body was racked with tears, and the sobs finally burst forth.

"Oh, no. Jess," Darby murmured. She sat next to Jessica and pulled her into a hug.

Jessica went, leaning against her friend, and allowed the wave of hurt and sadness to overtake her.

She didn't know how much time had passed. It wasn't until she grew silent that Darby cupped her cheek and guided her head up.

"Now tell me. What brought this on?" Darby easily slid into her counselor role. She reached over to the coffee table and snagged a few tissues. She carefully wiped Jessica's face. "I thought you and Bradley was going out for lunch."

"We did." Jessica exhaled, taking the tissue from Darby's hand. She blotted underneath her eyes, sure her mascara and eyeliner were running. "It was another usual date with Bradly. He took me to the café where we met. He claimed that today was actually our two-month anniversary."

"That sounds sweet, but I don't understand the tears. Was lunch that bad?"

"Darby." Jessica elbowed her. She brought the tissues back to her face, trying to remain calm.

"I'm serious. Tell me. What happened?" Darby rubbed her back. It was no wonder her patients continued to return to her. She had a gift from God that allowed her to help people going through shit.

"I'll tell you what happened. One word." Jessica paused. She fell back against the pillows and stared at the ceiling. "Iker."

"Wait. Iker was there?" Darby gasped.

"Yes. Bradley and I were sitting at a table, and I look up and see him standing at the table with a coffee in his hand."

"No." Darby readjusted herself on the couch to face Jessica. "Tell me how seeing him made you feel."

Jessica fell quiet as she thought about everything that had raced through her. She hated to admit she had drunk him in at first. Those intense eyes of his had met her gaze.

That devilish twinkle that always appeared in his eyes before he did something stupid was blaring brightly.

Just looking at him had taken her breath away.

"I was shocked at first. He said he was in the neighborhood, but I don't buy that." He lived about a half hour away from downtown. Even when they were together, he never just came in that area unless he was specifically coming for her.

"I don't either."

"What cruel game could he be playing?" she asked the rhetorical question out loud. She knew Darby wouldn't be able to answer on Iker's behalf, but still, she wanted to put the question out there in the universe.

It had taken her about a year to feel comfortable with dating again. She had been so used to Iker that getting to know other men was hard. She had so many expectations it wasn't fair to some of the men who would never be able to live up to her standards. She would immediately compare them to Iker.

The first sexual encounter she'd had with one of the guys she'd dated had been a complete disaster.

"Well, I wouldn't put it past Iker for him to have been in the neighborhood checking up on you. He probably saw you with Bradley and then went into the café."

"But why? Jealousy? He left me," she snapped. She rubbed a hand across her face, emotionally drained. She wasn't built for mind-fuck games like this. Iker had never been cruel to her before, so why now? "If you don't want me, leave me be and go on your way."

"That would be too easy," Darby murmured.

"Easy? He didn't have an issue moving on." Jessica sniffed. Even with her eyes closed, the tears flowed again. Having him leave her had been tough, but then to hear he was already seeing other women devastated her. Her cousin, Winnie, worked at one of the bars where Iker hung out. Winnie had texted her, informing her when Iker came in and left with women.

After the fourth report, she couldn't take it. Jessica kindly told her cousin to stop texting her about him. She didn't want to know or hear about his shenanigans in the bar.

Winnie had meant well. She knew how much in

love Jessica was with Iker and thought she was helping.

Far from it.

It was doing more damage than good.

Just the thought of him with other women was like he had taken a dagger to her heart and ripped a hole in it.

"Men like Iker can't handle seeing the women they gave up, move on with someone else," Darby said.

"Again, then why break up with said woman? Why not just keep her?"

"So he could have his cake and eat it, too. I'm willing to bet my paycheck he's kept tabs on you. Bradley is your first steady boyfriend. I hate to admit it, but Bradley is everything Iker is not. He's a gentle-man, a financial genius, dresses well, and right now holds your attention. Why hadn't he appeared before now?"

Jessica stared at her friend. She was onto some-thing. Bradley and Iker couldn't be more different.

Iker had sized Bradley up. She'd watched the way his gaze had traveled over Bradley prior to dismissing him. She'd seen the look plenty of times.

Iker was a man who didn't like to share anything: headstrong, blunt, and rough around the edges. Hell, he was a SWAT officer, and they were the baddest men who carried a badge.

"I don't know," Jessica answered softly.

It wasn't like they didn't live in the same city. Not once had they run into each other. They had been together for almost four years. He knew her favorite stores, her favorite restaurants, where she worked...she smelled a rat.

He wasn't there by coincidence. It was planned. Son of bitch.

"What do I do? Bradley made me invite Iker to the show on Friday."

Darby's mouth dropped open. "He what?"

"Bradley apparently was oblivious to the tension in the air between me and Iker. He did ask how I knew Iker, and I gave a little white lie. I told him we were old friends." Jessica cringed.

"And Bradley thought it would be fun to invite him to your event?"

"I believe he said something along the lines that I could have more of my friends there for support."

"But I'm not even coming." Darby gasped. She shoved Jessica. "You didn't put my name on the list."

"You want to come? I will call them now and add you." Hope flourished in Jessica. If she had Darby there, then there would be a buffer between her and Iker.

"Oh, hell no. I don't even want to see what will go down." Darby shook her head. "I don't think I could stomach watching Iker sniffing around you. It's that alpha male mentality. I'm sure soon enough Iker will be pounding on his chest demanding you take him back."

Jessica snorted. Had he come running back to her two years ago, there was no doubt in her mind she would have taken him back.

Now, after piecing herself back together, she didn't know if she could. He had put her through so much, she had to protect herself.

She had learned a hard lesson. Losing herself to him had been detrimental to her health.

"Do you think he's really going to show up?" Darby asked quietly.

Jessica thought of the expression on Iker's face when he'd accepted the invite.

Oh, yeah, he'd be there.

"He'll be there."

"Then I suggest you show him what he lost, and what Bradley gained."

"Darby!" Her gaze flew to Darby's. Was she crazy? Jessica glanced around the living room for the first time, looking for evidence of her friend drinking. There were no wine bottles or glasses sitting out. "Are you crazy?"

"I'm as sane as a june bug." Darby giggled. "He wants to play a game, testing you, seeing what you are up to, then I say remind him of what he's given up. One man's trash is another man's treasure."

"What's on your mind?" Zain asked. He held the large red bag steady as Iker pounded his gloved fist into it.

Iker had needed a way to blow off some steam. There was nothing like beating away the stresses of the day.

The gym, Champions, was located a few doors down from the police precinct. Iker and Zain had joined a few years ago when the placed opened. A lot of cops were members of the boxing club. It was a place to learn the fundamentals of boxing, self-defense classes, and one-on- one training.

"Who said something is wrong?"

"You are defiantly taking out some aggressions on the bag." Zain winced.

Iker landed a double-punch combo on the bag. He stepped away. Sweat dripped down his face. He blew out a deep breath and nodded to the bag. They switched places with Iker holding it for Zain.

Iker tried to will his breaths to slow down.

"So, are you going to tell me or what?" Zain asked. He threw a few slow punches then glanced at Iker.

"I don't know what you're talking about." Iker glanced around the gym, taking in the men sparring in the ring. A few others stood on the outside shouting pointers and instructions.

"Bullshit. I know you, Iker."

The bag jerked from a solid two-hit combo.

"It's Jess," Iker responded softly.

Zain paused and peered around the bag at Iker with a confusion expression.

"I'm sorry, did I hear you say Jess, as in Jessica Horton? The woman who you were madly in love with then walked away from?"

Iker closed his eyes and leaned his head against the bag.

"The one and only," Iker muttered.

"The same one who caused you to go on a two-week drinking binge that I basically had to pull your sorry ass out of hell for?"

Iker winced.

Zain knew everything that had gone down between Iker and Jessica. There wasn't much Zain didn't know about Iker. They had met when they'd both joined the police department fresh from the academy. They had become friends and were as close as brothers.

Iker had been there for Zain when his wife left him. Same for Zain, he had been there when Iker had made the tough decision to leave Jessica alone.

Zain had never agreed with Iker's reasoning for leaving her, but he'd stood by Iker's side through it all.

"What is making you bring up her name?" Zain stood beside Iker, resting his taped-up hands on his waist.

"I went out the other day to take the new car for a joyride," Iker began. He shared how he'd somehow found himself parked outside her job.

Zain listened without interrupting him.

"When I saw her walking down the street with that boyfriend of hers, I don't know what came over me. Before I knew it, I was in the shop buying coffee and strolling over to their table."

"Shit." Zain tunneled a hand through this hair. That was one thing about having a close friend like

Zain. He knew Iker was unpredictable, and the look he gave showed it.

"What the fuck did you do?"

"Nothing at all. Said hello, introduced myself to the guy. Hell, I even shook the motherfucker's hand." Iker pushed away from the bag.

He couldn't believe he'd shaken the dipshit's hand.

"And that—wait. How the hell you know she had a boyfriend?" Zain stared at him.

Iker met his gaze, unashamed to admit he had kept tabs on her.

"I hear things." He shrugged. They did still share a few common friends who might have mentioned she was dating someone. "Okay, I might have been checking up on her."

"Really? What the fuck for?"

Iker wiped his forehead on the back of his gloved hand. He turned around and walked up to the bag. Zain grabbed it and held it in place.

He swung hard, slamming his fist into it.

Why was he coming around her?

He should leave well enough alone, but Jessica had never been a woman he could walk away from.

"I just wanted to see her." He stepped back, breathing hard. "I heard she was in a new relationship with some fucker, so I looked into him. He's a banker. Clean as a whistle. I wanted to make sure she'd be safe."

"And that was all?"

"The boyfriend, Bradley," he spat the man's name, "invited me to her art show thing on Friday."

"You're not going, are you?" Zain asked in disbelief.

"One more time. I'm going to go for support." Iker didn't know who he was trying to convince, him or Zain.

"Does she want you there?" Zain asked softly.

They stared at each other. Iker broke the gaze. His attention landed on a few women walking through the gym heading toward the other room where self-defense classes were held. One caught his eye and gave him a small wave, then dashed into the room giggling.

He wished he could really feel something for another woman.

All the women he had slept with since Jessica, half the time he was intoxicated, wanting to try to erase her from his mind.

If he had to honestly answer Zain's question, he'd say no. Her eyes said it all. He saw the shock, fear, hurt, and anger in them.

All of it directed at him.

He didn't even want to think of the hurt he had caused her.

"You still think they will come for her?" Zain's voice dropped low, breaking into his thoughts. He stalked to Iker, stopping inches from him. "You know that we would have protected her. Hell, we've all gone to war with the fucking gang to keep people safe. That is what we do."

Iker cut his gaze to his friend and jerked his head in a nod.

What Zain had said was true.

None of them would hesitate to answer a call from their teammates.

They would bleed for each other, kill for each other, and he knew it would be no different if something would have happened to Jess.

But he didn't even want to risk that.

"She's too great of a risk, man." He dragged gloved hand down his face again to keep the sweat from going into his eyes. His heart raced at the thought of one of those thugs putting their hands on Jess.

"Then you need to stay away from her," Zain warned.

That sure as fuck wasn't what Iker wanted to hear.

Zain moved over to where their stuff sat on a shelf, grabbing a bottle of water. He took a swig, turning to face Iker. "You go sniffing around her, then you'll draw some unwanted attention to her, and then what?"

Iker already knew the answer.

He wouldn't hesitate to put one of those motherfuckers down.

The shrill ringing of their cellphones went out simultaneously. There was only one reason why they would be going off at the same time.

SWAT was being called in.

⸺

"WHY DO THEY ALWAYS RUN?" Jordan complained. She knelt on the thug's back who'd tried to run from them and applied zip ties to him.

"Because he saw you coming." Zain snickered, jerking the man he'd tackled to the ground up onto his feet.

Iker rolled his eyes. There was no doubt that Jordan fit in with their team. She gave just as good as she got.

They were called in for a raid on a meth house out in the rural areas. The house was located about forty minutes outside of Columbia. Confederate flags and pickup trucks greeted them on the property.

The entire operation was run by hillbillies with plenty of weapons and firepower. The second SWAT breached the premises, and all hell broke loose.

While the three of them had taken off after the two runners, the rest of the team was rounding up the people who were in the house. The paddy wagon was out front waiting for them to put in the criminals.

"Fuck you, Roman," Jordan snapped. She stood and yanked on the guy's arms.

They had cleared the entire house, and the two were hiding underneath the small porch at the back of the house.

It had been Jordan who had heard a sound and gone to investigate. The second she'd stepped out onto the back porch, two figures took off running towards the woods in the back. Zain and Iker had followed behind her.

"Watch it," the guy yelped. He stumbled to his feet and glared at Jordan. He looked strung out on the drugs they had been making in the house. The scent coming from both men was enough to make a skunk gag. "You're going to get yours, you black bitch."

Zain and Iker froze in place.

"What the fuck you did you say?" Jordan threw her glove-covered fist, landing it on his lower back. The woman had a mean hook, and at the moment, the drug dealer's kidney was her punching bag.

"Shit!" He bent forward, groaning. "Y'all saw that, right? Ain't this considered police brutality?"

"Quit your bitching," Iker ordered. He knew better than to get in Jordan's way when it came to dealing with thugs. She was a woman who could hold her own. She was one of the strongest women he knew. He'd made the mistake once in trying to defend her, and it ended with him getting his ass chewed out.

"Let's go, asshole," Jordan grumbled.

"Baldwin. Roman. Knight. Where the fuck are you?" Mac's voice came through the comm. That deep growl trained toward them meant he was pissed.

Fuck.

"At the edge of the woods in the back. We caught the two runners," Iker replied. He fell in line behind

Zain and Jordan as they pushed the two men toward the house.

Iker glanced ahead. A figure was on the back porch. Mac stood with his arms folded in front of him.

"We didn't do anything," the guy being led by Zain complained.

"Shut up," Zain and Iker echoed at the same time.

"People who don't do anything don't run," Jordan said.

"Y'all came in with guns aimed at everybody. What do you think we would do?" the shorter one whined.

"Y'all good taking them to the paddy wagon?" Iker asked, eyeing Mac.

"Yeah, we'll be fine," Jordan said.

They made their way back to the house. Blue and red lights highlighted the darkened sky. This was an easy job for them, but Iker could see there was a stick up Mac's ass.

Jordan and Zain disappeared around the house. Iker walked up the stairs, securing his weapons.

"What's going on?" Iker asked.

His sergeant waved for him to follow him. They

went back into the house and took the stairs down into the basement.

"When Dec and I swept through this area, look what we found," Mac said.

The basement was filled with everything needed to make meth. For rednecks, they sure had a nice-sized operation going on.

Iker took in the tables, barrels, the shelves along the walls packed with supplies. One would think it was a chemistry lab at a top university in this basement.

"What am I looking for?" he asked.

"Walk along the wall. See anything familiar?" Mac asked.

Iker strode around one of the tables and took in the area.

He paused.

"Shit," he cursed. Someone had been doodling along the wooden table.

Demon Lord tags.

"Exactly. I had Sergeant Wilson hold off allowing anyone from coming in for a few more minutes," Mac said.

"So the Demon Lords are into meth now?" Iker asked. He glanced around the room and took in more insignias drawn along the wall.

"We'll need to confirm the relationship and make sure this isn't any wannabes," Mac said.

"I'd say when they confiscate the computers, have Brodie check into them."

"Planning to, but this isn't why I really brought you down here." Mac walked to the other end of the room and pointed to a pile of papers on the counter.

Iker went over to him and drew still.

"What the fuck?" He was staring down at photos of himself.

It had been months since Diego had been arrested. His trial would be starting soon, and the entire SWAT team planned to be there for it. Eyeing the photo had him wondering if Diego was still sharing secrets while in prison. The son of a bitch had pages of charges. Everyone wanted a piece of him. Internal affairs had gone through every case he had touched, adding charges daily.

"We're going to find out why your pictures are here," Mac said. He slapped Iker on the shoulder. "Don't worry, brother. They won't touch you."

6

"Jessica. How are you?" Bradley's smooth voice came onto the line.

"I'm fine. I was just thinking about you," she teased. She walked around her living room, dusting. The gallery was closed for the day so final preparations for the event tomorrow could be finished. Mr. Ablo wanted the gallery looking its best. A cleaning crew was hired to scrub every inch while the decorators were scheduled to come in and transform the building. "Are you busy?"

"Never too busy for you. All good thoughts, I hope," Bradley said.

"Of course," she breathed. It was true. She had been thinking of Bradley a lot lately. They were a couple, and she was a woman who had needs. She was sure, him being a man, he had them also.

Why were they waiting?

Jessica had come to the conclusion that she and Bradley would take the next step.

Tonight.

"So what do I owe the pleasure for this call?" he asked.

Jessica rolled her eyes at how polite he always was. She was starting to get used to his manners. "Well, I was thinking that I want you to come over after work. I'll cook for us, and we can stay home tonight for a date." She slid the duster along the top of her television. Dusting was something she enjoyed doing around the house. It was a way for her to relax.

"Really? What's on the menu?" he asked.

"It's going to be a surprise." She giggled.

Bradley was a man who loved seafood, just as she did. That was one thing they had in common. She had a couple of lobster tails, some jumbo shrimp, and steaks in the fridge.

"Well then, I can swing by after work. Want me to bring a bottle of wine?"

"That would be great." Glancing down at her watch, she saw that she didn't have much time. Jessica wanted to pull this off. If she played her cards right, she would be able to seduce Bradley and finally have sex with him. Their make-out sessions were nice, pleasant even.

She just hoped there was more spark to them once they went all the way.

When she and Iker had first started dating, the sexual tension had been thick, even on their first date. She had only been able to hold off until their third date then—

She blinked.

No thinking of Iker.

He was not in her life anymore.

"Good. I have the perfect bottle at my house. I'll grab it and be by around six." Excitement lined Bradley's voice.

"I'll see you then," Jessica said.

"Can't wait to see you," he said and disconnected the call.

Jessica glanced around her house. She needed to finish tidying up. She wanted to make sure everything was impeccable. If she was going to convince Bradley to sleep with her, she was going to have to set the mood.

Within the hour she was done. Her house was officially company ready. Everything sparkled, and the new candles she put out were burning, setting the perfect ambiance.

She had all of the meats prepped and ready, along with her sides. Walking out of the kitchen, she headed into her bedroom. She would need a quick shower.

If tonight would be the night, then she wanted to be dressed for seduction.

"JESSICA, THIS WAS WONDERFUL." Bradley groaned. He took a sip of his wine and placed his glass back on the table.

She beamed, happy he had enjoyed the meal. She did love cooking and didn't get to do it much since becoming single again. Preparing meals for one wasn't as fun.

"Thank you." She dipped her last piece of her lobster into the butter and popped it in her mouth. She glanced at him and smiled. So far, everything was going off without a hitch. Their conversation had flowed easily since he had arrived.

Jessica had taken great care to make sure her hair was flawless, and she was plucked and shaved. She had even splurged on new lingerie for the night. She was dressed in a simple black wraparound dress that hugged her curves.

Dinner by candlelight, and soft jazz music playing in the background was her ideal setup. Bradley had arrived with his bottle of wine and looking very dapper. He'd changed from his suit he probably wore to the office into something casual. His button-down shirtsleeves were folded up to reveal his forearms, and his slacks were tapered seamlessly. The scent of his cologne had hit her when he had brushed past her.

She was always a sucker for a man who smelled good.

Bradley was a man who took pride in his looks. They had received many compliments when they had gone out on the town.

She'd heard they looked like the perfect couple.

"Are you nervous about tomorrow?" Bradley asked. He reached for his napkin and dabbed his mouth.

"A little. Zakir is a wonderful guy, and I'm hoping he will blow up after this." She had a soft spot for underprivileged artists. That was why she loved working for Mr. Ablo. It was about the artwork and not the color of the person's skin. He trusted that

Jessica would continue to spotlight quality and eye-catching pieces.

"What is he expected to earn with the sales?" Bradley asked. He was very attentive to her when asking about her work.

"If he sells every piece, he stands to earn about fifty grand," she gushed. That was a big deal for an unnamed artist. "We have drummed a lot of interest in his works. He's showed me his latest works and he's going to go places."

"That's wonderful. He's a lucky man that you came across him." Bradley chuckled.

"That's what Mr. Ablo said." She reached for her glass and took a sip. The wine Bradley had brought over was exquisite. He had great taste and knowledge in wines.

"The man knows what he's talking about." He shrugged. "Want more?"

He reached for the wine bottle and poured himself a little more.

"Sure."

He picked up her glass and filled it halfway.

She took it back and sipped it. "What's interesting in the world of investments?"

Butterflies fluttered around in her stomach. She had only had sex with a member of the opposite sex a few times in the past two years. Having a drawer of toys was nice, but it didn't replace human closeness or intimacy.

She missed that.

She drank in his smooth brown skin that was free of any blemishes. His mustache and beard were kept close to his face. The candlelight highlighted his good looks. Bradley was certainly a handsome man who drew the attention of women young and old. She hadn't had any reasons to not trust him.

When they were together, she always had his full attention.

Jessica inhaled and tuned back in to what he was saying. She could at least have the decency to pay attention to him while he was talking.

His face became animated as he spoke about his job.

"They invited me to come speak at the conference," he said.

"Really? That's amazing. I'm sure you will do fine," she gushed.

"It's a little intimidating. Believe me when I say most times I go to these conferences, I'm usually one of few black men there."

She put her glass down and applauded and hooted. He shook his head, laughing at her silliness.

She was proud of him. She knew what it felt like to be the only person of color in a business that was not as diverse as it should be. In the art world, there were a lot of vendors or artists who were shocked when she arrived. Most were not expecting a black woman to represent an Italian-owned art gallery.

"Why don't we move to the living room." She pushed her chair back and stood.

He followed suit and reached for his plate.

"I can clear the table—"

"I don't mind helping. Plus, my mother would have my hide if I didn't help clear the table." He winked at her.

They had yet to meet each other's families. He'd shared plenty of information about his. From the sounds of it, he was close with his family.

"Fine. Don't say I didn't try to take care of you," she teased.

"Hey, it should have been me cooking for you. This weekend is going to be big for you." He trailed behind her into the kitchen.

"Don't worry. You have plenty of time to spoil me."

They worked together as a team. She rinsed dishes off and placed them in the dishwasher while he put the leftovers in bowls and stored them away in the fridge.

"I plan to." He came up behind her and placed his hands on the sink, trapping her between it and him. He leaned down, pressing a soft kiss to the nape of her neck.

Her heart skipped.

This was what she wanted.

To take their relationship to the next step.

"Really?" She cut the water off and spun around. She tilted her head back so she could meet his gaze. "And why is that?"

He reached up and trailed a finger down her temple and cheek.

"Because you are a beautiful woman who deserves to be treated to the finer things in life," he murmured. His large hand cupped her cheek while he closed the distance between them. "Whenever I'm around you, I find that I'm smiling all of the time."

"Laughing is good for the soul," she replied, leaning into his warm hand.

"It is." He bent down, kissing her softly.

Jessica opened her eyes when he pulled away. At some point her hands had held on to the counter behind her. She hadn't wanted to wet his clothes with them.

"Living room?" she whispered.

"Sure."

He stepped back from her, his dark eyes locked on her. She dried her hands then took his hand in hers. She led him through the dining room so they could pick up their wine glasses.

She tried to will her heart down to a normal pace. It had been a long while since she'd attempted to seduce someone.

They entered the living room where the ambiance was set. She had candles lit around the room, and the music was still playing through the wireless speakers located around her home.

Jessica guided him to the couch. He sat and took a hefty sip of his wine, his eyes not leaving her.

Well, here goes.

She sat her glass on the coffee table and moved to stand in front of him.

"What are you doing?" he murmured. He lifted his glass to his mouth then paused.

A small smile graced her lips. She reached for the tie on the side of her waist and undid it, allowing the dress to open.

"Getting comfortable," she whispered. The dress

slipped from her shoulders and drifted to the floor, leaving her in her black lace bra and thong. "I hope you don't mind."

Bradley's gaze slid over her body, taking her all in.

His audible gulp reached her ears.

"No. Not at all." He cleared his voice, his eyes growing wide.

"Good." Jessica strode forward and plucked the glass from his fingers and placed it on the coffee table next to hers.

She straddled his legs and slid onto his lap.

Something hard rested underneath her.

Biting her lip, she wrapped her arms around his neck.

"Jessica..." His voice was strained. His Adam's apple bobbed up and down.

"I figured since we've reached our two-month anniversary this week, we could take our relationship to the next level." She shrugged.

Bending down, she pressed a chaste kiss to his lips.

"Is that so?" He had yet to put his hands on her. They were resting on the couch next to him.

"Yes," she breathed. She slid her hands up to his shoulders and came to rest on his cheeks. She covered his mouth with hers, initiating another kiss. This time she pushed her tongue forward into his mouth.

He returned the kiss, his tongue stroking hers.

Her hips moved slightly, excitement filling her.

His impressive-sized hardness waited underneath her.

"Jessica." Bradly groaned. His hands came to settle on her waist.

Her pulse pounded in her eats. It had been a while, and she was excited to feel the touch of a man.

"What is it?" She peppered kisses on his face and down his neck. She breathed in his scent, her body taking notice that there was a man with a hard dick underneath her.

Her core clenched as if to ask if this was a drill.

Jessica bit back her giggle. She nipped his neck with her teeth.

"Jessica," Bradley called her name again.

"What?" She smiled, lifting her head so she could meet his gaze.

She froze.

He was staring at her with a distant sadness in his eyes. He reached up and cupped her cheek.

"Jessica. I know you had this night planned out for us," he began.

"Yeah." She nodded. Disappointment filled her. Was he really about to not take her up on her offer? "What's wrong?"

She leaned down to kiss him again, but he held her back. He closed his eyes for a moment, then opened them.

"I don't want to hurt you in any way," he sighed.

Jessica blinked, staring at him.

"But I can't."

She glanced down between them. If she wasn't mistaken, he had an erection—a very large one by the feel of it.

"What are you talking about? It feels as if it's working fine." She didn't want to appear desperate, but what man would resist a woman practically throwing herself at him?

"Believe me, I want to." He took her hand in his and kissed her inner wrist. "But I can't. Not tonight."

He carefully moved her off his lap and onto the couch next to him.

"Did I do something wrong?" she asked, flabbergasted.

"No, no. Please don't think that." He stood from the couch, running a trembling hand over his face. Her gaze dropped down to his trousers that were tented from his dick. "I promise I will explain. I just can't right now."

"We can talk now." She scrambled off the couch and snagged her dress from the floor. She slid it back on, tying it shut.

Jessica spun around to find Bradley backing away from her.

"I can't. I'm going to go ahead and leave. I promise I will explain later." He spun on his heel and headed toward the front of the house.

She scurried behind him, truly at a loss for words.

What the hell?

"Are you sure I haven't done anything—"

"I swear it's not you."

They entered the foyer.

He turned around suddenly where she almost crashed into him. He rested his hands on her shoulders, staring deep into her eyes. "Jessica, you are an amazing woman, and I appreciate everything you did in making this a special night for us. I do owe you an explanation, but just not right now."

He kissed her forehead.

She stared up at him, not sure what to say to that.

He moved over to the closet and took his sports

coat out of it. He faced her, and she couldn't read his expression.

"I'll call you." He kissed her cheek then opened the front door.

He closed it quietly behind him, leaving Jessica standing there, unsure of what just happened.

7

"This is probably one of the stupidest things I've ever done," Iker murmured. He guided his car to The Ablo Gallery.

But like a moth to a flame, he couldn't stay away from Jessica.

One more time.

He promised himself this would be the last time he'd go around her. After tonight, he would disappear from her life again. She had a new man and appeared to be happy with him.

Iker tightened his grip on the steering wheel.

She was happy.

Safe.

Without him.

Tonight, he would be the old friend, coming

out to support Jess at her big event. There was nothing wrong with him supporting her in her dreams.

This job of hers was something she had worked so hard for. He remembered the day she had received the promotion. She'd been all smiles and talking a mile a minute. They had celebrated.

All night.

Iker groaned. He remembered that night as if it were yesterday. They had spent the entire night making love. Both had been too spent to go to work the next day.

He chuckled.

Jessica had a voracious sexual appetite. One he hadn't had any trouble trying to sate.

Releasing a sigh, he pulled into the valet line for the gallery. Glancing around, he took in the long line and the people milling about.

This was some event. Everyone was dressed in formal wear.

Now he was glad he had gone shopping. It was rare for him to don anything other than jeans, but he had a feeling this night was going to require more than that.

Iker followed the direction of the valet waving him up through the orange cones in the street. He maneuvered his luxury sports coupe behind another car.

This new car was his pride and joy. He had splurged and purchased it on a whim. Hard work had paid off. The note was staggering, but the car was well worth it.

The car in front of him moved up. He followed, parking next to a young valet.

Iker put the car in 'park' and opened the door.

"Welcome to The Ablo Gallery," the young man said. He handed Iker a ticket while giving a low whistle. "Nice ride."

"Thank you." Iker pocketed the small piece of paper and walked around toward the building. Butterflies filled his stomach as he approached. There was a small line while security checked names.

Excitement was in the air.

All of this because of his Jess.

"Good evening," a gruff voice greeted him.

Iker turned to face the muscle in a suit at the door. A young woman stood behind a podium next to him. She was young and pretty, offering him a smile.

"Name."

"Iker Baldwin," Iker replied.

"Welcome, Mr. Baldwin." The guard nodded to him.

"Here you go, Mr. Baldwin." The woman handed him a few papers. "It you are interested in purchasing anything, please go over to that table and register. They will take your credit card information and put it on file."

"Have a good evening," Iker murmured. He hadn't planned on buying anything, but he didn't want to seem like the oddball. There were a few tables with guests in line to register. "Whatever."

He headed over to the tables, and within a few minutes they had him register.

"Now if you see anything you like, it's as simple as sending a text to the number on the brochure with the item number," an older woman with her silvery gray hair flowing around her shoulders said. She offered him a warm smile. "Enjoy your browsing, and I hope you find something you like."

"I'm sure I will." Iker tossed her a wink and headed inside the gallery.

It had been a while since he had last stepped foot inside Jessica's place of work. Someone had gone all out on the decorations. Classical music filled the air, and the gallery was transformed into an elegant place as if they were expecting royalty.

Tall tables wrapped with white tablecloths were situated around the rooms were people gathered, drinking wine and eating hors d'oeuvres. Servers dressed in traditional white shirts and black pants walked around with trays.

"Wine?" A young man stopped near Iker.

"Sure. Thanks." He took a flute and strolled around.

One hour and he'd leave. He was here for support only.

Iker went into the first exhibit room. He ambled around, observing the pieces on the wall. The room was filled with people gawking and excited about the artwork.

"Hello, sir." A young man dressed in a business suit walked over to Iker. "My name is Chris. Is there anything in particular you are looking for?"

"I'm just browsing. I take it this isn't the exhibit that is for sale?" Iker asked, motioning to the photo on the wall. It was a black-and-white picture capturing what appeared to be an intimate moment between a man and a woman. By the clothing, Iker could instantly tell it was sometime in the early twentieth century.

"Oh, no. This exhibit isn't for sale. That is going on in the main room located down the hall," Chris said. He turned to stare at the portrait. "This one is beautiful, though, isn't it?

"It is. Can you tell me about it?" Iker asked. He knew he was stalling. He would kill the hour and go. Just so he could say he'd supported Jessica. This was her night—along with whatever starving artist she was spotlighting.

"Of course. I would be happy to show you around this one." Chris grinned wide. He motioned for Iker to walk along with him. "I'm an art major and I'm interning, so me showing you around would help me use this degree that my father said I'm wasting money on."

Iker liked the kid.

"By all means, show me around." Iker took a sip of the wine and wandered along with Chris. He reminded Iker of a younger male version of Jessica. So thrilled to be able to talk about her passion.

"So this collection is titled a San Francisco Minute. It's street photography that captures the heart of San Francisco during the first half of the twentieth century." Chris waved his hands as he spoke. He guided Iker over to another photo which showed a group of women standing on a street corner, smiling. "Back then, there was no asking for permission, you just snapped pictures of people and moved on."

"Yes, times have certainly changed," Iker murmured.

"Most of the people in the photos probably aren't aware their pictures were taken." Chris laughed. He pointed to one where an older man sat on the curb of a road. He looked dog-tired. "This artist, James Katzel, was well-known in the photography world. These photos were snapped around the nineteen-thirties."

Iker quietly studied the photos. They came to one of a police officer standing next to his squad car. That piqued Iker's interest. He imagined living in that era and wasn't certain he would want to.

He thought of his life and how different it would be if he were back in that time period.

Hell, he and Jessica would probably never have met. Interracial couples weren't as accepted then as they were now.

Chris continued educating Iker on the art. His knowledge of the work was astounding, and it was a shame that his parents didn't see him in action.

Iker was lucky enough to have had a great relationship with his father. Right after high school, Iker had worked for him in construction, but knew he wanted to do more in life. Hank Baldwin had been proud of Iker the moment he had shared that he was going into the police academy.

"Later on, his most famous exhibit of his was his nineteen-sixties photography which captured a lot of the civil rights era. We haven't been lucky enough to book that one yet. I know Jessica had been working really hard to try to get them to allow us to show it here."

Iker hadn't realized they had went around the entire room until they stopped at the entrance.

"You know Jessica Horton?" Iker causally asked.

"Yes, my internship is through her. She's my boss here." Chris glanced at him. "Are you friends or a relative of hers—"

"Old friend. I'm here to support her event."

"You want me to find her for you? I'm sure she's in the other room," Chris offered.

"No need. I don't want to bother her. I'm sure she's busy." Iker sat his empty glass on the tray of a server passing by.

"Okay, well, it was a pleasure chatting with you. If you need anything, please don't hesitate to find me." Chris grinned.

The room suddenly had quite a few guests strolling around taking in the photos.

"I will. Good job, Chris." Iker gave him a salute and ambled on. It was a shame the kid's father wasn't more supportive. It left him wondering if Jessica had been met with the same resistance from her parents on her degree.

Walking through the gallery, he continued on, following the mass of people toward a room where he assumed the main event was taking place. Chatter amongst the guests was growing louder.

Iker managed his way into the room and was taken aback by the sculptures and paintings. Trying to blend in, he moved to a painting on the wall. He believed it was what Jess would describe as an abstract. The bold brushstrokes and odd angles were interesting.

Jessica certainly had an eye for talent.

The bright colors drew him to them.

A familiar laugh sounded not too far away from him.

Glancing over his shoulder, he took in Jessica standing with a group of people. Bradley was near her, standing slightly behind her.

Iker instantly picked up on what the guy was doing.

Giving her space and letting her shine.

Iker had done the same thing when he had attended an event such as this a few years ago.

He blew out a deep breath. Bradley had just earned a point in Iker's book. He quickly turned, not wanting Jess to see that he was there.

His heart fluttered. Unable to resist, he took another peek at her. She wore a black dress that hugged her curves. The scoop neckline exposed the column of her neck. Her short hair was styled with curls that he used to love running his fingers through.

It was something he knew she thought was professional, but it made him—and his cock—take notice.

She spun slightly to speak to someone who had joined the group. He inhaled sharply. The dress dipped low in the back, exposing her soft brown skin.

Iker scrubbed a hand over his face.

He moved through the crowd, taking in the exhibit, but he wasn't seeing anything. The image of Jess in that sexy dress was the only thing he saw.

This was a mistake.

"I shouldn't have come here," Iker muttered.

"Iker?" a voice gasped.

A long-legged blonde made her way to him. He paused for a second. She looked slightly familiar. His eyes flicked to Jessica who was still engrossed in a conversation with the people surrounding her. He swallowed hard, turning back to the woman who stopped next to him.

"You'll have to forgive me. Do I know you?" he asked. He pulled at his tie, suddenly feeling warm. He prayed this wasn't someone he'd had relations with since Jessica. He wasn't proud to admit he couldn't remember all of the women he had slept with. Now was not the time to run into one.

"We've met once. You look like you've seen a ghost." She fell into a fit of laughter. She petted his arm. "You are off the hook. I'm Tiffany. I work with Jessica. We went out for dinner and drinks a few years ago for a double date."

Iker relaxed. Now that he took another glance at her, he did remember her. He and Jess had gone out with Tiffany and her boyfriend. They'd had fun that night.

"Oh, yes. How are you?"

"I'm great. You're here to see Jessica?" She raised an eyebrow.

He could tell she wanted to ask a question, but she was holding back.

"I was invited and figured I would come to support."

"Do you need me to show you round? There are

a few pieces that haven't sold yet. This exhibit was a hit."

"Actually, I'm not staying much longer. I just came to browse." He slipped his hands into his pockets and glanced around. Too bad they were only servicing wine and champagne and no real alcohol.

What he wouldn't give for a beer.

"It was nice seeing you again," Tiffany said. "If you change your mind and see something you like, just come and find me."

"Will do." He nodded.

She went over to greet a couple.

Iker stopped by a sculpture sitting on a raised platform. It gave him the perfect vantage point to peek at Jessica.

His gaze landed on her.

The crowd who had been speaking with her had moved on, leaving her and Bradley. Iker was too far away to hear what was being said between them, but he could sense something was wrong.

Jessica backed away from Bradley with her hands raised. She brushed past him and headed out of the room.

Bradley glanced around as if to see if anyone had witnessed their small squabble. He adjusted his bow tie, snagged a wine glass from a server, and moved over to speak with a gentleman.

Iker found himself stalking out. He caught a flash of black heading toward the back of the gallery. If he remembered right, Jessica's office was located in that direction.

Iker paused at the end of the hallway and didn't see anyone looking his way. He ambled down the hallway after her.

8

essica's heels clicked on the marble floor. She just needed a moment to get herself together.

All night, Bradley had been trying to apologize to her. This was not the time nor the place for him to remind him of her embarrassing attempt to take their relationship to the next level.

Entering the area where the offices were located, Jessica felt relief to see her office door. Opening it, she dashed inside, closing it softly behind her. She walked over to her window and stood. She didn't have much of a sight but the back side of a building.

It was nighttime, and there wasn't much to see. She tried to massage the tense muscles of her shoulders.

She'd probably hurt Bradley's feelings when she'd cut him off, but at the moment, she didn't care. To bring up last night at her job was just uncalled for.

So far, tonight was going off without a hitch. The art pieces were selling left and right. If all of them sold, it would be a record.

Zakir would be a household name.

Zakir, his wife, and a few friends had come to the event. They had stood around and chatted for a moment, then he'd moved on to show off his work to his friends. It would also do well for the patrons to meet and speak with the artist. When the potential clients could connect with the artist, it created a relationship.

One that blossomed into repeat customers.

She stiffened at the sound of the door opening.

"Bradley, you don't have to apologize again. It's okay." She closed her eyes and exhaled.

"What the fuck did he do?" a familiar growl sounded behind her.

Jessica whipped around and certainly didn't expect to see Iker in her office.

Bradley had forced her hand in inviting him to the gallery. But she hadn't thought he would really come. Iker rarely dressed up, and he always complained that events like this were not his scene.

He always felt out of place around men in suits.

"Iker, what are you doing here?" She cleared her throat.

A dark storm rolled in on Iker's face.

"I'm going to ask you again. What did the fucker do to you?" His voice was low and chilling.

It sent a shiver down her spine.

It may have been two years since they'd been together, but she knew that tone. If she admitted Bradley had laid a finger on her, he'd be out that door beating the crap out of him in the blink of an eye.

Iker was much taller than Bradley, outweighed him, and was a boxer. A good one. He knew how to fight. Add that to his training as a SWAT officer, and her ex-boyfriend was deadly.

She crossed the room quickly, holding her hands up.

"He didn't do anything," she admitted. She came to stand before him, tilting her head back to meet his gaze. Seeing him dressed up in a suit did weird things to her. Butterflies entered her stomach.

He was drop-dead gorgeous.

The suit. The beard. The hair falling over into his eyes was a complete turn-on.

Jesus.

What the hell was she going to do?

The memory of him leaving her still felt like a dagger to the heart, but deep down she wanted to be held by him.

Be kissed by him.

The sex between them had always been explosive.

But the one thing she missed was their quiet intimate moments. On their off days, they would lie in bed with each other, talk, or watch movies. It was some of her fondest memories of their time together.

"Then why would he be apologizing to you?" Iker's intense gaze was locked on her.

It was moments like this when she would have sworn up and down he could see clear through to her soul.

"It's just—" She paused. *Oh, hell no.* She was not divulging to her ex the issues she was having with another man. Closing her eyes briefly, she shook her head. "Don't worry about it. I promise it's nothing."

He stared at her for a moment. His eyes roamed her body. Her heart raced as the intensity of his gaze grew.

"If he's touched you..." His voice faded off. He reached up and cupped her cheek.

"Iker, what are you doing here?" she asked, trying to distract him. She hated the sound of her voice shaking. Memories of how things were between them came flooding back. One touch from him, and her body would go up into flames.

"I needed to see you again," he admitted.

"But why?" She was at a loss. He'd left her two years ago, giving her some crazy excuse that he needed to protect her by walking away. She'd never understood what that meant.

If she had been in danger, wouldn't it have made sense for him to stay with her?

He closed the gap between them.

"This dress looks damn good on you." He apparently wasn't going to answer her. His hand skated along her torso and went around to her back.

She gasped, her body arching into him. His warm hand connected with her bare skin.

A growl escaped him.

He spun them around, pushing her against the door.

"Iker," she gasped.

"Ever since I saw you walking down the street with that asshole, I've been thinking of you."

"Were you stalking me?" she asked. Her traitorous body was turning on her. Her nipples beaded into tight little buds. Her core clenched as the aroma of his cologne surrounded her. She inhaled, the scent bringing back fond memories of when she had purchased it.

It had been his Christmas gift. She had been at the mall shopping, and while browsing, she'd come across it. She had fallen in love with the cologne, and when he'd first worn it, she'd practically jumped his bones.

"No."

"So you see me with another man and all of a sudden you can't stop thinking of me?" She tried to push him away from her, but Iker was pure muscle. This just didn't make sense. She wasn't going to bring up the fact she knew he had moved on with other women.

"I saw you and I remembered how good it was between us." He bent down and buried his face into the crook of her neck.

She bit back a moan at the sensation of his tongue running along the column.

His body pushing on hers felt damn good. A familiar hardness pressed to her stomach.

His cock. Jessica was all too familiar with his big member. Flashes of her riding him in the past came to mind.

A whimper escaped her.

"Iker," she moaned.

"I always did love it when you said my name." His hand found its way to her thigh at the edge of her dress. "Your body always was so damn responsive to me."

His teeth nipped her neck. She jerked, a gasp escaping her.

Dammit.

He remembered her spot.

He sucked on her skin while his hand disappeared underneath her dress.

"Iker, we can't." She was trying to keep her thoughts together, but one touch from this man and her brain turned to mush.

"Fuck. You and these damn sexy garter belts." His hand connected with the straps and hooks attached to her stockings. His lips continued to skate across her neck, licking, kissing, and nipping her. "I know if I check, I'm going to find your pussy drenched."

Jessica bit her lip and leaned her head back on the door. She half hoped he did slide his finger between her folds.

He'd find just what he was looking for.

Even after all of these years, he still got her going.

She had to put a stop to this. Anyone could walk back to her office searching for her.

Shit.

What if Bradley came?

As frustrated as she was at him for what had happened at her apartment, he didn't deserve to find her making out with her ex-boyfriend.

"Iker. Stop."

He froze.

His lips pressed a small kiss to her neck. He lifted his head.

Their eyes connected, and there was so much she wanted to say to him and ask him, but tonight wasn't the time.

If she was going to get closure, she was going to have to speak with him to get a better understanding of what had happened between them.

"I'm sorry, Jess."

His saddened eyes met hers. He bent his head down and softly kissed her lips. They automatically parted, but he stepped back. He removed his hand from under her dress, smoothing it down.

"I truly am. For everything."

He gently pulled her away from the door and opened it. With one longing glance as if to memorize her, he disappeared through it, shutting it softly behind him.

Jessica stood staring at it.

What had just happened?

THANK goodness Jessica had the notion to stop in the restroom before returning to the gallery. Her face had been flushed; she had the air of someone who had been caught in a heavy make-out session.

After fixing her makeup and her dress, she went back to the event with a wide smile on her face.

She was a going to have to push down all of her emotions and focus on Zakir.

He was the true star of the night.

"What in the hell was Iker doing here?" Tiff asked, coming to walk alongside her.

They were friends and had worked together for a long time.

"He ran into me and Bradley at lunch the other day, and Bradley invited him." She shrugged, trying to act nonchalant.

They arrived back in the main room. Jessica scanned it, her gaze landing on Zakir and his wife speaking with a guest.

"Did something happen? He beelined out of here like the gates of Hell had opened." Tiff turned her curious gaze to Jessica.

She couldn't look her friend in the eye.

"I'm not sure. Maybe he got called out." Jessica moved away and headed toward Zakir. She was sure Tiffany meant well, but now was not the time for twenty questions.

Jessica put on a fake smile, walking around the room to speak with the patrons. Her job was to ensure that this exhibit sold out.

She was already making a name for herself on finding talent. If she continued to sell out shows, more artists would be banging on her door to have her book them. The gallery got a nice percentage from sales being hosted. Events such as this allowed the other exhibits that were on show to have visitors.

She stopped by a couple who were members. The Redds frequently attended her shows and had made quite a few purchases.

"Miss Horton, you have outdone yourself with this event," Mrs. Redd gushed. Her cheeks were flushed as she waved a hand around. "I had to have Albert purchase two items that I fell in love with."

"Anything for the wife," Mr. Redd said. They came from old money, their families being very influential in the South. Mr. Redd's family dated back to one of the first settlers in South Carolina. Their family business had spanned centuries and was still doing well. His ancestor was one of the signers of the Declaration of Independence.

"Thank you. Which pieces did you snag?" Jessica asked.

"That beautiful owl sculpture. It just resonated with me," Mrs. Redd bragged. She tapped her fingertips on the expensive pearls resting around her neck. "And that painting of the man in the field. Love this artist's work."

"Those are amazing pieces." Jessica smiled. She caught sight of Zakir making his way to her.

"Why don't you share what you just told me with the artist himself." Jessica waved Zakir over to her.

He and his wife arrived. Jessica made short introductions. The Redds were captivated by the Crosses. She gave a small wave to the Redds while backing away.

There were a few more things she needed to check in on.

"There you are, my love." Bradley came to her side, wrapping an arm around her waist. He kissed her temple. "Where'd you disappear to?"

He guided her away toward a corner where they could have a little privacy.

"I just went and took a breather."

He studied her for a moment, jerking his head in a nod.

"I saw your friend, Iker, leaving. Did you see him?" Bradley asked. He reached up and brushed her bangs from her eyes.

"For a moment," she lied.

"That was nice of him to stop by." Bradley took her hand and brought it up to his lips. "Why don't I take you out tomorrow? I want to explain my behavior and make up for ruining everything."

"Okay." She would give him a chance to explain himself.

He relaxed and leaned over to place a kiss on her cheek.

"Good." He sighed. He tucked her into his side, escorting her back to the room. "I have something great planned. I'll pick you up at six—"

"Six?" she gasped. "In the morning?"

"Yes. You're going to love it. I promise."

9

"I don't know how I could ever repay you," Zakir said. He enveloped Jessica in a strong hug.

"You don't have to thank me. Your work speaks for itself." Jessica smiled, stepping back.

"But if this hadn't been for you, my husband wouldn't have sold out of all his pieces," his wife, Shawna, said. She curled her arms around Zakir.

Her loving gaze at her husband tugged on Jessica's heart strings.

This was why she scoured around looking for hungry artists. All most of them needed was a platform to showcase their work.

Bradley draped an arm around her shoulders and squeezed.

"Well, this was one crazy night." Jessica laughed.

She gazed around and saw the gallery staff cleaning. The last guest had left about half an hour ago.

It was going to be a late night of cleaning to return the gallery back to normal for it to reopen tomorrow.

Waylon, one of their full-time security guards, was helping to clear the room of trash. He gave a nod as he headed toward the back of the building with two bags in his hands.

"Let me see you two out." Jessica motioned for them to join her.

Bradley entwined their fingers and stayed by her side. They chatted while strolling through the gallery. They finally arrived at the door, saying last-minute goodbyes with the promise of Jessica calling Zakir on Monday.

"Enjoy the rest of the weekend," she said.

With a wave, the happy couple left through the door.

Jessica used her key to lock it behind them. They turned and waved one last time, walking down the street.

"You did it!" Bradley exclaimed. He wrapped his arms around her, hugging her tight. "I'm sure you just changed his life."

"I hope so." Jessica sighed. She glanced at her

watch. "Well, we should get ready to go ourselves. If you have a surprise for me that requires me to be up and ready at six in the morning, then I need my beauty rest."

"You are beautiful even if you had bags under your eyes," Bradley teased.

"Hey!" She scoffed, playfully shoving him. It was nice that the strain between them was gone. If there was something he needed to share with her, she would be patient until tomorrow. "You haven't seen me at my worst yet."

They began walking back when a knock sounded on the glass doors behind them.

They turned. A woman and a man stood at the door. They must be latecomers.

"I'm sorry. We are closed," Jessica called out. She hoped they heard her.

The man smiled, holding his hand up to his ear. It was dark outside, and a lone car passed by in the background.

"Crap, he didn't hear me." She released Bradley's hand and moved toward the door. "We are closed. The event is over. We open tomorrow at ten."

She froze in place as the man brandished a gun.

"Jessica!" Bradley yelled.

Her heart seemed to be in her throat as she

backed away. She spun around at the sound of the glass door shattering.

She screamed, dashing toward Bradley. He snatched her hand and swung her around in front of him, pushing her toward the main part of the gallery.

"Is the party over?" a deep voice yelled. "Don't run, or I'll shoot."

Jessica paused, spinning to the trespassers. Bradley pushed her behind him.

The woman entered, a very large shotgun in her hand. Her long dark hair flowed around her shoulders. Four men walked through the shattered door with their guns raised.

"What do you want?" Bradley asked, holding his hands up.

"That's for us to know and you not to find out," the woman snapped. A scowl was etched on her face. She jerked her gun toward them. "Turn around and walk. Hands where we can see them."

Jessica swallowed hard. Her heart pounded. She inhaled and tried to will her heart to slow down.

"Do what they say, Jessica," Bradley urged.

She jerked her head in nod and swiveled around.

"Everything okay out here?" Waylon jogged toward them, concern on his face. He slid to a halt at the sight of the group with guns. "What's going on?"

"Someone grab him. We don't want Mr. Security Guard to alert the authorities," the woman barked. Apparently, she was in charge.

Two of the men accosted Waylon, twisting his arms behind his back, and zipped tied his wrists together.

"You two with me," a man with a scar running across his chin snarled.

Jessica glanced around, at a loss for words as a few more people entered the building, all with weapons drawn. A van came to a stop outside the doors and parked.

Scarface tugged her arm and yanked him with her.

"Get your hands off her," Bradley hollered.

"Shut up, lover boy, before I make you." Another man joined them, pulling Bradley with him.

The gallery was in chaos as it was overtaken.

Jessica held back tears as she watched everyone who had remained to help clean up be ushered into a back storage room. All of their cellphones were stripped away from them. They were all restrained with their hands tied behind their backs.

Jessica was pushed from behind, and she stumbled into the room. Bradley put his body in front of hers to keeping her from falling.

"Guard this room. We need to be fast," a tall man with stringy blond hair ordered.

"Yes, sir," the younger man said. He shut the door, leaving them alone.

Silence fell around the room.

"Is everyone all right?" Jessica asked.

"Yeah," someone breathed.

Nods went around.

"What do they want?" Kate asked. She was one of the maintenance employees. Staying this late had been overtime for her. Most of them had volunteered to stay late to ensure the gallery would be ready for a regular business day tomorrow.

"I have no idea. Whatever they want, they can have. Mr. Ablo has insurance. I'm just glad no one was hurt," Jessica said.

She remained standing and leaned back against the wall. She closed her eyes, sending up a prayer that this would be over soon.

The Ablo had security cameras everywhere and hopefully would be useful for the police. None of the robbers wore masks, which worried Jessica. She had watched enough television shows to know either the robbers didn't plan for them to make it out alive or were dumb.

She hoped it was the latter.

"Hey, Jess." Tiffany moved over to her. "I was able to trigger the silent alarm when I was in the front room."

A collective sigh went around. A few years ago, some other art galleries and museums had been robbed. After hearing this, Mr. Ablo had installed state-of-the-art security measures around the building.

It would be only a matter of time until the boys in blue arrived.

Sounds came from outside the room. Jessica just hoped that soon the robbers would take what they wanted and leave.

The door swung open, and the dark-haired woman stood in the entryway.

"Who's in charge here?" she demanded.

No one said a word.

Jessica swallowed hard and took a step forward.

"I am."

⌒⌒

"YOU HAVE GOT to be shitting me," Iker grumbled. He swung his car and busted an illegal U-turn in the street. SWAT was being called in.

After leaving the gallery, he aimlessly rode

through the city for about an hour. He had no destination in mind, he just needed to get away. Both windows were down, and the wind blew through his hair. The music was on blast as he mindlessly drove around. He had to get the taste and feel of Jess out of his mind.

He had meant what he'd said when he had apologized for everything.

He had tried to tell her she was better off without I'm and this was the only way he could guarantee her safety.

But tonight, he had grown weak.

Iker had just planned to go to one of his favorite bars when Mac's call came through.

Going after bad guys would certainly be better than getting wasted. There was nothing better than going hunting with his SWAT brothers and sister.

He pressed down on the gas, and his heart raced.

Maybe this was just what he needed.

Soon he was pulling his car into the parking lot of the precinct. He killed the engine and got out. He hurried and made his way into the building. He had a change of clothes in his locker room. There would be no way he'd be able to go out on an assignment dressed in a suit.

He threw open the door to the locker room,

finding his teammates in there getting dressed.

"Well, look what the cat dragged in." Ash chuckled.

A sharp whistle cut through the air.

Iker bit back a grin. He should have known they were going to give him shit about being dressed up.

"Where the hell are you coming from, pretty boy?" Myles asked.

"None of your damn business," he muttered, arriving at his locker. He opened the door and tossed his keys onto the shelf.

"Did someone have a date?" Brodie snickered. He leaned toward Iker as he passed. "Fellas, he even has on cologne."

The room fell into a fit of laughter, jokes, and teasing.

Iker rolled his eyes. He could take the heat. If the tables were turned and it was anyone else, he'd be leading the pack. He quickly changed, ignoring his teammates who continued to crack jokes about him.

"Y'all keep up a lot of noise when you should be getting dressed," Mac's hard voice cut through the air.

The laughter faded with him walking through the locker room. Iker pulled his ballistics vest over his head and secured it.

Mac stopped at the corner of his row where he and Zain were standing. "Don't worry, fellas, after we complete the briefing, Iker's going to share where he's been."

Iker cracked a smile. Even Mac was in on the jokes.

"Yes, sir," Iker murmured.

"All right, men. Meet outside in five." Mac spun around on his heels and walked out of the room.

"Yo." Zain hit Iker on the arm. "You went, didn't you?"

Iker slammed his locker closed. "Do I really need to answer the question?"

"You did." Zain shook his head.

They filed out of the locker room and headed out back where the BEAR was parked. It was their ride to all missions that required SWAT.

"It's about time you fellas joined me out here," Jordan goaded them as they arrived outside. She stood with her arms folded in front of her. A scowl was on her face.

"Whatcha worried for?" Iker sniffed. "You could take out all the bad guys on your own."

"You're damn right I could. You lazy bastards took forever getting dressed." She rolled her eyes.

"Glad you showed up when you did." Declan smirked. "She was going to leave you guys."

Declan pointed to the BEAR sitting outside the garage already idling.

"Hey, who drove my baby?" Zain reached the BEAR and patted the truck. He eyed Jordan who flipped him off. "They didn't hurt you, did they?"

"All right, SWAT. Gather around." Mac motioned for everyone to stand close. It was time for the briefing, and everyone grew serious and listened to their sergeant.

Iker shifted his attention to Mac.

For some odd reason, dread filled Iker. He wasn't sure why, but something was wrong.

Shaking it off, he focused on Mac and Dec who stood next to each other as usual when giving details of the upcoming mission.

"We received a distress call today from The Ablo art gallery," Mac announced. "A silent alarm was tripped."

Iker was gutted. He staggered back as if hit in the solar plexus with a bat.

"What?" Iker croaked. All eyes flew to him. "I was just fucking there."

"What the hell were you doing there?" Brodie asked quietly.

Ash nudged him with his elbow, shaking his head.

Iker drew a haggard hand across his face.

"What happened?" Iker demanded. His muscles grew tense as he waited for the reply.

"Calm down, Iker." Mac held up a hand. His sharp gaze didn't miss anything. He was well aware of the reason why Iker was about to lose it. "Dispatch called the gallery to confirm the need for assistance, but there was no answer."

"Two patrol cars drove by and were the target of fire when they approached the front door," Declan intervened. The look on his face was grim. "According to the officers, the front glass door was shattered. The art gallery was taken by force."

Iker growled low. He sent up a prayer that Jess wasn't still in the building, but knowing her and how hard she worked, she was probably part of the cleanup crew.

"She'll be okay," Zain murmured. His strong, firm grip rested on Iker's shoulder.

"What was going on there tonight to attract the attention of robbers?" Myles asked.

"A starving artist sale," Iker replied automatically. "The art gallery had spotlighted a local artist."

"Most transactions I'm sure would be credit,"

Ash said. "There wouldn't be any cash there."

"Doesn't matter at this point. They aren't bringing us in to investigate. We're being brought in to do what we do best and safely retrieve the hostages," Mac said.

Iker's heart raced, his anxiety increasing. He wouldn't be able to settle until he knew Jess was safe.

"We'll continue the briefing on the way." Declan clapped. "Load up."

Iker spun on his heels and went over to the BEAR. He got in and sat back without a word, waiting for the rest of this team to get in.

All he could see was Jess's face when she'd stared up at him when he had her pressed against the door.

He'd walked away from her to keep her safe.

He had risked everything he had loved that day when he had made the decision.

"If she's there, we'll get her out," Myles said.

Iker looked up at his friend and jerked his head in a nod.

The BEAR rocked as it moved out. Zain was driving while the rest of them would ride in the back like they normally did.

Only this time the mission was hitting close to home for Iker.

It involved someone he loved.

"How the fuck did the police get called?" the woman snarled. She dragged Jessica behind her as they moved toward the warehouse side of the building. Shipping and receiving was located in the far depths.

"I don't know, Halle," Scarface replied.

"You." Halle swung Jessica around, pointing her handgun at her face. "Who called them?"

Jessica eyed the gun, her heart racing a mile a minute. She had to think quick on her feet.

"The door," she gasped.

Halle's hand tightened on her arm.

"The shattering of the glass set off the alarm. This is an art gallery with every expensive items."

Halle stared at her for a moment.

"Boss, we haven't found it yet." Another goon came up beside Halle.

A sense of dread overcame Jessica, for she knew what they were looking for.

"Where is the vault?" Halle asked. She stepped closer to Jessica, pushing her gun into Jessica's side.

"The vault?" she asked, trying to stall.

"Don't play dumb with me, bitch." Halle shoved the gun hard into Jessica's side.

Jessica yelped from the pain. "It's in the basement," she mumbled. She glanced around at the goons staring at her. She didn't know what they would want out of the vault. None of them appeared as if they were art collectors.

"Stall the cops," Halle shouted at a few of her men standing at the end of the hallway. "Make sure they know we have hostages and are not afraid to use them."

An icy chill slithered up Jessica's spine.

Using hostages?

What the hell did that mean?

"You're coming with us," Halle snarled. "Lucho and Miguel. With me."

They dragged Jessica to the stairwell and down the stairs. Jessica prayed the SWAT team would be dispatched.

Jessica stumbled down a few stairs.

Strong hands lifted her practically off her feet as they continued to the lower level. The man, Lucho, eyed her, placing her back down on her feet on the landing.

"Hurry up, bitch," he snarled.

She continued on to the last sets of stairs. Her heel got caught in the last one. She flew forward, pain exploding in her ankle. She landed with a thud on the concrete floor.

"Dammit." Halle moved to her side and attempted to yank her up by her arm. "Get up."

"Wait. I twisted my ankle," Jessica insisted. Her ankle throbbed. She didn't think anything was broken, but it would be hard to stand on it.

"Take those damn heels off." Halle snapped her fingers.

Miguel bent down next to Jessica and removed her left shoe. Jessica swallowed hard at the strange glint in his eye. She was immediately uncomfortable watching him pull her right one off. His hand snaked its way up her calf.

"Miguel," Halle called. "Help her up, you sick fucker. We don't have all day for you and your fucking foot fetishes."

Jessica jerked her leg out of Miguel's hold. She

scooted away from him and stood on her own. She tested out her foot and would be able to walk. With a limp, but she'd be able to do it.

"Lead the way." Halle motioned to Jessica with her gun.

Jessica gave her a nod and opened the doorway that was located at the bottom of the stairwell. She limped the entire way, going slower than she probably would have had she not twisted her ankle.

There was no way she was going to show them weakness. The longer she stood on the foot, the more her ankle screamed. She'd be damned if one of the creeps would carry her.

She led them past the freight elevator and to the room located across from it.

Inside was the large vault where extremely expensive items were kept. There were other areas in the basement where items were stored.

But anything that required its own insurance policy was stored inside the vault.

Only the robbers did not do their research very well. It was quite obvious to Jessica.

If they had, they would have known the location of whatever they were searching for. If they knew it would be in the vault, they would have known where it was located.

The round opening was the size of the entire wall. The black metal door had steel bars that went across it. On the wall near it was the electronic panel that controlled the vault's door.

Jessica paused in front of the door and stared at it.

"Well, what are you waiting for?" Halle asked. She shoved her gun into Jessica's back.

"You want me to open it?" Jessica asked, turning to look at her.

"What the hell you think we brought you down here, so we can admire it?" Halle ordered.

"Well, I figured you would just break into it." Jessica shrugged. By the looks of it, none of them were equipped to do that. Mr. Ablo had purchased the latest state-of-the-art contraption to house the most valuable art pieces.

This allowed them to be able to receive fine art from all around the world and guarantee its safety.

"Why would we do that when we have you?" Lucho asked, his words heavily accented.

"I won't be able to open it. After hours, it locks everyone out. It is only accessible during certain hours, and right now, the only person who has the override code would be the owner himself. I wasn't given that type of access."

"What?" Halle hollered. She stalked around Jessica to stare her in the face. "So there's no way to get this open?"

"At the moment? No."

"Son of a bitch." Halle stalked to the vault's door, studying it. "There's no way in hell we would be able to get this open."

"We need to go," Lucho murmured. He touched his ear, and it was then Jessica saw a small communicator in it.

Halle swung around and moved toward Lucho.

"They've called in the SWAT team," he said.

Jessica's heart leaped.

They were going to be rescued. She could have wept tears of joy, but she held back. She didn't want to draw any more attention to herself than needed.

"Then it looks like we will need to use the hostages to make a run for it," Halle declared.

⁂

"BALDWIN. Do you need to sit this one out?" Mac stood next to Iker.

"No, sir. I'll be fine," Iker claimed. His focus was on the building where Jessica worked. Not too long ago he was in there holding her against him. He bit back a curse.

He shouldn't have left.

Kept an eye on her and made sure she was safe.

Iker could kick his own ass. He hadn't wanted to leave, but if he had stayed, he would have made a damn fool of himself.

"We've confirmed there are about twelve employees and with an unknown amount of bad guys," Declan announced. "We have spoken with the owner who gave us a list of names of people who may still be here."

The team processed the information, and there was no doubt they would be successful tonight. They had practiced this scenario repeatedly to ensure they were the best at what they did.

"Everyone good with the plan?" Mac asked.

They stood outside the gallery. The red and blue lights of the patrol cars lit up the night sky.

"Lock and load," Dec said.

Iker ensured his MP5 was ready to go. He slid his mask into place, hiding half of his face. Zain moved to stand near him. His friend didn't say a word. Some of the team were in the dark on what was going on. He would have to explain later, but just now, he needed his team to be on their top game.

"All right, SWAT, let's hunt," Mac growled.

The plan was to split up. Four through the front while the rest would go through the back.

Declan, Iker, Zain, and Jordan would go through the back entrance. Mac and the others would breach the front door.

With guns drawn, they followed Declan in a tight formation through the alley next to the building.

Iker centered his breathing. His heart slowed to a steady beat. He allowed his training to take over him.

Declan raised his fist sharply once they reached the edge of the building. He motioned for them to continue. Iker brushed past him, with the others behind him. Declan would pull up the rear.

Iker aimed his weapon true as he approached the back entrance. They stayed close to the building. Iker paused when he arrived at the door. He peered inside the glass and didn't see any movement. It was made entirely of glass, just like the front entrance, giving them wide visibility.

"We're at the door," he murmured into his comm link.

"Roger that," Mac's low voice came across the line.

Zain moved in front of him, working the lock

located next to the door handles. A light click echoed. Zain swung the door open.

"We're going in," Iker murmured, hefting up his weapon.

They filed inside in single file.

It was eerily silent before all hell broke loose.

Gunfire reverberated from the front of the building.

Iker tightened his grip on his weapon. They passed by a door that according to the plans would take them to the basement.

A ding of an elevator chimed in. Footsteps rushed forward, and two men appeared.

"What the fuck?" One with a scar cursed. He immediately went on the attack toward Iker, his fist flying forward, knocking Iker's gun toward the ground. The gun swung down to his side, the strap tightening around his chest.

"Shit," Iker muttered.

He was too close. The guy rushed and slammed into Iker. His teammates flew forward toward the other people coming out of a freight elevator.

Shouting ensued around them.

Iker raised his fists, bringing them down onto the guy's spine. He grunted and fell to one knee.

Iker raised his leg, whacking it into the robber's

face. His head jerked back as he sprawled onto his back while holding his face.

A scream sounded.

Iker's eyes flickered up to the sight of Jessica being flung on the floor by a dark-haired woman. Jordan engaged the woman, who turned out to be no match for Jordan.

Zain and Declan had the other guy on the floor, zipping his arms behind him.

"You broke my nose—"

Iker rammed his fist into the guy's face. He fell back, with Iker not wasting any time securing his wrists behind him.

He ignored the pain in his knuckles and dashed over to Jess. He knelt over her. Her wide eyes glanced up at him.

"Jess, are you okay?" he asked, ripping his mask off.

"Yeah, I'm okay." Tears streamed down her cheeks. Pain crossed her face when she moved her leg.

"What's wrong? he asked. It was then he noticed she was without shoes. Her ankle appeared to be swollen. "Did one of these motherfuckers do this?"

Red clouded his vision.

Someone had hurt his Jess.

"No." She grimaced. "My heel got stuck on the stairs, and I fell down them. You know me, heels and stairs don't mix."

"I'll carry you, babe. It doesn't look good." He eyed her ankle again. She was going to need an X-ray to check if it was broken.

"No, I can—"

"Shut it." He scooped her up into his arms and held her close to him.

It was then he took notice that the gunfire from the front had ceased. He turned around and found Jordan staring at him like he'd grown a third head.

"The back entrance is secured," Declan announced into the comms.

"Front is secured." Brodie's voice came through.

"I thought you said this would be an in-and-out job," the robber who'd attacked Iker muttered.

"Shut up, Miguel," the woman snarled. She glared at the man while the other one remained silent.

"Are there any more of you back here?" Jordan demanded, kneeling by her.

"Fuck you," she snapped.

"Oh, fuck me? I see." Jordan bent down and yanked her up to her feet by her wrist.

The woman screeched and tried to buck against Jordan who held her.

"Unless you want your ass kicked again, I'd suggest you stop struggling." Declan smirked.

He and Zain helped the men to their feet.

"Where are the others?" Iker asked Jessica. His heart thundered. He was trying to not read too much into the way she appeared to lie against him. Her arms came up to wrap themselves around his neck.

"In the storage room around the corner." Her big brown eyes stared up at him.

"Dec," Iker called out.

"Got it. We'll get them. Take her out to the EMTs to get checked out." Declan gave him a salute.

"Iker's coming out with one of the hostages who needs a medic," Zain announced through the comms. "Make sure the EMTs are ready."

Iker jerked his head in a nod of thanks to his friend. He headed toward the back doors. He didn't want to take her through the building. With the sign of a gunfight up front, he didn't want to chance going past any casualties.

He exited the building and retraced his prior steps toward the alley.

Jessica sniffed.

"What is it, babe?" he asked softly.

"I was so scared back there," she admitted. Her arms tightened around him. "When they separated me from the others, I wasn't sure what was going to happen to me."

Iker held her closer to him. He didn't like the fact that she had been afraid for her life. He had half a mind to go back there and beat both of those men's asses and let Jordan loose on the woman.

"It's all right. We got you."

She winced again. He quickened his steps, making his way down the alley.

"Can I admit something to you?" she whispered.

He stepped from the alley and beelined toward the ambulance. The uniforms were swarming the building. Chaos ensued outside. The media had arrived, and there were some nosey onlookers gathering around the yellow safety tape.

"What is it, babe?"

"I prayed you would come and rescue me."

Iker's breath was snatched from his chest.

The EMTs jumped from the ambulance and opened the back doors. They pulled out the stretcher and lowered it to the ground.

"Put her here."

Iker sat her down carefully, unable to get a word

out. She gently reached up, palmed his face, and released him.

"Thanks, Iker." She smiled softly. The EMTs hefted the stretcher up into the vehicle then climbed in behind her.

His name was called off in the distance. He glanced over his shoulder. Mac waved him over. Iker was torn between staying with Jess and doing his duty.

"Go, Iker. It's okay." She nodded. "I'm safe. Go do your job."

"I'll find you later," he promised.

"Jessica!" a voice shouted.

Iker stiffened. Bradley was making his way toward the ambulance. Iker had forgotten about the boyfriend.

Bradley arrived next to Iker.

"Iker, I heard you rescued our girl." Bradley held out his hand to him.

Iker glanced down at it, taking it in a strong hold. Bradley grimaced, but he didn't back down.

"Of course. Jess is special," Iker murmured, his gaze flicking to hers.

"Are you her significant other?" the EMT asked Bradley. "We're going to have to get going. You can ride back here with her."

"I am and will. Thanks," Bradley answered the EMT. He turned and slapped Iker on the shoulder.

Iker narrowed his gaze on him.

"Thanks again, man."

Iker backed away while watching Bradley climb in with Jess. The other medic jumped out of the back and shut the doors. He jogged over to the driver's seat and got in.

Iker took another step back with a lump in his throat.

Hearing someone else claim his woman brought a fire to his chest.

Jessica was his woman.

It was time for *Brad* to move on.

Iker was back in Jessica's life, and he was here to stay.

11

Jessica leaned back as comfortable as she could be on the emergency room stretcher. The mattress was hard and unforgiving. Jessica had a conspiracy that they did this on purpose so people would not want to stay long. The stark white room was small, with only one chair, a sink, displays on the walls, along with some equipment they had used to monitor her vitals. The curtain to the room was drawn, giving her a little privacy.

She had been poked, prodded, and had plenty of pictures taken of her ankle. She leaned her head back and relaxed against the pillow.

A detective had already stopped by to take her

and Bradley's statements. He made a promise to follow up with her in a day or two.

The nurse had just come and removed the electrodes from her chest. Aside from her ankle, she was given a clean bill of health. They were waiting for the results of the X-rays to come back and for the orthopedic surgeon on call to come chat with her. The ankle was swollen to at least three times the normal size. They had given her something for the pain.

Her gaze fell on Bradley sitting in the chair next to her. Because he was also a hostage in the robbery, he was made to be checked out, too. He was, of course, deemed healthy with no injuries and released by the hospital.

There was an expression on his face she was unable to read.

"Are you okay?" she asked softly.

He focused his eyes on her and blew out a deep breath. From the moment they had entered the hospital he'd appeared uncomfortable.

Now this look, she didn't know what it meant.

"I should be asking you that." He scooted closer to her and took her hand. He raised it, kissing her inner wrist. His eyes closed momentarily, then opened and landed on her. "I felt so helpless when they took you from the room."

"It's okay—"

"No, it's not. I don't know what I would have done, but I should have done something."

"It's okay. Had you tried, they probably would have hurt you." She squeezed his hand.

He was a businessman, not a badass SWAT officer who fought bad guys every day.

The memory of Iker taking on Miguel would be forever etched into her brain. Even though his face had been covered, she would recognize him anywhere.

His movements were fluid and swift, disabling the guy without breaking a sweat.

"You're right. Those people were really scary." He grew quiet. Something flashed across his face.

Jessica sat up higher. She had to know what was bothering him.

"Seriously, Bradley. What's wrong?" She turned her biggest puppy dog eyes on him.

He stared at her and exhaled softly.

"Okay, um..." He swiped a trembling hand along his face.

Jessica was growing concerned. She'd never seen him like this before. He swallowed hard, abruptly standing. He walked toward the exit, then turned back around to face her. "I don't like hospitals."

Jessica blinked.

"A lot of people don't," she replied slowly.

He slid his hands in his pockets and stared at the floor.

"I spent a lot of time in a hospital when I was a teenager," he admitted.

Jessica's breath caught in her throat.

"I'm so sorry. What was wrong?" she asked. Her heart went out to him imagining a younger version of himself being confined to a hospital.

"I was fourteen years old, and like many others, I was bullied as a kid." He moved over to the wall and leaned back against it.

Jessica's heart pounded as she waited for him to continue. Dread filled her with what she was sure was going to be a horrific story.

"We lived in a predominately white area. I was one of few kids of color who lived there. The neighborhood bullies always taunted and teased me for being a nerd. Most days I could ignore them, but this one day in particular they just wouldn't leave me alone." He fell silent for a moment.

Jessica wasn't sure if he was going to finish before he pinched the bridge of his nose.

"I was walking home with this girl who I liked. Her name was Cassandra. She was pretty, smarter than me, and lived a few doors down the street from me. It was innocent. I remember we were talking about comic books."

Jessica smiled softly, watching him fall into his memories.

"Her older brother was one of the kids who picked on me. He and his friends didn't appreciate I was walking Cassandra home. They jumped me. Beat me bad. I can still hear her screaming for them to stop. One of the guys carried her away, which I'm glad they did. They dragged me to this abandoned field, tying me up to a metal fence. The punks poured lighter fluid on my jeans."

"Oh my god." Jessica's hand flew to her mouth. Tears blurred her vision at the imagery that came to mind.

"I'll spare you the details, but let's just say they tossed a match my way. The jeans went up in flames." He rubbed his hands over his eyes, exhaling. "It was ruled a hate crime. The kids who had tormented me were white and hated I was in their good area. Apparently, even in our day and age, I should not have been speaking to Cassandra. I'm black and should have known my place," he spat.

The tears began to fall. Even today, hate crimes still existed. Reports of such violence was reported on the news almost daily.

"The reason I freaked out the other day was because thirty-six percent of my body is covered in burns. I've had relationships with women. Some are able to stomach what my legs look like, some can't, and I didn't want to see the pity or disgust in your eyes. So, I just left."

The room fell quiet.

Jessica brushed the wetness from her face. Just imagining what he'd been through broke her heart.

"Thank you for sharing with me," she whispered. Jessica waved him over to her.

He came, his eyes red as if he were holding back tears. He sat on the edge of the stretcher and folded her in his arms.

Jessica squeezed him tight, feeling sorrow for all of the pain he had been through. She lost track of time of how long they sat there. He pulled back first, wiping the tears from her cheeks.

"Jessica, I really like you. A lot. I know we've only been dating for two months, but I want our relationship to work. I don't want my disfigurement to ruin things between us."

His solemn gaze tore at her heart. She knew she

wasn't like those other women who may have been disgusted with him. He was a sweetheart, and after hearing the tale, how could anyone treat him bad for something he had no control over?

"There's no rush, Bradley." She sniffed. "Whenever you're comfortable, we can move forward. I can't imagine what you lived through. I'm sure it was hard to share with me, or anyone for that matter."

"How did I get so lucky to meet you?" he asked wistfully. His lips curled into a small smile. He reached up and caressed her cheek. "You are the perfect woman."

"I am far from perfect."

"Don't tell me how I see you," he murmured. "You are everything I've ever dreamed of. To me, you are."

Jessica's cheeks warmed at the sentiment. She tried to keep from smiling but was unsuccessful. Bradley had a way to make her smile. That was the one thing that had drawn her to him when they'd first met.

"Well, since it looks like you won't be in any shape to have a fun-filled day today, I'll reschedule what I had planned for us for another day."

"Oh, I'm sorry."

"Don't be. None of this is your fault. We can wait until you are in better shape."

Jessica lifted her leg to try to shift in the bed and grimaced. Her pain medication was starting to wear off. She'd have to ask for more soon.

"Do you need me to get the nurse?" he asked, looking worried.

"No, it's just tender." She shook her head. She'd wait a little longer before requesting the medication. It made her a little nauseated.

"I hate to ask, but do you think you will be up to going to my cousin's wedding next week?" he asked.

"Of course. I'll just have to adjust my shoe choice to match the outfit I bought."

They shared a laugh. He had asked her around a month ago about the wedding. She had found a cute dress. There was no way she'd miss the wedding. It was going to be the day she'd meet his parents and family.

"I could use some coffee," Bradley announced and cleared his throat. He pulled back and patted her on the leg. "Want something?"

"Not sure if you can find anything right now." Jessica looked at her watch and cringed. "But if you can find something, I'll take the strongest of whatever they have."

"Knock, knock," a singsong voice called out.

"Come in," Jessica answered.

The curtain moved to the side to reveal a team of doctors standing in the doorway. A short African-American woman, with dark-almond skin wearing dark-blue scrubs and a white lab jacket with a surgical cap on her head, led the team.

"Hello, I'm Dr. Andrews. I'm from ortho." The woman gave a warm smile. She came to stand beside the bed.

She looked extremely young to be the staff physician, but Jessica wasn't going to say anything.

"Hi. So, what's the verdict, Doc?" Jessica asked, trying to remain calm. "Will I live?"

Chuckles went around the group.

"Oh, you most certainly will. I reviewed the films of your ankle, and the good news is that it's a hairline fracture. I don't think you need surgery," Dr. Andrews said with a wide grin.

"That is good news," Bradley muttered. He reached over and squeezed Jessica's hand.

Jessica was relieved it wasn't worse.

"What we're going to do is prescribe you wear a protective boot, rest, ice, and elevate it," Dr. Andrews advised. "You're also going to want to try to stay off of it for a few days until it doesn't hurt as bad. For the pain, you can use anything like ibuprofen."

"Okay, that sounds easy enough." Jessica hadn't had a chance to speak with Mr. Ablo yet, but she was confident he would make her take time off work.

"I'll see if one of the residents can find an appropriate boot for you. I want to see you in my office in a week." Dr. Andrews handed Jessica her business card. "Call my office in a day or two to set up the appointment."

"Thanks so much, Dr. Andrews." Jessica waved to her.

Dr. Andrews and her team left her room, closing the curtain again.

"That's not so bad news." Bradley blew out a deep breath.

"I know. I was praying she wouldn't say surgery." Jessica held the card to her chest. She would call first thing tomorrow after she woke up.

"I'll go get our coffee." Bradley stood from his perch on her bed. He leaned over and kissed her forehead, before exiting the room.

Leaning back, Jessica blew out a deep breath, utterly confused.

Here she was with a nice guy, who had lived through horrors she could never imagine, but yet, she had wanted a certain man to come and rescue her.

Was she wrong for praying for Iker to come to her rescue?

The second he had lifted her into his arms, she had felt at home.

But yet, he had walked away from her. Tore her heart to pieces and disappeared from her life.

Bradley was sweet, intelligent, and a true gentleman.

Iker was rough around the edges, fierce—

"She's sleeping," a loud whisper announced.

Jessica's eyes flew open to find Zain, Iker's friend, standing in the doorway. He had been there, too, as part of her rescue mission. He was a goofy nutball, and she liked him.

"Zain, how the hell are you?" She laughed.

He stepped into the room with a few other teammates.

If he was here, then that would mean—

Iker.

He crept into the room behind Mac.

It had been a long time since she had seen the guys. She took in the group and saw a couple new faces.

"I'm doing well, girl. If you wanted to see us, you

could have just called. Didn't have to go be in the middle of a robbery gone wrong." Zain rolled his eyes and came over to her.

Jessica burst out laughing.

Zain apparently still didn't have all of his marbles.

"It's been too long, Zain." She returned the hug. She glanced around the room. "Mac, Declan, Myles. Y'all look good. Where's Ash?"

"He had to run. The baby is teething and been driving Deana crazy," Declan said.

"Baby? Ash?" she squeaked.

Chuckles went around.

"We'll have to catch up sometime." Myles laughed.

"This I need to hear." Her gaze landed on Iker who remained in the back of the group. "Who're the newbies?" She jerked her chin to the woman and man she didn't know.

"Jess, this is Brodie and Jordan. They are the most recent recruits to our team," Zain introduced them.

"Hello." Jessica waved. Her gaze landed on the female SWAT officer. Jessica was impressed. These guys were badassess, and if this woman could hang with them, Jessica knew they would get along just fine. "Thanks for helping. That Halle chick was a real bitch."

"Not a problem at all." Jordan snickered. "It was my pleasure. I'm a professional bitch handler."

Jessica grinned at her.

Yes, they would get along just fine.

"We just wanted to check in on you," Mac said. He leaned back and folded his arms in front of his chest. "My wife is the manager of this department. If you're still here when she gets here in the morning, I'm sure she'll stop by."

"Wait a minute. Wife? Mac, you done went and got married?" Jessica was truly floored. In the two years she'd been separated from Iker, a lot had apparently changed.

Mac cracked one of his rare smiles. "And had a baby. A little girl. Her name is Nia."

Jessica's eyes couldn't grow any wider. She was in shock. Mac was married with a daughter?

"That's wonderful. I can't wait to meet them," Jessica said. She looked around the room. "Who else is married?"

Declan raised his hand. It was then she saw the wedding ring on his finger.

"Engaged," Myles announced, grinning.

Myles settled down?

Hell had officially frozen over.

"I know you don't know me, but engaged." Brodie chuckled.

"Still happily single," Zain muttered.

"Single here." Jordan laughed, fist-bumping Zain.

"So what's the verdict with the foot?" Myles asked.

"Hairline fracture. Someone should be coming by to put me in a boot." She grimaced, adjusting her leg. Her ankle throbbed. "Rest and relaxation are being prescribed by the good doctor."

"Well, we don't want to keep you." Zain patted her on the shoulder. "Follow doctor's orders and stay in touch. Just because you and the big guy over there aren't together, don't mean you get to forget about us."

Murmurs of agreement went around. Jessica felt horrible. She had figured that since she wasn't with Iker anymore, the guys wouldn't have wanted her around.

"Thanks for stopping by." She smiled and waved to the new members. "Nice to meet you."

Everyone filed out.

Except the tall, scruffy man with intense green eyes that were locked on her.

Iker.

She'd forgotten how good he looked in his all-black and that damn vest with SWAT on the front. It gave him a total badass appearance and completely took her breath away.

He stalked toward her. The way he moved reminded her of a predator.

"Jess," he began. He sat on the edge of the bed.

She scooted over to make more room for him. He focused on her and took her hand in his.

"What are you doing, Iker?" she whispered.

"I thought I was doing the right thing." He stared down at their entwined fingers.

Jessica bit her lip, immediately knowing what he was referring to.

"It's been two years. I haven't seen or heard from you until you —" She got choked up and closed her eyes for a moment. Panic filled her. She didn't want to break down again, and in front of him. She'd cried enough to fill a river. "You appear out of nowhere. What do you want from me?"

"You."

Jessica froze.

Their eyes connected. In his, she saw torture, doubt, and fear burning bright in his green orbs. Her heartbeat thundered in her ears. She was sure the same was reflected hers.

His thumb slowly stroked her skin, sending tremors through her body.

"Iker, what we had was in the past. You made the decision for us," she murmured.

"Jess, baby. I am willing to do whatever I have to do to get you back. I know you are with that guy, but I'm gonna prove we belong together." His steady gaze held hers.

Why now?

She had yearned to hear these words coming from him, but now it was two years after he'd walked away. They couldn't just turn back the hands of time and resume where they'd left off.

"We are two different people now, Iker," she said. Tears welled up in her eyes again. She blinked them back while shaking her head. "When you left me, that broke me, Iker. It took a long time before I was able to piece myself together. I'm not sure I want to go through that again if you change your mind."

"I'm so sure, Jess. Give me another chance."

"Say I do take you back. Then you leave again? I won't survive two heartbreaks, Iker."

He tried to gather her to him, but she held up a hand. There was no way she was strong enough to resist him once she leaned into him. That she already knew.

"We can go somewhere to talk. We can find neutral ground for us to just have a long conversation. I'll be an open book and tell you anything you want to know."

"I don't know, Iker." She exhaled, confusion clouding her better judgement. It was tempting because she wanted to hear him out.

"Jess, please. I need you."

A knock sounded, breaking the tense moment. The curtain pulled slightly to the side, revealing Bradley. His gaze flickered between Iker and Jess.

She was still in shock at Iker's declaration.

Iker glanced over his shoulder, a sad smile appearing on his lips.

"Good ol' Bradley's here," Iker announced. His voice was full of sarcasm and venom. He pushed up off of the bed and stood.

Their hands slowly slid apart. Jessica immediately missed the warmth of his hand.

"Later?" The intensity of his stare increased.

She knew what he was asking.

Her head jerked in a nod before she could even think.

Iker spun around on his heel and stalked from the room.

Jessica hesitantly met Bradley's gaze as he walked in. He sat her coffee cup down on the small bedside table next to her bed.

"I take it that there is more to him than him being an old friend." Bradley sat in the chair.

Jessica's shoulders slumped. Reaching for the coffee, she picked it up and took a sip without looking at him. "Yup."

12

"Brodie, please share what you found out," Mac instructed. He stood behind the podium in their briefing room.

With everything that had recently happened with Jess, Iker had forgotten his photo was found at the meth house.

It had been a couple of days since the kidnapping. After this meeting, Iker was going to look for the detective working the foiled art gallery heist. He needed to know who those people were and if they would be a danger to Jess in the future.

"One thing for sure is that house is definitely tied to the Demon Lords," Brodie announced.

The room grew silent. The gang was a pain in

their side. It was no surprise that the gang would be dealing with a meth house operation. They had their hands in a lot of the drug trade in the south-east.

"Tell us something we didn't already know," Ash muttered. He tipped his chair back, leaning on two legs. A scowl played on his face. Ash had been one of the unlucky ones in the room. The Demon Lords had it in for him. The dangerous group had kidnapped Ash one day when he was leaving the precinct. Lucky enough, their team was able to rescue him before he was executed.

"One thing I don't know is why good ol' Iker's photo was in the house." Brodie blew out a deep breath. He ran his hand through his thick hair, obviously stumped. It was rare for him to not find an answer.

"It's okay, man. They want some of me, they are welcome to try." Iker scoffed. He wasn't worried at all. He could protect himself just fine. Leaning forward, he rested his forearms on the table in front of him. "Don't stress yourself out."

"We need to figure this out," Mac snapped. His cold eyes turned to Iker. "We have too much bad blood with this organization. We need to be a step ahead of them."

"We don't want to risk anything, Iker," Dec commented.

"What do you want me to do? Hide in my house forever?" That was the last thing he would do. If the gang wanted him, he was sure they knew where he lived. They had caused enough troubles for him and his teammates.

"Well, we know that will never happen," Zain uttered. He shoved Iker with his elbow. "This son of a bitch is too damn stubborn for his own good."

Chuckles filled the air.

"Just like all of you. Don't act like any of you are any different," Iker said, glancing around.

Not one of his teammates disagreed with the statement. They all knew he was speaking the truth.

That's what made them all so damn tough.

They refused to take shit and would go down fighting.

"Brodie, keep working on it. I'm sure you'll figure it out," Mac said. He glanced down at the podium at the papers in front of him. "The task force the mayor and captain are putting together needs an ambassador. Any volunteers?"

The room became so quiet a pin could have dropped onto the floor and it would have been heard.

"What does the position entail?" Jordan raised her hand.

"First, you would represent SWAT and meet with other members of other divisions. They are wanting to ensure coordination with other departments is fluid. Maybe even work together on additional projects and missions."

"If no one else wants it..." Jordan casually looked around.

Everyone avoided her eyes.

"Job is all yours." Myles snickered.

"Pussies," Jordan teased. She turned back to face Mac. "Put me down. I guess I'll do it."

Applause went around. She held up her small middle finger, flipping them all off.

"Don't be like that, Jordan," Zain scoffed. "We knew you were the best person for the position."

She held up the finger again, not even looking in Zain's direction.

"Settle down." Declan eyed them. He stood and went over to the podium that Mac had abandoned. "Now, Officer Cruz's trial starts next week. We have been granted special permission to attend."

The room fell deathly quiet.

This was serious business. Their fellow officer

had been leaking sensitive information to the Demon Lords. They had never understood why the gang always appeared to be a step ahead of them. The gang had information that was only provided to the cops, and it led to them doing their own investigation on who was the precinct's mole.

"With all the dirt they found on him, this trial shouldn't even take long," Brodie said.

"Right," Ash said. "One day should be all they need."

It was a shame that a fellow cop had turned bad. The reasoning behind it was horrific. The gang had been holding the cop's sister hostage, drugging and prostituting her out. Cruz had thought if he did as they asked, he would have been able to save her sister. In the end, he had been too late.

"I'm sure justice will be served," Declan announced. "Any questions?"

Iker tuned out the rest of the conversations. He became lost in the memories of Jess in the emergency room. Those few moments they'd had alone, he'd tried to make her see how sorry he was, almost ended up begging.

He was willing to put his pride to the side to get her back.

Iker had meant every word he'd said.

I need you.

Those three words came from his soul.

He did need her.

A plan formed in his head. He was going to get his Jess back. He knew everything there was about her and planned to use it to his advantage.

He wasn't a patient man, but she was worth it.

"If there is nothing else, you're dismissed," Mac's voice broke through Iker's thoughts.

Iker stood. He needed to run over and find out who was overseeing Jessica's case.

He headed for the door, pausing when his name was called.

"Yo, Iker. Where you bolting off to?" Zain walked over to him.

They exited the room and walked down the hall toward the bullpen.

"I need to find someone," Iker muttered.

"It wouldn't have to do something with the art gallery investigation, would it?" Zain asked.

"Brother, you know me too well." Iker slapped him on the back.

"Well, hell. I better come with you."

Iker grinned. He always could count on his friend.

"I WANT you to take two weeks off, paid." Mr. Ablo's voice came through the line.

"I don't really think I need that much time, sir," Jessica sputtered. Her boss was wonderful and was pushing for her to rest and relax, just as the doctor had ordered.

How dare he be such a wonderful man.

"I'm serious, Jessica. We are going to keep the gallery closed for another few days. I have a security firm coming in to make the gallery safer," he announced. The robbery had unfortunately made the news, and it could do some damage to their reputation.

Jessica was already planning for when she returned to work. They would have to go on damage control and call the vendors who were schedule to lend the items to the gallery.

"Let me come in. I will stay off my feet and sit in a chair to help—"

"No. Absolutely not." Mr. Ablo's firm voice cut her off. "This is fully paid. I feel horrible that you all went through that experience. I don't know what I would have done if someone was terribly hurt, or worse, killed."

Jessica slumped back against her couch. She glanced down at her foot encased in the gray boot which sat on her coffee table. It wasn't the most fashionable thing she'd worn, but it would have to be on for now.

She grimaced, her calf muscle itching.

"None of this was your fault, so please don't feel guilty," she said. Her eyes fluttered shut briefly. "Fine. If you want me off of work, let's do at least a week, then we'll reassess how I'm doing."

"Jessica, you are one stubborn woman." Mr. Ablo exhaled sharply. "Fine. One week, then we will talk. I don't want see you at the gallery or hear from you until seven days from now."

"Yes, Mr. Ablo." Jessica grinned. She pumped her fist in the air, knowing she would be back to work in about a week. She wasn't going to push it before then with her ankle still being tender, but seven days should be just what she needed.

It wasn't like she couldn't do research for her next artist spotlight.

She didn't have to be in the office for that.

"Talk you in a week." He disconnected the call.

Jessica sighed and dropped her phone onto her couch.

Seriously.

What the hell was she going to do for a full week?

The doorbell sounded.

"Are you shitting me?" She groaned. Who the hell could that be? She wiggled to the edge of the couch and slowly stood. She tried not to put too much weight on her bad ankle. She hobbled down the hallway to her front door.

"I'm coming," she called out. She glanced at the iced-glass windows and was able to make out the figure waiting behind the door.

Darby.

She made it to the door and opened it.

Her friend stood there with a wide grin on her lips.

"Hey, girl! I'm here to look after you." Darby flew into the house. Her hair was currently plaited into two braids that disappeared down her back. In her hands were a few grocery bags.

"Who said I needed a babysitter?" Jessica closed the door and tried not to smile. She loved having her friend over, and if she wanted to come to hang, then she was all for it.

"We are having mimosas and fruit." Darby held up the bags and headed farther into the house.

Jessica trailed behind her, watching her disappear into the kitchen. The sounds of cabinets opening and shutting greeted her as she walked in.

"You don't have to work today?" Jessica asked. She made her way slowly over to the island and took a seat.

Darby flew around the room grabbing everything she needed. She was no stranger to Jessica's kitchen.

"Not today, so I figured I'd come over here and see what you were up to and if you needed me to do anything for you."

"That's sweet of you." Jessica leaned her forearms on the island.

"I'm just so glad that you are okay. I couldn't believe it when I heard the gallery was robbed. Did they get anything?"

Jessica shuddered, the memories of that night just refusing to go away. Since she'd come home from the emergency room, she hadn't really gotten much sleep.

"Nothing of extreme value. The couple who were able to get away took a few paintings, but insurance will pay for them."

The detective who had come to speak with her had shared with her that he would be contacting her later to show her some photos of potential suspects to see if she could point any of them out.

She didn't think she could, but she would try to help.

"Here you go." Darby slid Jessica's drink across the way to her. It looked much lighter than the mimosas she was used to ordering when they went out for brunch. "Cheers."

They clinked glasses.

Jessica drank hers and sputtered.

"Girl, this is basically all champagne." Jessica laughed.

Darby tossed her a wink and took a sip of her drink.

"You know my recipe calls for champagne and the aroma of orange juice," Darby joked.

Jessica shook her head at her friend. Darby placed a platter of mixed fruit in front of her. It was filled with berries, melons, and watermelon.

"What am I going to do with you? Jessica popped a piece of watermelon into her mouth. The flavor exploded on her tongue. It was sweet and juicy. Just the way she loved watermelons.

"So, what's new besides the you know what?" Darby used air quotes with her question.

"Well, if you must know, Iker showed up at the event." Jessica reached for another piece of watermelon.

"He did?" Darby gasped. "What did you do?" She flew around the island with her drink in her hand and took the seat directly next to Jessica.

"I know I had originally said he would be there, but I didn't really think he would show up." Jessica sighed. She took another sip of the bubbly drink and stared off into space. "But boy did he show up."

Her memories took her back to her office and him pressing her against the door.

"Oh, no. You can't stare off like that and not share the details. Something happened between you two." Darby nudged her with her elbow. "Fess up."

Jessica rested her head in her hands. She was so confused and didn't know what she wanted at the moment.

There was no way she would share the intimate details of what had occurred in her office. She had to draw a line somewhere.

"One hand, I know I should leave that boy alone. I won't be able to handle another breakup should he leave me again," she began. She lifted her head and glanced at Darby. "I have a boyfriend. A good one, but he had me so confused until the other night when we were in the emergency room."

"Y'all had sex in the hospital?" Darby gasped, a grin spreading across her face.

"What? God, no!" Jessica giggled. She realized she hadn't told Darby what had happened the other night when she had planned the date that had gone wrong. She quickly went over her embarrassing ordeal.

"In the middle of you putting the moves on him, he gets up and leaves?" Darby's mouth was practically on the floor. "What kind of man does not take advantage of a woman throwing herself at him? So what gives? He's still holding on to that V-card?"

Jessica broke out in a fit of laughter at her friend's expression. Darby was never one to hold any punches.

"No, according to him, he is not a virgin. Hell, he had me thinking it was me." Soon she grew serious, thinking of the story he had shared with her. "Apparently, he was the subject of violent bullying. His attackers tied him to a fence, poured lighter fluid on him, and set him on fire. He's burned pretty bad on his legs."

"Have you seen him yet?" Darby asked quietly, her smile faded.

"No. I haven't." She shook her head. "He just admitted that was the reason he had done the hundred-yard dash out of my house."

"Okay, Miss Thang. What else?"

"What else?" Jessica's eyebrows rose.

"You're keeping something else from me."

"You know me so well." Jessica sighed. She finished off the champagne, sitting her glass down. "Well, Iker and the guys had stopped by the emergency room. Once the team left, Iker stayed behind."

"Oh, goodness. Hold on. I need another drink." Darby hopped down off her chair and raced to the other side. She eyed Jessica's empty glass. "Want a refill?"

"Sure. Why the hell not? It's not like I have to go to work or be driving anywhere today." Jessica giggled. She pushed her glass across the counter to Darby. "Anyway, Iker basically told me he wants me back."

"I told you so!" Darby exclaimed, jumping up and down in place. She turned to the fridge and placed the juice inside it. She flew back to her seat, sitting their glasses down on the counter. "What did you say?"

"I don't know." Jessica's shoulders slumped. She blew out a deep breath and reached for her glass. She took a sip of the chilled drink. "I'm just confused."

"Don't pressure yourself. Follow your heart." Darby rested a hand on Jessica's arm. "No one can make you make a decision. Only you know what will be best for you."

"That's the problem, even I don't know what the best option is."

"Well, I for one don't pity you. A woman with two handsome men, who are complete opposites, vying for you must be a hard life to lead." Darby snorted.

"Darby!" Jessica laughed, elbowing her friend.

"Where is your boyfriend? Why isn't he here taking care of you?"

"He had to go to Daytona for business."

Bradley had felt guilty for leaving. She had encouraged him to go. It was for his job and important. She was fine. Her parents and brother were going to be stopping in to make sure she had everything she needed.

"He should be gone for two days, and then I'm sure he'll be here."

The doorbell sounded.

"You sit here. I'll go answer it." Darby got up and headed out of the kitchen.

Darby's words rang again in her head.

Follow your heart.

But where would it lead her?

Sounds of laughter filled her house. Her family

was here. With a grin, Jessica slowly stepped down from her chair and headed toward the voices.

Seeing her family was what she needed at the moment.

Her heart? She'd worry about that later.

13

Iker sat in his truck and stared at Jessica's house. He wasn't sure what he was doing, but he had to speak with her.

He had spoken with the detective who had been assigned to the robbery. Detective Clayton Best had been on the force well over twenty years. He was one of the officers who had taken Iker under his wing when Iker first joined. Iker was pleased that someone he trusted was handling the case.

Clay informed him the suspects who had been apprehended were not talking.

It would seem they were after a valuable painting that was locked up in the vault. The owner of the art gallery had shared with Clay what was inside. The black market was hot, and it was thought they would have stolen the painting and sold it for big money.

Who the thieves worked for, they were still in the dark. Clay had promised Iker he would keep him in the loop once Iker explained to him the relationship between him and Jessica.

Iker glanced over at the bag resting on his passenger seat. Memories of her sitting in that hospital bed had stayed with him the entire weekend. It had taken everything he had not to go to her house. He figured Bradley or her family would be there.

Today, he could no longer stay away.

He'd brought something he knew she wouldn't be able to resist.

Glancing back at her house, he saw there weren't any cars in her driveway.

Good. He didn't feel like dealing with the boyfriend. He had meant every word he had said to her the other night.

He wanted her back and would be willing to do whatever he needed in order to succeed.

Snatching up the bag, he exited his vehicle. He slammed the door shut and walked to her house. The yard was well-manicured, as always. Jess loved working with her hands. Her flowers and plants were a joy and a stress reliever for her.

He jogged up the stairs and paused at the door. He slid his shades to the top of his head and sent up a prayer.

When you left me, that broke me, Iker.

The painful tremble in her voice had just about put him on his knees. Leaving her had been the hardest thing he had ever done in his life.

Mentally he had entered Hell. Being without Jessica had torn him to shreds. He couldn't function, he couldn't think, only living on autopilot.

Work had been a blur. He hadn't cared about the risks they were taking. He dove in, headfirst.

When his brothers needed help when it came to dangerous off-the-book missions to save loved ones, he was one of the first to volunteer.

Being in her presence again showed him how much of a mistake he had made.

Iker drew in a deep breath and pressed the doorbell.

His heart raced with the thought of seeing Jess again.

How had he lived this long without her?

The door swung open.

"Iker?" Jessica gasped. She stood there with a surprised look on her face.

Iker's tongue stuck to the roof of his mouth. He couldn't take his eyes off her. She was as beautiful as always. Her short hair appeared as if she had combed her fingers through it. Her large brown eyes were locked on him.

She had on a pair of black leggings, a short t-shirt that showed off her midriff, her lone foot encased in a soft boot cast, the other one bare showing off her white-painted toenails.

It was a simple outfit, but fuck.

His cock was taking notice of her.

Anything Jess wore turned him on.

"Jess." He cleared his throat and held out the bag. He felt like a big goofball, staring at her.

She glanced down at it first then took it from him.

"I thought you might need this," he said.

She opened the bag and peered back at him. A small smile played on her lips.

"Ben and Jerry's ice cream?" She leaned against the doorjamb and eyed him. "Is this supposed to be your peace offering?"

He jerked his head in a nod. His heart thundered. Would she let him in, or would she shut the door in his face?

"Those are your favorite flavors," he murmured.

A car went down the street. It pulled into the driveway a few doors down.

Jessica paused for a moment. Her gaze slowly roamed his body. Iker held back from puffing his chest out. He knew what she saw in front of her. He had spent as much free time as he had working out. He took great pride in his appearance, and it had paid off.

Heat flared in Jessica's eyes.

He knew that look.

It was the same one she used to give him before they'd fuck each other until they could barely move.

Without a word, she pushed the door open and moved back.

Iker celebrated on the inside. This was a step in the right direction.

He brushed past her and went inside. She closed the door behind him.

"Just because you come with Ben and Jerry's, doesn't mean you will be getting what you want," she said. She walked past him and headed toward the kitchen.

He grinned.

Jess was just as stubborn as he was.

"It at least got me in the door." He chuckled. "I was half expecting you to greet me with a gun."

Iker had purchased her a Glock 19 which was just the right size for her. He'd taken her to the shooting ranges multiple times to ensure she was comfortable with it.

She had loved tagging along with him to go to the gun range.

"I had thought about it, but then I would have had to go get it out of the safe," she replied haughtily. "With this thing on my foot, I'm not as fast as I once was."

He leaned back against the counter watching her try to choose which ice cream she wanted. He had purchased four pints of the stuff. Jess was addicted to chocolate, and when it was in ice cream, she was in love. She finally picked one and put the other three in her freezer.

She opened the pint and pulled a spoon out of her drawer. Taking her first bite, she rested against the island and stared at him. Those brown eyes were shooting daggers at him.

He was a big man and would take whatever she dished out to him. She had every right to be pissed off at him.

"You wanted to talk." She took another bite and motioned around the room with her spoon. "This isn't neutral ground."

"That I did offer. Up to going somewhere with me?" He glanced around the kitchen. "Or is your little boyfriend going to be coming to take care of you?"

Iker wondered where the dipshit was. Why wasn't he here taking care of Jess? Had it been Iker, he wouldn't have left her side after what had just happened.

"He's out of town." She scooped another spoonful of the chocolate ice cream into her mouth.

"After your traumatic experience four days ago and he's not around?" Iker smirked.

"That's none of your business." Her chin rose slightly. Her brown eyes narrowed on him.

Jess was brandishing her claws.

Iker pushed off the counter and ambled over to her. She stiffened, eyeing him warily. Resting his hands on the ledge behind her, he trapped her between him and the island.

"You are my business," he murmured. Iker wasn't above using his size to get what he wanted. He always loved how much smaller she was in comparison to him. The heat that flared in her eyes told him everything he needed to know.

She was still attracted to him. She casually sat her ice cream and spoon behind her. Her head tilted back to allow her to meet his gaze.

"Not anymore."

Oh, yes, Jess had her claws out. Her glare would have pushed back a weaker man, but not Iker. He was here for the fight to win her back.

"Last I checked I was with Bradley."

"Really?" he snarled.

His control snapped.

He shot his hand out, gripping her neck. Her nostrils flared, desire blaring in her eyes.

He bent his head down, his mouth brushing her ear.

"Where is he?" He closed the gap between them, pressing his pelvis to her stomach. His cock was long and hard, straining against his jeans. Her audible gasp fueled the need to possess her. "If you were mine, I would never have left your side. I'd be right here with you."

"Iker," she groaned.

"I'd show how thankful I was that nothing happened to you, by worshiping your body." He slid his tongue down the column of her neck. A tremor racked through her body. He nipped her skin with his teeth. "We wouldn't leave the bed until I was sure there wasn't one inch of your body marred. I'd bury my cock so far into you that we wouldn't know where either of us began or ended."

"Iker," she repeated. Her small hands rested on his waist, digging into his top of his jeans.

He trailed kisses on her jawline, ending on her lips. He brushed her mouth with his. Her lips immediately opened for him.

The kiss was one of carnal passion.

Iker's chest rumbled his pleasure at the feeling of Jessica in his arms again. Her soft whimper met his ears. He tilted his head to the side, deepening the kiss.

It wouldn't take much for him to pick her up and carry her to her bedroom. He remembered the layout of her home.

But why waste time?

Sex in the kitchen was always a favorite of his.

He tore his lips from her mouth. She remained still, her lips swollen, her eyes closed.

Iker bent down again, pressing a hard kiss to her lips.

He nuzzled his face into the crook of her neck, breathing in her scent.

"He doesn't know what to do with this body of yours." It angered him to think that Bradley-boy has touched Jessica's curvy body intimately. Iker vowed to erase all memories of the other man from her memory. "I can't stand the thought of another man's hands on you."

Jessica stiffened. Her hands slid between them, pushing with all of her might.

Iker stepped back, confused.

"You can't stand what?" She gasped. She stared at him with wide eyes, her chest rising and falling fast.

Fuck. What did he say?

His heartbeat was thundering in his ears.

"Jessica," he murmured, reaching for her, but she sidestepped him.

"Correct me if I'm wrong, but you just said you can't stand the thought of another man's hands on me. So let me ask you, Iker Baldwin. Were there any women after me?" Her eyes filled with rage.

He was in trouble.

Iker rubbed his face. There was no point in trying to lie. If he was going to earn her trust again, he was going to have to come clean.

"I will never lie to you, Jessica," he began. He closed his eyes briefly before reopening them.

Tears flowed down her cheeks as she waited for the answer he felt she already knew.

He reached for her, but she brushed his hands away.

A hiccup escaped her.

"Answer me. Were there other women?" She bit out the question through clenched teeth.

"Only after we broke up," he admitted. The cry that tore from her almost brought him to his knees.

"Why?" she screamed. She swung on him, the blows landing on his chest.

He took every one, knowing he deserved it and more. He knew she wasn't asking why there was women, but why had he left her.

He swept her in his arms, refusing to let her walk away from him. He held her tight as her body was racked with sobs. She continued to struggle, but he held on until she finally slumped against him as if the fight had left her. His own eyes became scratchy.

Iker just held on to Jessica. He refused to give her up.

They would get through this.

He'd be damned if she didn't take him back.

Iker lost track of time of how long they stood there. He rubbed his hand on her back, trying to comfort her as best as he could.

She finally quieted. Iker reached down and tipped her chin up so she could meet his eyes.

"Jessica. There is nothing I can say to make up for of the hurt and pain I've caused you." He was sincere in everything he said. If he could take away the pain, he would. He wiped the trails of tears from her face.

A shudder passed through her.

"Ever since you left, it bothered me. What did I do for you to decide to just leave me?" She blinked again, fat tears spilling from her eyes.

He blew out a deep breath. He cupped her cheeks in his hand, staring into her eyes.

"Not a damn thing," he admitted. It was never anything Jessica did. He had to make her see why he'd made the choice he had.

Two years ago, when he had left, he had been scared of her becoming a mark to the Demon Lords. Now, he knew he wouldn't have anything to worry about. His brothers and sister in blue would ensure she remained safe, just like all of the other SWAT spouses.

"Come with me," he said. "We'll go somewhere to talk. Please?"

She studied him and jerked her head in a nod.

"Let me get my purse."

14

Jessica opened her eyes feeling the truck slow to a halt. Soft country music was playing on the radio. She didn't know how long she had slept.

The second Iker had merged onto the highway, with the wind in her hair, her eyes drifted shut.

She gently wiped at her mouth to make sure she wasn't drooling. She pushed up higher in her seat and peered out the window. Iker guided the vehicle onto a small road.

"Where are we?" she asked.

"Welcome back to the land of the living." Iker smirked, glancing over at her. "You don't recognize where we are?"

He pulled into a parking lot and found a spot.

"Lake Murray?" She brushed her bangs from her eyes. Her heart skipped a beat. It had been one of their favorite places to come. There was so much to do here where they could get outside and experience nature.

"Bingo." He exited the vehicle and made his way around to her side.

Jessica didn't know what to expect from this day. She had sworn she wouldn't have a meltdown in front of him, and before she knew it, she was sobbing in his arms.

Way to go, Jess.

Iker opened the door and held out his hand.

"Are you okay?" he asked. He pushed his sunglasses to the top of his head, his green-eyed gaze landing on her.

"Yeah." She placed her hand in his and allowed him to help her from the large truck. She rested the strap of her purse across her chest, allowing it to hang at her side. Jessica looked around. She hadn't been here since they had separated. "What do you have planned today?"

"I figured once we got here, we'd play it by ear. We could go on a gentle walk, grab a bite to eat, or whatever you want to do."

Jessica loved the nature trails. It would be nice

and allow them to have that conversation he'd promised. She would try her best to hold back on the waterworks.

"Well, I'm glad I wore sensible shoes." She pointed down at her sneaker and the other boot-covered foot. "How about the nature trails first then get something to eat?"

"Sounds good to me." Iker stepped forward and bent down. He kissed her lips. He withdrew slightly, his eyes boring into her. "Thank you for coming with me, Jess."

She nodded.

He took her hand in his and led her down to the park. Walking together, hands entwined, almost felt as if they were still together. The path he chose for her would be the easy one. He must not want her to experience any pain. It was one families with little kids took.

They finally made it to the trail. Jessica loved it because it allowed them to see nature undisturbed. They opted to take the one trail that put them closer to the lake's edge.

It was a beautiful day, and there were plenty of people taking advantage of the good weather at the lake. They strolled along in silence. Birds flew overhead, while the sound of nature surrounded them. Tall trees and blue skies was the perfect backdrop.

"We're on neutral ground now," Jessica said, breaking the silence.

"That we are." Iker tightened his grip on her hand. He exhaled and drew her closer to him. "A few years ago, SWAT was in deep. A war was starting between us and the gang, the Demon Lords."

Jessica's head flew to face Iker. What the hell did that have to do with their relationship?

"Okay," she murmured. Confused, she just decided to let him continue.

"The gang is extremely dangerous and don't give a shit about anyone but themselves. We've tangled enough with them that they put a target on each member of SWAT."

"What? Are you sure?" This was getting crazy. It sounded like something from a movie.

"Oh, yeah. I'm quite sure. I've been a cop for a long time and have been threatened before. But this was different. The Demon Lords don't just come after you, they come after everyone you love."

Iker halted, facing her. He brought her hand up to his lips, pressing a kiss to the back of it. They stood beside a wooden fence next to a sign that provided some educational material on the trees and flowers nearby.

"My gut feeling was they would come for me, by going through you."

"Iker—"

Her heart raced at the pure torture on his face.

"We were at war with a gang who is one of the most dangerous organizations in the country. We're talking human trafficking, drugs, murder, extortion. Every time we raided them, we caused them to lose a lot of money. In the millions of dollars. Me and every member of my team knew what we are getting into when we put on our vests." He released her hand and stepped away. He shoved a trembling hand through his hair and took a few steps away from her.

Jessica began to understand the sacrifice he had made. Her heart hurt for their lost relationship, the promises they had made to each other that were broken, and everything they had dreamed of that didn't come to fruition.

"I didn't want them to use you to hurt me," he said. His stared down at the ground. His shoulders slumped.

She moved to him, unable to remain away from him. She stopped at his side, gently touching his arm.

He lifted his head and stared at her. "I had to

distance myself from you so they wouldn't link you to me. If they would have come for you and took you from me…" His voice trailed off, ending on a hitch.

"Oh, Iker." She went into his arms. His warm embrace surrounded her. She held on tight, lending him her strength.

He pressed his lips to the top of her head.

"I would give up everything to make sure you remained unharmed. I'd lose my fucking mind if they hurt you." His lips brushed her hair as he spoke. He tipped her chin up, forcing her to look up at him. "That's why I walked away from you. I was willing to give you up so you could have a long, safe future."

"Iker, this is the conversation we should have had two years ago. I love that you were thinking of me, but there was one problem with your plan," she whispered. Tears blurred her vision. She blinked them back as a shudder raced through her.

"What is that?" he asked.

"You constructed and designed a plan you thought would work, but you didn't even ask what I wanted. You didn't even give me a chance to make a choice about my future—our future. You just took it upon yourself to decide what was best for me."

"Jessica—"

"Let me finish. Because you felt leaving me was

the only way to protect me, you never realized how much your leaving me would hurt me. You caused me more pain than anyone ever could." She was practically shouting by this point.

Jessica stepped away from him. She covered her mouth with her hand to keep from screaming her frustration.

Iker was an intelligent man, a highly decorated police officer with the awards to showcase it, but when it came to their lives, he'd made a rash decision that had put them both through hell.

"Jess, baby. I made the wrong decision. I know that. It wasn't easy for me either." He rested his hands on her shoulders.

She opened her eyes and stared out at the landscape before them but didn't see any of it. Memories of her days after he left surfaced. There had been days she hadn't wanted to get dressed or eat, but Darby was there to kick her ass and make sure she did.

"Your decision changed our lives forever," she whispered. "You had no right to do that. We were supposed to be a team."

"I know, and there is nothing I can do to change the past. I went to a dark place when I left. I didn't recognize the man I had become. There were days I was drinking every day. So much so that I would black out and wake up not remembering anything from the night before. Looking back, I don't know how I didn't get fired or demoted."

She spun around and took him in.

"Iker." She sighed.

"You asked me if there were women after you. Yes. Do I remember them all? No." He shook his head. He reached up and cupped her face in his large hand. "None of them meant anything. I was spiraling out of control, and it was Zain who pulled me up from Hell. He kicked my ass good, too."

"I'm glad he was there for you," she admitted. "Darby refused to give up on me."

"Both of them are more stubborn than we are." Iker chuckled.

Their laughter broke up the tension. They stared at each other, lost in their own world.

"So where does this leave us?" he asked.

"I don't know, Iker." She shook her head and backed away slightly from him.

A family walked along the trail. The couple were holding hands while their two small children ran ahead. A small twinge of jealousy coursed through Jessica. She had hoped at her age, she would have at least started her family by now.

"I want you back, Jess. I'm not going to stop saying it until I have you."

"Iker, have you forgot about Bradley?" she asked. She was in a relationship with a man who was trying to do everything he could to please her. Just because Iker came back into her life demanding to have her back, it didn't mean she would come running.

The night at the ED, when Iker had left, she'd shared everything with Bradley. He'd taken it in stride and nodded. He only had one question for her.

Was she going to go back to Iker?

She had responded no.

But now, she was here with Iker.

What did this all mean?

Iker scowled and moved closer to her. He slid a fingertip over her cheek, trailing it down to her neck.

"Wanna grab lunch?"

Jessica's stomach chose that minute to rumble. He smirked at the sound. She fought a smile, rolling her eyes instead.

"Sure. I'm famished."

He took her by the hand, leading her toward the path that would take them to the restaurants.

"This isn't the end of this conversation, Jess. I intend to win you back."

IKER HELD Jessica's hand as they walked through the restaurant. Even dressed down in leggings, a t-shirt, and a sneaker, she was turning heads. Iker tossed a few frosty glares at men sitting at the bar on their way past.

He didn't like the way they were staring at her.

The protective nature he always had around her was at full force.

"Oh, my goodness. That was so good." Jessica patted her belly and sighed.

"I could tell you enjoyed yourself." He grinned.

"Hey!" She slapped his arm with the back of her hand. "What is that supposed to mean?"

He gave a nod to the hostess at the front and guided Jessica through the door. The fresh air met them as they exited the building.

"I'm just kidding. I always loved how you enjoyed food."

She rolled her eyes, walking alongside him.

Iker felt they had made a breakthrough today. The conversation over their early supper flowed well. They were able to catch up on their families and their lives. Iker shared with her everything about him, his SWAT buddies.

It felt good to just talk with her. It was something he had truly missed. She had a way about her that when he spoke about anything, she made him feel as if he were valued and appreciated.

He glanced over his shoulder casually.

The entire time they had been at the lake, he hadn't wanted to let on that someone was following them. Whoever the men were tailing them, must be observing them only. They had yet to get close to them or approach.

If they did, Iker would be ready for them. It was rare he left the house without weapons concealed on his body. With all of the events that had happened over the past few years with his teammates, he wasn't chancing getting caught slipping.

"Anything else you want to do while we're here?" he asked.

Jess tilted her head to the side as she decided. Iker loved how cute she was.

"Let's go down to the marina and watch the boats sail by." She turned her big brown eyes on him, and he was lost in them.

"Sure thing, pretty lady." He pulled her the direction of the marina. One of the restaurants located on it had an open deck that allowed them an upfront and close view of the water and the boats. They had a nice bar and played music.

They made their way through the place and headed out to the deck. There were tons of people enjoying the music and sitting at the bar. Jessica laughed, rushing as fast as she could with that boot on to get a good spot near the wooden railing.

Iker stood beside her, barely taking in the view. He was captivated by Jessica's beauty. Her genuine smile, her short dark hair blowing in the wind. She leaned forward with her eyes shut and inhaled.

"I've missed coming here," she murmured.

"Yeah, me, too." He turned away and took in the sailboats gliding by out in the distance.

The atmosphere was a fun one. Popular music blared through the speakers. There was a small crowd of people dancing on the deck having a good time.

Iker scanned the deck, and off in the corner on the opposite side, he caught sight of the two men who had been chaperoning from afar.

Iker took his phone from his back pocket and acted as if he were taking a selfie. He snapped a good picture of the two before they even realized it.

He pulled open a text and sent a message with the photo to Brodie.

Check these boys out for me, will ya?

Brodie immediately responded.

What the hell are you up to?

Iker shook his head. He didn't have time to explain. He didn't want Jess to worry.

I'll explain later. They've been tailing us all day.

He slid his phone back in his pocket and turned back to Jess. She was swaying to the music as she observed the boats sailing by.

Unable to resist, he moved behind her and rested his hands on the railing, trapping her in his arms. The move hid her from the prying eyes of the men watching them.

"Iker," she sighed.

He closed the distance between them. It felt so good to have her back in his arms.

"What?" he asked. He dropped his face forward and nuzzled the crook of her neck. "I'm not doing anything inappropriate."

His cock certainly wanted to. He was as stiff as a board and wasn't hiding it from her. Her ass swayed slowly, teasing him.

"But I know how your mind works." She leaned back into his embrace.

He celebrated on the inside with her unconscious move.

"Is that so?" He wrapped his arm around her, holding her in place. "Tell me what I'm thinking."

She twirled around and faced him. She grinned and shook her head.

"Oh, no. You want me to say dirty, nasty things that will lead to nothing but a world of trouble."

Her cheeky smile had him grinning back at her. He brushed her bangs from her eyes and saw the heated look of desire in them.

He was weakening her defenses.

It would be only a matter of time until she submitted to him.

"It won't lead to trouble, Jess," he murmured. He popped a chaste kiss on her lips. "It will lead to us to a bed and not leaving for at least twenty-four hours."

"You don't have to walk me up to the door." Jessica pulled her key from her purse.

Iker took her hand and assisted her up the stairs.

"Are you serious? You do know how dangerous it is to walk from the car to your door, right?"

They fell into a fit of laughter. Jessica would admit she would have thought she would be nervous at the moment. Him walking her to the door made it feel as if they were on a date.

They arrived at her door. It was getting late with the sun almost setting. Deep down, Jessica didn't want the day to end, but it must. There was no way in hell she could invite Iker inside.

If she did, she knew where it would end up.

Her pushing him down on her bed so she could strip his clothes off.

There was only so much teasing she could take from him. Iker knew exactly what he was doing.

Taking her to their favorite place.

Good food. A few drinks.

Kisses. Touches.

Dammit!

She had to think of something to calm her damn body down.

Bradley's face came to mind.

Crap!

It was like a splash of cold water on her face. She stood to her full height and smiled up at him. No, she wouldn't be inviting him in.

"Today was interesting," she began, folding her arms in front of her.

"That it was," Iker replied. He took the keys from her hand and slid them into the door.

"Iker, I don't think—"

"I'm not." He shook his head. He leaned down and kissed her.

Jess gasped, shocked at the gentleness of his lips. She fell into the kiss. She gripped his shirt. His mouth slid over hers slowly. A moan slipped from her, and before she knew it, he was pulling away from her.

"I have to go."

Jessica stood there in shock. All she could do was nod and step into her house. She gripped her purse strap in her hand.

He must have to go into work. A few times she'd watched him get text messages and took a call away from her.

"Be safe out there," she said. She cleared her throat, coming to her senses. It was best for him to leave.

"Always, babe. Now close the door and lock it." His steady green eyes were on her.

Deep in them, she saw the promise of what was to come.

Her stomach clenched.

Shutting the door, she remained there. She brushed the lace curtain aside and watched him jog back to his truck.

His lean form was God's gift to women.

He hopped in the truck. The lights flashed on, and he backed out the driveway. With a honk of the horn, he went flying down the street. Jessica continued staring off in his direction until she no longer saw his brake lights.

"What am I to do?" She leaned her head against the window, and a sigh escaped her.

She glanced down at her watch and decided she'd take a nice hot bath and find something on the television.

Her schedule was all screwed up since she didn't have to go into work. It was nice to be off, but she'd rather be out scouting the town for new artists.

After grabbing a very tall glass of wine, she headed into her bedroom and stripped her clothes off.

Within minutes her bath was ready. The bathroom was set for someone needing to relax. Candles lit, soft music paying on her phone.

"It's time for me time." She sighed, sliding deep into the bubble bath. The warm water felt marvelous on her ankle. It was slightly tender.

Reaching for her wine, she took a sip of it and relaxed back against her bath pillow.

There was so much on her mind, she needed this time alone. No work. No family or friends over. Just the quietness of her house—

The music playing on her phone was interrupted by it ringing. She knew who it was without looking since she liked to give everyone their one special ringtone.

Sitting forward, she snagged her phone from the small table next to her tub.

"Hello?" she answered. She hit the speakerphone button and placed her phone back down.

"Jessica. How are you?" Bradley's smooth voice greeted her.

"I'm doing well." She sipped on her wine again. "How is the trip going?"

"It's just work. I've been missing you and wanted to see what you have been up to."

She stared at the ceiling. She didn't really want to share with him where she had gone and who she had spent the day with.

But she wasn't a liar either.

If anything, her boyfriend deserved to know the truth.

Well, at least most of it.

"I had lunch with Iker today." Her words were greeted with silence at first.

"I thought you said you weren't getting back together with him?" Bradley's voice dropped a few decibels.

She was sure this wasn't an ideal time to bring this up, but she needed to share this with him.

"We are not, but I need closure. I'm sure this isn't what you wanted to hear, but he was a big part of my past, and the way our relationship ended, I truly never understood what went wrong. Or if it was something I did. You know Darby is a counselor and she helped me through that period in my life. She had said one day we would need to have the talk. I would need closure, and that should help me move on."

There was a pregnant pause, then he spoke again.

"Darby sounds like a smart woman." He gave a dry chuckle.

Bradley and Darby had met a few times. Bradley was aware he wasn't Darby's favorite person, but he was trying to get in on her good graces.

"She is and she was right. Talking with him today helped me see that it wasn't me."

"Of course it wasn't," Bradley snapped. His voice softened. "Iker was a fool to leave you. I guess I should be thanking him. If it wasn't for him leaving, it would never have opened the door for me to meet you."

"That's true." She smiled. "Tell me all about Daytona."

She needed to get them off the subject of her and Iker. It wasn't fair for him to be putting in the work to make their relationship work and she was still hung up on her ex. She was going to find a way to keep Iker at arm's length.

Those lips and hips of his were too dangerous. Whenever she was around him, her brain went haywire.

"Well, it's not much to tell. Business meeting after business meeting. I did have dinner at one place that I would be willing to go to again. Food was wonderful." Bradley went on to speak about the conference and the presentation he'd given.

The water was beginning to cool, so she began washing up while he spoke.

"This cousin of yours who is getting married, are you guys close?" she asked. She lifted her leg and ran her sudsy loofa along it.

"We grew up together. Jessica, are you taking a bath?" Bradley asked, his voice suddenly becoming husky.

Jessica grinned. Men were all the same. He'd heard one sound and zeroed in on it.

"I certainly am. I was in the middle of having some me time, soaking and relaxing in my bubble bath."

"Why didn't you say something?" He cleared his throat. "I would have called you back."

"Nonsense. I wanted to hear about your day. I'm sure you had more fun than me." She chuckled.

"I'm not so sure."

"Oh, please. I'm sure you were down there being wined and dined by that company. Rubbing elbows with rich bankers. How can that not be fun?"

"You are too silly, Jessica," he murmured. He exhaled slowly. "I do miss you. I was worried about you and that foot in a boot."

"I'm doing fine. It will take more than falling down some stairs in heels to keep me down." She finished bathing and stood, reaching for her towel.

"Honey, do you want me to let you go?" Bradley asked.

"Not unless you want to," she said, wrapping her towel around her body. She quickly got out and opened the spout to drain the tub. Today was a bit much on her body and on her brain.

Scooping up her phone and empty glass, she padded into her bedroom. She sat them down on her nightstand and grasped her nightgown. It was soft and delicate. The smooth silk slid over her skin.

"What are you about to do?" he asked.

"Well, I had planned to put on my jammies and find a good movie to watch." She winced, walking around the bed, and got in. Her ankle was tender.

Not enough to medicate for, but she was definitely going to prop it up with pillows while she watched her movie.

"I wish I was there with you," he sighed. "Holding you and watching a movie would be much better than being in a hotel alone."

"Aw, you poor baby." She laughed. "You'll be home tomorrow, right?"

"And it can't come soon enough. There are a few meetings, and then we will be done for the day. I'll be checking out and heading back to you."

She should have felt pleased or excited about Bradley returning home. At the moment she didn't know.

All she *did* know was that she was one confused soul and was going to have some thinking to do. As much as she was afraid to trust Iker again after what he'd done, she just didn't know if she could give him her heart again.

Was it fair to lead Bradley on when she wasn't even sure what she wanted?

Go back to Iker or let him go, forever?

"WHO ARE THEY?" Iker ran his fingers through his hair. It had taken everything he had to be able to walk away from her tonight. The kiss they'd shared had rocked him down to his core. He'd seen in her eyes that if he had insisted on going into her home, she would have let him.

But Brodie had responded that he had something.

Hence why Iker had left Jessica at her home with a puzzled look on her face.

He couldn't believe he had left either, but this was too important.

Those men had been following them, and he wanted to know why.

"And you are sure they were trailing you?" Brodie's finger flew across his keyboard as he stared at the computer monitor.

"I am one hundred percent positive they were following us. They tried to blend in, but I spotted them immediately." Iker leaned back on the couch in Brodie's home office. "When is Ronnie supposed to have the baby?"

"She was due a week ago. They are going to induce her tomorrow." Brodie glanced up from what he was looking at and grinned.

"That's awesome."

Mac and his wife, Sarena, had welcomed their daughter a few weeks ago. Iker shook his head at how much his teammates had grown. He was proud of everyone who had found someone to share their lives with.

A weird feeling swirled in his chest, and he was surprised to see it was jealousy.

Had he stayed with Jessica, he would probably be a family man now. He and Jess had wanted to have kids. They had talked about it. Even spoke of marriage at one point.

But he had allowed the fear that lived in the back of his mind to come forward and take over. The thought of losing Jessica had consumed him.

After they'd separated, the nightmares had begun almost immediately. Dreams where men had abducted her and he was too late to save her.

It had fucked him up and was part of the reason he began to drink.

"Thanks, man. Means a lot," Brodie said, breaking through Iker's thoughts. He typed out a few commands and settled back in his chair.

Iker didn't like the look that passed on his face.

"What is it?" Iker grew tense, waiting to hear the news.

"Thanks to my buddy, I was able to get a version

of the advance facial recognition programs the FBI and CIA are using now." Brodie grinned and held a finger up to his mouth. "Don't tell anyone."

Iker laughed. Brodie had a college buddy who was a tech genius who had contracts with almost every military branch and was always sharing with Brodie so they could trial things at the local level. Many of the toys Brodie got to play with had come in handy and had meant the difference between life and death.

"What did you find?" Iker groaned. He didn't give a rat's ass about the toys Brodie had. Who was he going to tell? Hell, they all looked forward to the things Brodie's friend shared with him. It helped the SWAT team out plenty.

"Well, the guys you sent me a picture of are brothers. Floyd and John Boy Rogers."

"Seriously, John Boy? Are you pulling my leg?" Iker asked.

"I wish I was. Those are their government-issued names." Brodie snorted.

"Anything special about them. Any tickets? Have I arrested either of them?" Iker rattled off questions.

"Hold your horses. Now it would seem they both

have been arrested, but you weren't the arresting officer," Brodie murmured.

"Then what is it? And don't you tell me that I'm being paranoid and it was just a coincidence," Iker muttered.

"Well, I'll be." Brodie paused and lifted his head. His gaze met Iker's.

"What is it?" A sense of dread swept over him. He sat forward on the couch and rested his elbows on his knees.

"Their father is Duke Rogers. The owner of that meth house we busted recently."

Iker's heart slammed against his chest.

What. The. Fuck.

His picture was found in that house. What could possibly tie him to a meth house? One that may or may not be in cahoots with the Demon Lords?

Iker didn't like the sound of this. They were going to have to get to the bottom of it.

Fast.

"You're getting slower in your old age," Jordan teased.

Iker hit the ground hard. He stared up at the sky.

Jordan's face came into view. "I didn't hurt you, did I?"

"I want a new partner," Iker hollered. He laughed and rolled to the side and pushed up off the ground. Today was the team's workout day. As dangerous as their jobs were, they had to maintain top shape and ensure their training continued.

There were times when they may have to engage in hand-to-hand combat against the enemy. Mac and Dec were drill sergeants when it came to training. It might have to do with the fact that they both were former SEALs.

They were out at their training facility where all of their training and SWAT tryouts were held. The sun was high in the blue sky. The meteorologist had called for perfect weather this weekend.

Tomorrow morning, he had plans to meet up with his brother at their mother's house.

"At least I'm not the only one she can put on their ass," Zain shouted, pumping his fist in the air.

"Stop your whining, Baldwin," Declan called out. He walked past with a smirk on his face.

"I don't see you over here sparring with her." Iker rested his hands on his waist, trying to catch his breath.

"I ain't that crazy." Declan barked a laugh.

"Come on, Baldwin. I'll go easier on you this time." Jordan rested her hands on her knees. Her eyes twinkled with mischief.

He was glad to be on her side. Jordan was one tough chick.

"You like dealing out pain," Iker muttered. "You're one sick bastard, Knight."

"Ha!" She fell into a fit of laughter. "Let's get this over with."

They practiced their maneuvers, holds, and takedowns. This time Iker was able to use his size and strength to get Jordan on the ground. He held her arms behind her as if he was going to cuff her.

Iker stood and held out his hand for her. She took it and stood just as Mac blew his whistle.

"Laps!" Mac called out.

"He's trying to kill us." Jordan groaned.

"Always." Iker patted her on the back and motioned for them to head over to track.

Myles, Ash, and Brodie were up ahead while Zain, Mac, and Declan fell in behind them. They'd do a mile before they should be done for the day.

They fell into a steady pace, jogging around the track.

He loved their team workouts. It gave him a chance to sharpen his skills. Each of his teammates were in top shape, and their skills were the reason they'd made the team.

"Brodie said you've been having some problems?" Jordan asked.

Iker glanced at the back of Brodie's head and smirked. Of course his teammates couldn't keep secrets when it came to each other's safety.

"A slight problem." He updated her on what was going on with the stalkers and his photo being found at the meth house.

"You think it's the Demon Lords?" she asked.

"I wouldn't put it past them. But I don't know what the hell they would want."

"What's going on between you and Jessica?" she asked.

Iker felt her gaze on him, but he refused to meet it.

"It's complicated," he admitted.

"I figured that out when I met her boyfriend in the hospital's cafeteria getting coffee," Jordan said.

"He's too soft. She's going to eat him alive," he muttered. His gaze took in the area and found there was distance between them and the others. It looked as if everyone was tired and out for a Sunday jog. Usually someone threw out a dare and bets would be flying around.

"So why aren't you with her instead?" Jordan asked softly.

"That is very complicated." He reached up and wiped the sweat from his brow. "Let's just say it was a big mistake on my part."

"What did you do, cheat on her?" Jordan gasped. She sped up slightly and turned around, jogging backward. She glared at him as if he'd done her wrong. It would appear that Jordan was ready to defend her fellow woman.

"What? Hell, no. Jess means everything to me."

"I was about to kick your ass. She appears to be a sweet person." Jordan rotated and came back to run alongside him.

"You would like her."

They ran in silence for a while. The steady pounding of their feet on the pavement echoed around them. Off in the distance, the sound of an ambulance siren pierced the air.

"My ex cheated on me," Jordan said. Her eyes remained forward as they ran. As each day passed, Jordan was relaxing around them more and more, sharing tidbits about herself.

"Are you telling me that me and the boys need to take a trip over to Atlanta?" Iker joked. But really he wasn't. If she said the word, Columbia's finest would be on a road trip to Atlanta in search of a son of a bitch needing an ass-whooping.

"Don't worry. That was already taken care of."

That he believed.

"If you need anything, you know you can call on any of us," Iker said. He wanted her to know that. She was new to their team, but already they had taken her under their wing as a sister.

"I know. Being around you guys let me know I definitely made the right decision. I didn't have this closeness with my last unit or really felt as if my back was covered when the shit hit the fan." She turned her big brown eyes to him and smiled.

"Well, that's how we roll here. We all bleed blue and are family."

"I see that and I love it."

They rounded the corner and didn't have much farther to go. The guys up ahead were already walking around the track to cool down.

"But I mean it. All you have to do is call on one of us, and we all will be there."

"Thanks." She nodded. "But getting back to you and Jessica. If she means something to you, then why is she with the other guy?"

"Oh, that won't be continuing. I don't share," he growled.

"Does she know that? Only she can make that decision."

"Yes, I told her I want her back," he said.

"Well, like I said, she is going to have to make that decision. It might not be what you want to hear, and then what?"

Damn, Jordan didn't hold any punches. She was like the sister he'd never had.

He sighed, slowing to a walk as they made it their

distance. Jordan walked with him, keeping up with his long strides.

"If she chooses him, then I'll step aside. But until then, I'm not going nowhere."

"HELLO?" Jessica's voice came on the line.

Iker settled back against his pillow. It was late, and he hadn't figured she'd answer. Ever since his talk with Jordan, he couldn't get Jess out of his mind. He had made the decision that he was going to win her back, but what if she didn't take him back?

A lump had sat in his throat with the fear he wouldn't be able to convince her to give them another chance.

He had to hear her voice.

He knew calling her this late there may be a chance she wouldn't be alone. Hell, if he was with her, she would be too busy to answer the damn phone.

When she'd picked up, he was actually taken aback by surprise. He had rehearsed a message he was going to leave her.

"Jess. Baby, how are you?' He cleared his throat. He reached for the remote to his television and turned the volume down. An old movie was on the screen, but he hadn't seen one moment of it due to him thinking of Jessica.

"Iker," she breathed.

The sound went straight to his dick. It stiffened painfully, demanding relief. He heard the sound of her blankets rustling and closed his eyes briefly.

"Why are you calling so late?"

"Did I wake you?" he murmured. He cleared his throat again. It was constricting for some odd reason. "I didn't wake Bradley, did I?"

It was a childish move, but he had to know if the son of a bitch was at her house.

Jessica's deep throaty chuckle filled his ear.

"Are you trying to find out if I'm alone?" she asked, her sassiness shining through. "I know the big, bad Iker isn't afraid of having competition for my attention."

"There will never be competition," Iker said.

"Really?"

"Keep playing, baby, and I'll show up at your fucking door."

The sound of her breathing greeted him. Iker could be dressed and out the door in under five minutes.

"You are crazy enough to pull some shit like

that." Jessica blew out a deep breath. "Not that it is any of your business, but yes, I'm alone tonight."

"Really? Your boyfriend couldn't hang with you?" He knew he was pushing it. Did he want to know about the other man putting his hands on her? Enjoying the pleasure of her warm, curvy body.

Fuck no.

"That again, Iker, is none of your business."

He ghosted a hand over his bare chest. He was so wound up that if she were here, he'd probably blow his load the second she touched his dick.

"Don't get your panties in a bunch," he murmured. The last thing he would want was to piss her off and have her hanging up on him. He was trying to get back in her good graces and couldn't afford to fuck this up.

"Iker. Iker. Iker. You know I don't wear panties to bed."

A tremor rippled through him. He swallowed hard as the memories rushed forward.

Fuck yeah, he remembered. There had been plenty of nights and mornings where he was able to taste what was between her thighs and didn't have any barriers to fight against.

"Jess, don't tease me," he warned. His hand slid

to his abdomen and disappeared underneath his blanket.

"It's not teasing. Just a reminder."

Her soft giggle sent an electric current through his body.

"Are you in the bed, baby?" he whispered.

"I am. It's after eleven, Iker. Where else would I be?"

"You should be here with me," he grumbled. His cock was thick and heavy with need. He palmed his shaft and ran his hand along it. His breath caught in the back of his throat. It wasn't his hand he wanted stroking him, but it would do for now.

"Iker—"

"It's the truth," he cut her off. He didn't want to hear anything about the boyfriend or anything else tonight. Right now, he just wanted to speak with her.

Hear her voice.

"Iker, what are you doing?" Her husky voice shared that she already knew what he was doing.

"Do you really want me to tell you that I'm stroking my cock?" A sharp intake of breath reached his ears. His cock was sensitive, and the sensation of his calloused hand running along it sent a shiver through him. "Jess, touch yourself."

"Iker, we shouldn't be doing this," she breathed.

"Why not? You're at your place and I'm at mine. You can't play with your own pussy?"

"Of course I can," she whispered.

"Then do it, Jessica," he rasped. He closed his eyes and imagined her lying in her bed with her nightie pulled up around her waist. His breath hitched in his throat at the sound of her faint moan. He set a steady pace of his hand moving along his shaft. "Tell me, Jess. Are you wet?

"Drenched."

Fuck.

He had half a mind to rush over to her place. He could be there in twenty minutes flat, breaking every speeding law there was.

Iker squeezed his cock, putting a little pressure on it as he continued to stroke himself.

"Jess, baby. Are you playing with your clit or fucking yourself with those little fingers of yours?" His body heated at the imagery he was imagining.

"Rubbing my clit." A throaty moan, this time louder, escaped her.

"Jess, baby. Do you still have your drawer of toys?" he asked.

"Hmm..."

He took that as a yes. Jessica Horton was a woman who loved taking pleasure in life. There were plenty of nights where toys had joined in their love-making. Anything he had to do to get that woman to scream his name, he was all down for.

"Reach in there and pull out whatever dildo you've got hidden in there." He may not be there with her at the moment, but he was going to make sure they both reached their climax together.

Iker paused his hand, his orgasm creeping toward him. He wasn't ready to explode yet. He pushed off the blanket, his body overheating.

"I have it." Her voice was thick with desire.

"Good, girl," he praised her. "Run it though your pussy, baby. Get it wet."

He had to hurry because he wasn't going to last long. It had been a while since he had released.

Just imagining her using her fake cock had him strung tight. He hissed, his calloused hand moving along his erection again.

Her breathing was becoming more labored.

"You do it yet, baby?" he asked.

"Yeah."

"Push it into your pretty pussy," he encouraged.

Her moan grew louder. He shut his eyes tight, his hand quickening.

"Fuck. Jess, I wish I was there with you."

"Iker," she whimpered.

The sweet sound of his name on her lips while she fucked herself sent a tremor coursing through his body.

"Keep going, baby." Iker shuddered. His muscles grew tight as he applied more pressure to his cock. His hand slipped up and down his length faster.

A vibrating noise sounded with Jess's moans. He would give his left nut to be able to be in the room watching her right now.

"God," she cried out.

"Fuck," Iker muttered. He teetered on the brink of his climax, refusing to release until she did. His hand tightened on his phone. He didn't care if he cracked it. He was spiraling out of control. "Go ahead, baby. Let me hear you come."

"Iker," she chanted his name repeatedly. Her cry turned into a scream when she reached her climax.

Iker joined her, a growl ripping through him, his seed spewing from his cock, landing on his stomach. His body trembled as he continued to stroke himself until no more came from him. He fell back against his pillows, spent.

His body was covered in a fine sheen of sweat while his breaths remained labored. He listened to Jess' rapid breaths.

"Baby, you still there?" he whispered.

"Hmmm..."

"I need you, Jess. So you need to do something about Bradley," he urged. He drew in a ragged breath. He opened his eyes and stared at the ceiling. "You belong to me, and he needs to get the fuck out of my way."

17

"Jessica, darling. Bradley didn't tell us how beautiful you are," Bradley's aunt, the mother of the bride, paused by her.

Right before the wedding had begun, Bradley had introduced her to his parents. The Berrys were a sweet, blue-collar family. His mother had gushed about how much Bradley had spoken of her. They even made Bradley promise to bring her by for lunch.

"Mrs. Richards, you are too kind." Jessica forced a smile at the older woman.

Bradley stood by her side with his arm lightly around her waist.

She turned to him. "Did you tell them I was ugly?"

"What? No," Bradley sputtered.

His aunt fell into a fit of laughter. She practically glowed. From what Bradley had shared with Jessica, this was the last of her children to get married off.

"You are absolutely gorgeous," he said.

"Oh, honey. I'm just playing. You two make a good-looking couple." Mrs. Richards motioned to the both of them.

Bradley was dressed in a dark suit with a tie that matched the lavender in her dress. She had worn an off-the-shoulders lavender-and-gold dress that high-lighted her curves. She would have completed the outfit with a pair of gold heels, but due to the ankle injury, sandals it was.

Jessica felt guilty for putting him on the spot like that. They were at the reception, and he had been making his rounds to speak with his family.

The wedding was absolutely beautiful. All of the festivities were being held outdoors. The weather was perfect. Warm and sunny.

Jessica had shed a tear or two watching the bride walk to her future husband. Their personal vows had opened the floodgates.

Jessica wanted that.

The emcee announced it was time for the couple's first dance.

"Come on, Jessica. I'll see you later, Auntie." He kissed Mrs. Richards on the cheek then turned to Jessica and guided her away.

They joined the crowd who gathered around the dance floor. He leaned over to her, his lips brushing her ear. "Cici was never a dancer. From what my mother told me, her and Deon had to take dance classes for this day."

"Really?" Jessica turned a curious gaze to where the people surrounding the area parted.

The bride and groom were a handsome couple. Cici's dress was breathtaking, with an off-the-shoulder neckline. Crystals adorned the fabric that flowed around her ankles.

The structure they were in was decorated quite tastefully. The white tent top had vaulted ceilings with strands of tiny white lights crisscrossing above them. They'd spared no money outfitting the place to be fit for royalty.

White tablecloths and glass centerpieces with flowers decorated the tables. Whoever had chosen the decor, they certainly had an eye for style.

Their song began to play. Deon swept Cici into his arms, pulling her close. If Bradley hadn't shared that neither of them could dance, she would never have known it.

Her vision blurred. She blinked back tears watching the couple as they danced. Their bodies swayed in perfect harmony.

The way they gazed upon each other brought a lump to Jessica's throat.

She wanted that.

To have someone look at her as if she were their last dying wish. As if the sun wouldn't be as bright if she were not in their life.

Bradley tightened his arm around her and held her close to him. He rested his chin on the top of her head as if he sensed how emotional she was watching his cousin.

She blinked back the tears, the desire to have someone she could grow old with.

Iker's face flashed in her mind.

As much as she wanted to resist him, she knew that she couldn't, and it was unfair for her to remain with Bradley.

She would break it off with him so he wouldn't continue to waste time on her. He deserved a good woman who would love him unconditionally.

Someone not still hung up on their ex.

The rest of the wedding party joined the happy couple. Jessica reached down deep and pulled another smile out.

"Are you okay?" Bradley whispered into her ear.

She glanced up at him and nodded.

"Yes. Why?" she asked.

He drew her close and shrugged. "You just seem distant today. Like something is bothering you."

"I'm okay. The ankle is a little sore," she lied.

That wasn't it at all. She couldn't shake the memories of last night from her mind. A shiver rolled through her. She shouldn't have engaged with Iker at all, but she couldn't help herself. It had only taken her a moment to realize he was getting started with his individual pleasure.

She quickly found herself joining him. It had been a while since she'd had a hard orgasm. Not that it was an excuse, she could have taken care of the problem at any time.

But the image that came to mind when his voice hitched a certain way had her following his instructions.

The sound of Iker's growls and commands had helped her reach completion. She had been seconds from telling him to come to her house. Had she issued the offer, the man would have been breaking down her door.

"Are you cold?" Bradley asked.

She shook her head, pressing her lips together.

She needed to push the thoughts of last night from her mind. She was already growing aroused just remembering.

"Come," he said. "I want to introduce you to someone."

He took her by the hand and tugged her through the throng of people watching the bridal party.

"This is a beautiful wedding," Jessica said. She scanned the area, taking in so many people smiling and laughing. The atmosphere was one of celebrating. Everyone appeared to be having a good time.

"It is. Cici has been dreaming of this day since she was about ten years old," Bradley said.

"Really?" Jessica sighed. She didn't think she'd been thinking of getting married at that young age, but she definitely knew she wanted to.

"How about yourself? Ever think about tying the knot?" he asked, tossing a curious glance her way.

"I have. I'm sure the perfect person will come along." She chuckled.

"Is that so?" he murmured.

Bradley guided them over to a group of guys. They weren't dressed up as fancy, but she could tell they had wanted to look nice for the wedding. They were standing at the edge of the tent, each with a drink in their hands.

"Look what the cat dragged in," one of the guys kidded.

"You got jokes." Bradley laughed. He moved forward and embraced the guy in a strong manly hug. "Where you been hiding, Jevonne?"

"You know where. The same ol' block." Jevonne grinned. His lewd gaze landed on Jessica.

She tried not to fidget as he checked her out.

"I see why we haven't seen you in a while."

Bradley grinned and came back to Jessica. He wrapped an arm around her waist. She offered a small smile to each of the men staring at her.

"Jessica, this is Jevonne, Reno, and Troy." He pointed to each one of them.

Jevonne smiled at her. A gold tooth in the front of his mouth shined. Reno was tall, bald, and a little round in the waist while Troy was short and had his dark hair in cornrows.

"Hello, gentlemen." She nodded to each of them.

"Where you find her at?" Reno joked. He stepped forward and took her hand.

She tried not to stiffen.

"And do she have a sister?"

"Down, Reno." Bradley brushed Reno away from her. He laughed, turning to Jessica. "I swear he has home training."

"That's okay," she sighed.

Bradley pulled her back to his side. "These are my cousins that I grew up with. I swear my life wouldn't be anything without them," he said.

Jessica instantly knew what he was referring to. They must have been the ones who'd stood at his side going through his treatments.

"Well, I thank you." She patted Bradley's chest with her hand. She wasn't sure what that meant, but she shrugged it off. She had no intention of doing anything to harm Bradley.

"We've heard a lot about you. Make sure you treat him right." Jevonne winked at her. "He's like a brother to us. We'd do anything for him."

"I will." She laughed, but internally she was a little weirded out.

Talk about family intimidation.

"Leave her alone, fellas. Jessica is a sweetheart. I'm lucky to have her." Bradley planted a kiss on the top of her head.

"Bradley, honey. Can we grab some wine?" she asked. If she was going to have to deal with more bizarre family members, she was going to need alcohol.

Lots of it.

"I HOPE YOU HAD FUN TONIGHT," Bradley said.

They walked through the parking lot toward his car.

Jessica reached up and held on to Bradley's jacket which was covering her shoulders. Bradley, being the gentleman he was, had seen her shiver and offered her his jacket.

"I did. I learned so much about your family," she replied.

"That sounds like a bad thing."

"What? No. It's just that it's the first time meeting your family. Usually when dating someone, one would meet the parents and immediate family first before the entire family." She chuckled. Tonight, she'd met every relative he had who attended the wedding. There was no way she would remember everyone.

"Was it too much?" He turned to her, stopping at his car.

"A little, but only because I'm not going to remember everyone. You have a huge family."

He stepped forward and took her hand in his. The music was floating through the air from the tent.

The party was still going on strong. The happily married couple had left about an hour ago.

Bradley stepped closer to her. He tipped her chin up and gave her a soft smile.

"You look beat. Let me get you home." He led her to the passenger door of his vehicle and assisted her in. He shut the door once she was settled in.

Leaning back in the chair, she buckled up her seat belt and relaxed. Her eyes fluttered closed. She might have had too much wine. Every time someone had mentioned how beautiful she was, she'd taken a gulp of wine. She had one hell of a buzz. Her eyes flew open at the sound of the driver's door opening. Bradley slid inside and glanced at her.

"Yeah, you definitely need to get home." He laughed.

"I'm sorry." Her words slurred together.

"Nothing to apologize for. I'm just happy you enjoyed yourself." The engine roared to life. He put the car in reverse and pulled out of the spot.

Jessica allowed her eyes to close again while the sway of the car soothed her. Soft jazz music filled the car.

A sudden overwhelming sensation overcame her.

Everything about her and Bradley was wrong. She couldn't keep up this charade any longer.

Her eyes opened, and she shifted in her seat to stare at Bradley. In the dark car it was hard to see his features. He was a handsome man and deserved someone who would put him first and love him like he deserved.

"What is it, honey?" Bradley glanced over at her. "Are you okay?"

"You've asked me like a hundred times today." She smiled softly. He was caring, and she didn't deserve him.

"I'm just concerned. You've looked like something has been bothering you all day." He focused on the road.

"I've been thinking," she began. She didn't know how to word it, so she just decided to wing it.

"About what?" His hands tightened on the steering wheel. He gave a nervous cough and flicked his gaze to hers.

"Us."

The car grew quiet. Only the music could be heard.

"I'm not sure I like the sound of this," Bradley murmured.

"Bradley, you are such a nice guy, and I don't want to hurt you. I've been thinking about this and I think it would be best for us to not see each other anymore." She kept her voice low, in an attempt to soften the blow.

"You're breaking up with me? Did I do something? Did I offend you—?"

"Honey, it's not you." She cringed as soon as the words escaped her lips. "What I mean is that I'm just in an emotional state right now. I don't think I'm really ready for a steady relationship yet. I don't want to waste your time, so I think it's best we stop before we move ahead."

Bradley didn't say anything. His arms were stiff as he guided the car into a turn. Jessica stared out of her window, sadness filling her.

They drove in silence for a while.

Bradley finally responded. "It sounds as if you have thought long and hard about this."

She jumped at the sound of his voice.

"I just need space right now." Jessica sighed. She leaned back against the headrest, turning her attention to him.

"Space. So just a temporary separation? Or we can see other people?"

"As in, we should remain as friends for now," she said softly.

"Jessica." Bradley reached over and took her hand in his. He brought her hand up to his lips and kissed the back of it. "If you think this is what's best."

"I do. I'm so sorry, Bradley. I just don't think I'm the right one for you and I'd rather move aside to give you the opportunity to find the right woman."

"You're a good woman, Jessica." He entwined their fingers together. "I think you are perfect for me."

"Oh, Bradley—"

"But I hear you. I'll give you the space you need." He squeezed her hand and tossed her a sad smile.

"Thank you, Bradley. I'm really sorry."

The rest of the drive was in complete silence. They finally arrived at her home. Bradley exited the car first, leaving it running. He came around the hood to her side and helped her out.

They walked toward her front door. Bradley held her hand the entire time. She was riddled with guilt but knew the best thing for her to do was to break it off with him.

She had to decide what she wanted to do with her life.

They arrived at the door. She reached inside her clutch and took out her keys.

"Thank you for a wonderful day." She tried to ease the fact that she was dumping him.

He stared at her with a sadness that was breaking her heart. He was too good for her. Anyone else would have put up a fuss, yelled, begged, but not Bradley. He was a classy man, as always.

"Anytime, Jessica." He pulled her close and kissed her lips. He stepped back, studying her as if he were memorizing her features.

She turned around and slid the key into the lock. She opened the door and stepped inside. She gave him a little wave and shut the door. She leaned against it and exhaled.

It was as if a heavy weight was lifted from her shoulders.

"It was the right thing to do," she stressed to herself.

Pushing off the door, she went into her house and headed toward her bedroom.

Now she had to figure out what she was going to do with her life.

18

"In light of the recent update in this case, we will break for recess." The judge slammed her gravel down. "Counselors, please report to my chambers. Now."

There was a slight murmur from the audience. The judge stood and was escorted through the door in the corner.

Iker and the SWAT team were sitting together in the back of the courtroom. Today was a hard day for them all.

Office Diego Cruz had betrayed the Columbia Police Department deeply. He'd turned on his brothers and sister in blue

Cruz was the mole.

Anything done in the dark was bound to come to light.

Per the captain, the entire SWAT team was granted permission to observe the trial. Dressed in their Sunday best, each member attended. Straight-faced and stoic, none of them showed any emotions when the trial had started, but suddenly it would seem Cruz was now willing to accept a plea deal the prosecutor had placed on the table.

"Can you believe this shit?" Zain whispered, leaning over to Iker.

"Actually, I can't. He's been snitching this long, what's a little longer?" Iker shrugged.

A fucking plea deal in exchange for Cruz testifying against members of the Demon Lords who were currently sitting in prison.

The main man the prosecutor was going after was Victor Huff, the former leader of the Demon Lords.

Once the judge was escorted out of the room, the bailiffs removed Cruz as well. When he was gone, the other bailiffs gave the audience permission to rise and exit from the courtroom.

Mac stood, and the rest of the team followed. They left the room and went out in the hallway. The crowd was thick with reporters and the other people who had attended the trial.

They moved over to a corner of the hall away from the door. There were other courtrooms located in this area of the building, but only this one was drawing attention. It had been a long while since a cop in the city was arrested for something as heinous as what Cruz had done.

It was making national headlines.

"He's going to be a sitting duck in jail," Myles murmured.

Iker nodded. That was his thoughts exactly. Plenty of people had gone after the head of the Demon Lords many times but were unsuccessful. Either they backed down and gave up, or they disappeared and were found dead. Victor hadn't been in charge of the gang for long. He had been the right-hand man who had taken over when Declan had shot and killed the last leader, Silas.

That had solidified the war against the SWAT team and the gang. Victor had praised them for getting Silas out of his way, but in the end, the war continued.

It was because of their team that Victor sat in prison at the moment.

"They aren't going to be able to keep him in the

general population," Ash said. He slid his hands in his pockets, shaking his head.

"He'll be dead by sundown if they put him back there," Brodie chimed in.

"The media is going to have a field day once they find out he's going to testify," Iker announced.

"Which would be like nailing the coffin shut," Declan added.

Iker scanned the hall, taking in the few people who lingered. He was sure the news channels were already broadcasting what was just heard in the courtroom. He almost felt sorry for Diego. If his family member had been taken and held hostage, Iker didn't know how he would react.

But to put the lives of others at risk for him or his family, he wasn't sure he would go that far.

There were always other ways, and Diego did not use the resources that were readily available to him. As a long-time decorated officer, he could have approached any of the teams, and they all would have bent over backwards to help save his sister.

Instead, he'd acted on his own and fell into the gang's clutches and broke the law. He went against everything his badge stood for. There were a substantial number of charges brought up against him. A plea deal would be the only way he wouldn't be spending twenty to thirty years in prison. As a former cop, he would never survive that long behind bars. Someone would end him, putting him out of his misery.

"I need some air," Iker mumbled. He speared a hand through his hair, feeling confined in the building.

"I'll come with you." Zain moved over to him, adjusting his tie. He walked past him, grumbling, "It's like a noose around my neck."

"I'm coming, too," Jordan murmured.

"We might as well take a fucking field trip," Mac muttered.

Iker chuckled as he and his team strode through the hall. A few members of the media eyed them.

They exited the building and jogged down the stairs. The streets were lined with news channel vans and trucks. Security was thick around the building. This was a high-profile case and had been pushed back a couple of times to allow both sides to prepare.

"Looking good, Knight. Not sure we've seen you in a dress before," Zain teased.

Jordan rolled her eyes and flipped him off. She wore a black dress and flats. Her hair was left down, and she wore makeup. It was rare they all were dressed up together, but with most of the team getting engaged and married, it was happening more often.

"You don't know what I do when I'm not on the clock, Roman," she retorted.

They all shared a laugh while walking to a large tree near the side of the building. There was a lawn with a couple of benches surrounding it. The branches and leaves provided some shade and allowed them a vantage point of everyone entering and leaving the building.

"How long before you think the Demon Lords will get their hands on him?" Iker eyed his team. It was a grim question, but one that they all knew the answer to.

"I give him a month," Brodie bet.

"They'll torture him. I say two months," Ash added.

"However long it is, he won't get to testify against Victor Huff. Unless Victor's trial starts tomorrow, there's no way he's going to make it," Mac said.

They all fell silent for they knew that was the truth.

Diego Cruz was a dead man walking.

JESSICA COULDN'T STAY AWAY from the one thing she loved.

Art.

She had got a tip from an old friend on social media about an artist showcasing her work at the library downtown. Unable to resist, she had gotten dressed and used her ride-sharing app to hail a car to drop her off.

It had been a few days since her breakup with Bradley. He'd checked on her via text, just making sure she was okay. She had thought he would be more overbearing, but as promised, he was giving her space.

Jessica strolled through the library and headed toward the basement stairs. She arrived at the top and stood for a brief moment; the memory of her tumble during the robbery came to mind.

Turning on her heel, she walked over to the elevator.

"We're playing it safe today." She hit the button. The door immediately opened. She stepped inside and a minute later she was on the lower level. The building was old and held a musty smell of ancient books. There were a few people milling around outside the door down the hall where she suspected the exhibit was located.

It was a warm day outside, and she had chosen to wear a spaghetti-strapped maxi dress that went to her ankles. It had been perfect for outside, but now that she was in the library, the central air was springing goosebumps on her skin.

Rubbing her arms, she hurried down the hall.

"Hello, are you here for the exhibit?" a young woman with her hair plaited into two braids asked. She couldn't be no more than fourteen years old.

"That I am. How are you?" Jessica greeted her with a smile.

"I'm well. There is a charge of two dollars." The kid pointed to the sign on the wall.

Jessica reached into her purse and pulled out a five-dollar bill and handed it to the young lady.

"Keep the change."

"Thank you." She put the money into a belt bag and picked up a flyer. "Here is some information about Mystelle's work."

"Appreciate it. By chance, is the artist here?" Jessica asked. She glanced down at the flyer that shared Mystelle's background and her area of interest. Her bio spoke of her being raised by her single mother and growing up poor. Her aspirations were to become a household name where many people would seek to have a piece of her collection in their homes.

"Oh, yes. She's my older sister. She and my mother are inside." She pointed behind her toward the door.

"All right. Thank you again." Jessica smiled and made her way past the table. She entered the room and immediately was captivated by what she saw.

The room was one of the smaller conference rooms the library rented out for events.

It was filled with beautiful paintings of African tribes. The bright colors, the depiction of the men and women of Africa, and the passion immediately snagged Jessica's attention. She took her time strolling around.

There were others present, but Jessica was lost in her own world and might as well have been alone.

She tuned all the chatter out as she stared at one piece.

It was a painting with bold strokes of yellow, purple, and red for the sky. A family: a man, woman, and child walking together. The woman balanced a bucket on her head while the man carried wood. The child, tiny, carried one stick.

The depiction of the family touched a part of

Jessica. She stepped closer to it, enraptured by the passion of the family flowing through the piece.

"Beautiful, isn't it?" a voice asked.

Jessica jumped, having not heard the person who'd joined her. A woman with deep-brown skin, with beautiful dreadlocks stood beside her.

"Yes, it. The artist is certainly talented. Are you Mystelle?" Jessica asked.

The woman laughed and shook her head.

"Oh, no. I'm her mother, Odessa." The women held out her hand.

Jessica smiled and took it in her hand.

"Wow, how old is Mystelle?" Jessica laughed. The woman didn't look a day over forty.

"She's sixteen." Odessa waved a young girl, dressed in jean shorts and a t-shirt, over.

"Yes, Mama?" Mystelle joined them.

Jessica studied her, and it was amazing that someone so young was so talented. She immediately grew excited about what she could offer them.

"I want you to meet someone. She loves your work," Odessa said. She motioned to Jessica. "I'm sorry, I didn't catch your name."

"I'm Jessica," she said. She shook Mystelle's hand. She motioned to the room. "This is some amazing work. What's your inspiration?"

Odessa smiled and motioned for Mystelle to answer.

"You probably will laugh." Mystelle smiled.

Jessica was captivated by her innocence and youth. She remembered being that young and passionate about art. Mystelle reminded Jessica of herself when she was that age.

"Try me." Jessica returned her smile. She was very interested to know how Mystelle came up with her imagery and topics.

"Well, most of them come to me in dreams. I keep a sketchbook by my bed, and the minute I wake up, I'm drawing what I saw so I don't forget. Then later I paint them." Mystelle bit her lip as if expecting Jessica to not believe her.

"Do you know how many other artists are inspired by their dreams? It's been a proven fact that our mind continues our creativity even when we are sleep. You are definitely not alone with this," Jessica encouraged.

Mystelle's lips curled into a bright smile.

"I'm just blown away by the detail, the colors. I feel as if I can touch the soul of Africa from these." Jessica waved around at the room.

"Thank you, ma'am," Mystelle said.

"According to this, you want to become a well-known artist who people seek to have your work in their homes." Jessica held up the flyer.

"Yes, ma'am." Mystelle nodded, a shy smile playing on her lips.

Her mother gave her a one-armed hug while dropping a kiss onto the top of her head. "My daughter has big aspirations, and I'm going to do my damnedest to make her dreams come true," Odessa said.

Jessica smiled and took another look around. She reached down into her purse and pulled out her business card.

"Ladies, I'm impressed. Let me officially introduce myself. My name is Jessica Horton, and I am the head artist liaison for The Ablo Gallery."

Odessa and Mystelle gasped.

That confirmed they knew of the gallery.

"I would love to feature you in our gallery." She handed Mystelle her card. "I organize a starving artist sale—"

"We've heard of it. Your shows be the talk of town," Mystelle gushed. She squealed and danced around in place.

Odessa appeared stunned, tears forming in her eyes.

Jessica blinked back her own because she knew

she was about to change their lives. This was what she lived for. She loved helping the less fortunate. It wasn't her giving handouts, she just gave them a platform to showcase their work.

"Do you have more?" Jessica asked.

"I do." Mystelle nodded.

"All this girl does is draws and paints when she's not doing schoolwork," Odessa said.

"I want you two to call me sometime next week. I shall be back in the office soon, and we can talk more details."

"Yes, ma'am." Mystelle nodded. She flew forward and wrapped Jessica in her arms. "Thank you."

Jessica smiled and returned the hug. She looked over Mystelle's shoulder and tossed Odessa a wink. The woman's tears were streaming down her face. Jessica stepped back and grinned at Mystelle.

"It's my pleasure. Now don't lose my card."

"Believe me, I won't." Mystelle slid it into her pocket.

Jessica grabbed another card from her purse and handed it to Odessa. With a wave, she spun around on her heel and made her way out of the library. She couldn't shake the grin off her face. This was the one part of her job she loved.

Once outside, she pulled her phone from her purse and placed a call to Mr. Ablo. She needed to know if everything was well at the gallery.

Come next week, whether he approved or not, she was going back to work.

19

I ker was staring off in the distance as his teammates talked and joked around. The recess should be ending soon.

"Y'all want to go grab a bite to eat afterwards?" Ash asked.

"Yeah, I'm famished." Myles rubbed his stomach.

"Didn't you just have two hot dogs from that vendor?" Jordan asked with wide eyes. She nodded over to the man on the corner of the street with his cart.

"He's a bottomless tank," Brodie said.

Iker chuckled, feeling a little hungry himself. He could certainly go for something.

Since Diego was going to accept the plea

bargain, the trial would be shortened. No point in continuing since he was going to take a lesser sentence in order to work with the prosecutor's office.

"Hey, ain't that Jessica?" Zain slapped Iker on the arm.

Iker looked in the direction his friend was pointing.

It was.

What was she doing out here?

"I'll be back," he announced. He headed over to where she was walking down the street. She wore a long dress with thin straps that showcased her shoulders and skin. Her warm brown skin appeared to be kissed by the sun.

She strolled down the street holding on to her purse as she gazed upon the storefronts.

"Jess!" he called out.

She turned toward him. She had oversized sunglasses on that hid her eyes. He waded through the traffic and jogged over to her side of the street.

"Iker, what are you doing down here?" she asked. A small smile played on her lips.

"Me and the team are at the trial of a police offi-cer," he admitted. Iker drank her in now that he was near her. She looked even better up close. The dress clung to her top, highlighting her full breasts. He knew what was hidden under there.

He resisted the urge to adjust his stiffening cock.

"I did hear about that on the news. Did you know him?" Her eyebrows rose high.

"Long story, but yeah." He blew out a deep breath.

"I'm sorry."

"Don't be. He deserves everything that will be coming to him," he muttered.

"Iker!" she gasped.

"Believe me, if I were to tell you how what he's done affected me and my team, you'd be saying the same." He shook his head. He didn't want to talk about Cruz, he was curious as to what she was doing. "What brings you down here?"

She licked her lips, and he was immediately drawn to them. He swallowed hard; the memory of their sexy phone time from the other night surfaced.

The sounds of her cries of passion echoed in his head.

"You know me. Catch a lead on a new artist and I needed to go investigate." She shrugged.

"I thought the doctor ordered rest and relaxation?" He stepped closer to her. The aroma of her perfume filled his nostrils. It was a scent he'd recognize anywhere.

"He did. Going to view artwork is relaxation."

"Bullshit. That's work for you." He snorted.

"It is, but then again, it isn't," she replied haughtily.

"How'd you get down here? You drive?" He looked around. He didn't see Bradley coming or walking with her.

"I called for a car. I didn't want to have to worry about parking. Since the exhibit was in the library, I figured I'd enjoy the weather and walk around a little before heading home."

"I can give you a ride home," he offered. He cleared his throat. "Unless Bradley is coming to get you."

Jessica motioned for him to move to allow a few women to get past them on the sidewalk. He gave them a nod and turned his attention back to Jess.

"Um, Bradley isn't coming to pick me up." She pushed her sunglasses to the top of her head. Her gaze dropped to her fingers which were entwined with each other. "I sort of broke up with him."

Iker's heart leaped.

It was about fucking time she kicked that ass to the curb.

"Is that so," he murmured. He closed the gap between them and took her into his arms. He couldn't care less that they were standing on a public sidewalk.

This was the best news he'd heard all day, and he wasn't going to waste any time.

"Iker," she breathed.

"I have to return back to the courthouse soon. Why don't you take my truck to get home?"

"I don't want to impose—"

"It's fine. I can have Zain drop me off to come get it." He tipped her chin up so she could meet his gaze. Her eyes widened at the feel of his cock pressing forward. "We need to finish what we started the other night."

Her audible swallow wasn't missed by his hearing.

"Iker, I'm not sure we should—"

"What? Finish what we both wanted?" He looked at the people milling around the stores. Laughter filled the air from a few people as they lingered at the corner of the street, chatting. Iker leaned down, his lips brushing Jessica's ear. "It was my name you were calling as you fucked yourself with that dildo."

A shiver passed through her.

He had her.

Without a doubt, she was just as turned on as he was.

"Do you want me, Jess?" he whispered. He snagged her the lobe of her ear with his teeth briefly, then let it go.

"Yes," she whispered faintly.

"I didn't hear you." He chuckled. Her small fingers gripped on to his waists. "Do you want me to fuck you? I promise my cock will feel much better than that damn toy."

Heat flashed in her eyes.

"You know I do."

A growl escaped him.

Finally!

This was the breakthrough he had been hoping for.

He had half a mind to ditch the rest of the trial and drag Jess off to either of their places.

Hers was closer.

"Take my truck. Go home, and I'll meet you there." He reached inside his blazer pocket and pulled his keys out. He handed them to her.

She glanced around him and waved to someone behind him. Iker saw Zain waving to her.

"I better go say hi to the gang. I don't want to get in trouble." She put his keys away in her purse.

"Sure. Zain would complain if you didn't," he muttered. At the moment, he didn't want to share her with anyone else. Now that he didn't have to worry about Bradley, he wanted her all to himself.

Taking her hand, he escorted her across the street. They made their way over to the tree where everyone was lounging.

He'd let her greet the team for a short moment, take her to where he'd parked, and then he'd come up with an excuse for him not to go out to eat with the team.

He had more important things he had to attend to.

He was fucking elated Bradley was no longer in the picture.

Iker wrapped a possessive arm around Jessica's waist once they made it across the street.

"Iker." Jess paused on the sidewalk and turned to him. She moved closer to him, her lips tilting up in the corners. "Will you be here much longer after I leave?"

Fuck.

The mischievous glint that appeared in her eyes had his cock growing impossibly harder.

"Baby, I promise I won't be too long behind you."

"I'm going to hold you to it." She spun around and walked ahead of him to the team.

His gaze dropped down to the gentle sway of her hips.

Hell. He might as well start coming up with an excuse to leave now. There was no way he was going to go back in that courthouse.

He took notice that the melee of the media that had been outside the building was dispersing. Court must be getting ready to be back in session.

Jess had made it over to the team and was already hugging and greeting everyone.

Zain caught his eyes. He raised a single eyebrow, and Iker immediately knew what he was asking. Without even asking, he was sure the guys and Jordan had watched him and Jessica across the street.

Nothing ever got past any of them.

Iker jerked his head, confirming.

They may not have that conversation yet, but it was just as good as done.

They were back together.

"It's so good to see you guys on the street in normal clothes." Jessica laughed.

"Baby, let me show you where I parked." He wrapped an arm around her waist and drew her back to him.

Iker didn't miss the way Mac's eyebrows shot up, as did everyone else's.

"Okay. It was nice seeing you all." Jess waved to everyone.

"Are you good with dropping me off at her house once we're done here?" he asked Zain.

"Sure," Zain said. He winked at Jess. "I'll have him there at a decent time."

Jess blushed and swatted Zain's arm. "Boy, bye."

"I'll be back," he said to his teammates before he took Jess by the hand and led her away.

"You basically just announced to your entire team that we'll be having sex later." Jessica leaned against his arm and wrapped hers around his.

"And? You got a problem with that?"

"Nope. Just making sure you're okay with them knowing why you may not be showing up to work tomorrow," she replied playfully.

A growl escaped from him at her words.

"What I tell you about teasing me, babe?"

"Iker, honey. I'm not teasing you. I'm just giving you a warning." Her voice grew husky.

The sound went straight to his dick.

They reached the sidewalk in front of the court-house. His truck was located in the parking lot across the street.

Suddenly, a scream sounded.

Iker's head jerked toward the noise coming the front entrances of the courthouse. People scurried out of the doors in a panic.

A loud bang filled the air while the ground rocked from an explosion.

***

"GET DOWN!" Iker hollered, tackling Jessica to the grass.

The ground shook as another blast rocked the building. Iker rolled off her. She lifted her head and found him with his gun in his hand.

"Shit," he muttered. He stood from the ground and helped her up.

"Oh my god," Jessica cried out, watching the scene unfold.

Men and woman rushed from the building, bloodied and dirtied.

Smoke was drifting up into the sky from the doors and windows of the first floor of the court-house. Sirens could be heard off in the distance, drawing closer.

Iker pushed her behind him, shielding her with his body. She held on to the back of his jacket. He kept one hand behind on her as if to make sure she remained in place.

"Jessica. I need you to get to the truck. It's parked right over there. Second row." His eyes were narrowed on her. A fierce expression crossed his face.

"What? No, I'm not leaving you." She shook her head, gripping him tight to her.

"Baby. I need to go. I'll be fine." He cupped her face. He swooped down and laid one hell of a kiss on her.

She fell into him, her knees growing weak. Iker lifted his head, his deep-green eyes boring into her.

"Go, Jess. I need you somewhere safe."

"Okay." She backed away from him and made her way through the throng of people trying to get away. She crossed the street and made it to the metal fence that surrounded the car lot.

She turned around and watched Iker join his team. Each of the SWAT officers rushed toward the burning building.

A lump formed in her throat.

This was what he did for a living.

Saving people.

She sent up a prayer that he and the others were safe as they helped the people in the building. She spun around and pulled his keys from her purse. She hit the button and heard the chirp in the direction he had pointed.

Rushing to the vehicle, she arrived and hopped in. She slammed the door shut and sat still for a moment. Her body shook with adrenaline. Her gaze took in the building. Whatever bomb had gone off wasn't large enough to do structural damage. The front windows were all shattered.

Jessica glanced around at the street and knew she had to go. If she stayed any longer, the police would have the area blocked off and she'd be trapped.

She started the truck.

"Shit," she muttered. She had to adjust the seat. Iker was so much taller than her, she was like a kid playing around in her daddy's car. After putting the seat and mirrors in a better position, she threw the vehicle into 'drive.' She made it to the street and swung a left, away from the craziness.

She tried to get one last glance at the building but was unable to see Iker.

I need you somewhere safe.

Inhaling deep, she pressed down on the pedal.

As she drove away from downtown, there were tons of police, ambulance, and fire trucks flying to where she had just left.

Jessica gripped the steering wheel tight. Her heart was still racing a mile a minute. How had she forgotten how dangerous Iker's job was?

This was something he'd dedicated his life to.

Serving and protecting the public.

She didn't know where running into a burning building fit in, but apparently it was in the small print.

The rest of the drive went by in a blur. Before Jessica knew it, she was pulling into her driveway. She put the truck in 'park' and killed the engine.

Leaning forward, she rested her head on the steering wheel. The day had been going well. She had left her home to go downtown to inquire about the artist; she'd planned some window browsing and possibly lunch at one of the cute little cafés. Running into Iker had been a bonus. As much as she'd tried to put up a fight and not give in to him.

A touch.

Dirty words of what he wanted to do with her.

One brush of his lips on her earlobe, and she was a goner.

Her body had made the decision for her.

She wanted him.

Needed him.

Now he'd better make it back to her in one piece.

Lifting her head, she ran her hand through her hair. This morning before she had left, she did a quick wash-and-go since her hair was so short. Her curls were close to her head and framed her face perfectly.

She glanced into the rearview mirror and grimaced. She had dirt and grass in her hair. She didn't even want to know what her clothes looked like after Iker had pushed her down on the ground.

He hadn't hesitated in covering her body with his.

Her breath caught in her throat.

That man.

His instinct had been to risk himself for her.

Jessica was an emotional mess. The thought of something happening to him tore her up inside.

Had she ever stopped loving him?

Grabbing her purse, she exited the truck and went into her home. It was quiet and calm. After the past hour, that was what she needed.

She went into her bedroom and cleaned herself up. A quick shower and fresh clothes, she felt a little better. With no plans to leave, she had put on her jammies, a soft tank top with matching cotton shorts. She'd washed her hair, threw some leave-in conditioner in along with her oils, allowing her hair to curl into its natural state. This was one reason she kept it only a few inches long. She didn't want to deal with a lot of hair.

Her stomach growled.

"I know," Jessica muttered. She went into the kitchen and warmed up some leftover spaghetti she had made the other day.

She headed into the living room with her bowl and flopped down on the couch. Turning on the television, she wanted to get updates on what the hell was going on.

She flipped through the local news stations while eating her early dinner. All of the stations were reporting on the courthouse bombing and were all saying the same thing.

There were no suspects yet.

No motives.

There was speculation that the target was the officer on trial.

A shiver went down her spine. If the target was potentially that officer, Iker and his team was supposed to be in the courtroom, too.

"Don't think bad thoughts," Jessica said. "Everything is going to be okay."

Jessica scanned the videos of the scene, looking for any sign of Iker. Blowing out a deep breath, she sat back, prepared for him to come to her as promised.

essica stretched, unsure what had woken her up. She sat up and rubbed her face. She had grown tired after watching hours of the news, but she had refused to go to bed. She'd grabbed a blanket and curled up on the couch. There had been no word from Iker. She must have fallen asleep while waiting.

The sound of her doorbell snagged her attention. Iker.

She scrambled off the couch, throwing the blanket on the floor. She rushed to the door as fast as she could. After she'd showered, she had left the boot off since she wasn't going anywhere.

Arriving at the door, she moved the curtain and flipped on the porch light. Her parents didn't raise a fool. She was going to look first before just opening the door.

It was Iker.

She flung open the door and practically vaulted into his arms.

A truck backed out of her driveway, blowing its horn as it sped down the street. Zain must have dropped him off as promised.

"Iker!" she cried. "I was so worried about you."

"I told you I would be fine." His voice was gruff, but he enclosed her into a tight embrace. He gave her a kiss on the top of her head. "Come on, let's go inside."

He ushered her in and shut the door behind him.

Jessica took him in, and there was something about him. Her breath caught in her throat as his gaze landed on her.

"Are you okay?" she asked.

He toed off his shoes and jerked his head in a nod, not saying a word.

She swallowed hard, her breaths becoming labored.

His hands moved to his shirt, and he began unbuttoning it. He walked toward her. She had never seen him like this before. The intensity was radiating from him.

It turned her completely on. Her body was responding to the sexual tension building in the air.

"Iker," she whispered, walking backwards. Thankfully, she knew the layout of her house pretty well. "What is it?"

"Those fucking bombs." He yanked the shirt off and dropped it to the floor. He reached down, pulling his undershirt over his head.

Her mouth watered at the sight of his perfectly sculpted body. The man didn't have an ounce of fat on him.

"What about them?" she asked.

He backed her up to the wall near the stairs. He pressed his hands on the wall, trapping her. She tilted her head back to meet his gaze. She had no idea what time it was, but now that he was here, she was wide awake. A shiver rippled its way through her body. Her nipples painfully pushed against her cotton shirt while her core was drenched.

Iker's hand cupped her cheek. He lowered his head and rested his forehead on hers.

"They could have harmed you." His voice grew husky.

The agony on his face took her breath away at the magnitude of how much he cared for her.

"Took you from me when I just got you back."

"Oh, Iker. I'm not going anywhere," she promised. She covered his hand with hers. "I'm right here with you."

A growl tore from him.

He slammed his mouth down on hers. She gasped, leaning into the kiss. It was one that was passionate and possessive. Iker was making his claim on her, and there was nothing she could do to stop it.

She belonged to him.

There was no doubt in her mind.

She skated her hands up his warm chest and entwined them together at the base of his neck.

He bent down and lifted her. She wrapped her legs around his waist. He moved to the stairs and carried her up them.

The door to her bedroom slammed open. She had left the nightstand lamp on earlier after she'd taken her shower. He marched across the room, all the while not breaking the kiss.

Iker slowly lowered her to her feet beside the bed. He tore his lips from hers. Their breaths were coming fast as they stared at each other.

She stood there while he stripped her clothes from her. His anger at the world radiated from him. Jessica was confident he would never hurt her.

"Jess, you are so fucking beautiful," he muttered.

He pushed down her shorts and helped her step from them. His gaze roamed her body. The hunger in them was like a caress to her skin. Goosebumps appeared on her arms. Her nipples beaded into tight buds.

"And you still have your pants on," she replied haughtily.

He smirked at her cheekiness.

He took his wallet out, tossed it to the night-stand, and turned back to her.

"Well then, take them off."

He didn't have to tell her twice. She'd seen the tortured look in his eyes when he'd walked into her house. She would erase it.

They had so much to make up for, she refused to allow the events from earlier to interrupt them. Tomorrow they would speak of what happened.

Now, it was all about them.

Jessica bit her lip and closed the gap between them. She undid his belt, then the button to his pants. She slowly unzipped them, her eyes still locked with his.

Moisture collected at the apex of her thighs. Her body was craving this man before her, but she was going to force herself to wait just a little longer.

Sex with Iker had always been explosive.

They were equals.

"It's just me and you tonight," she said.

He gave another nod. His chest was rising and falling fast.

Her hands shook as she slid them inside the tops of his pants. She gripped them and shoved them down. They fell to the floor. He kicked them away. His boxer briefs were dark, and his erection tented the cotton material.

Jessica bit back a groan at the size of his cock. She hadn't forgotten this part of Iker. She'd had plenty of fun with his fat cock.

Jessica pushed his underwear down. His cock sprang free. It was long, angry-looking with its purple and wide mushroom tip.

"Get on the bed, Jess." His curt words broke through her devious thoughts.

Ideas of what she wanted to do with his cock had flooded her mind.

"What?"

"On. The. Bed." He bit the words out through gritted teeth.

She almost said no. She wanted to see what he would do if she disobeyed him. Her core clenched at the thought.

At the moment, she wasn't as brave.

She sat on the bed and scooted back to the middle. He knelt on the bed and crawled over her, forcing her to lie on her back.

Iker leaned over her and captured her mouth in a kiss. A moan erupted from her as she turned all of her pleasure to Iker.

His tongue slipped inside her mouth, stroking hers. Iker dominated the kiss, controlling every part of it. He tore his lips from hers and trailed hot kisses on her jawline and down to her neck.

She gasped at the sting of his teeth sinking into the hollow of her neck. He smoothed the area over with his tongue. Her hands rested on his shoulders. She moved them, exploring him. He appeared larger than the last time they had been together.

Her fingers found their way to his hair and threaded their way into his thick strands.

Iker was going on an exploration of his own. He captured her nipple in his mouth. She cried out from the pressure of his suction. His other hand teased her other bud, pinching and rolling it. He switched to using his teeth to gently nip her bud, then swopped over to the other one. He took his time with that one until she was writhing.

Nipple stimulation always enhanced her arousal.

Looked as if Iker remembered.

He continued on his journey south, licking and kissing a path down to her core. Her legs fell apart, opening herself to him. The liquid heat inside her rolled through her body. Her soaked pussy was anticipating his arrival.

"Iker," his name came out a moan.

He nipped her inner thigh. A deep throaty chuckle came from him.

"Patience is a virtue," he murmured, his lips brushing her thigh.

"Not right now, it isn't," she whimpered.

Did he want her to beg him to put her out of her misery? At the moment, she'd do it. Just to feel his mouth on her.

"Jesus." His finger slid through her slit. His heated gaze met hers. "This is all for me?"

He held up a finger, showing it coated in her honey. Jessica jerked her head in a nod and groaned, watching him lick his finger clean.

He pressed a kiss to her slit. Jessica lifted her hips to offer herself up to him. A cry escaped her when his tongue made the journey through her parted lips. A feral growl vibrated from him. His hands urged her thighs to open wider.

Iker covered her pussy with his mouth, and Jessica could have wept. Her body shook while he feasted upon her. He captured her clit, and her body bucked off the bed.

"Where are you going?" He pushed her back down with one hand.

The flat of his tongue bathed her clit, capturing it with the sweetest pressure. Jessica's breaths were labored as an electric current flowed through her body. Her nipples, sensitive from his attention, tingled. Her skin was on fire. It wasn't going to take long for her to peak.

Iker introduced a finger inside her while suckling her swollen bud.

Then a second one was introduced, stretching her walls.

She cried out, unable to contain what he was doing to her.

He fucked her with his two fingers, all the while focusing on her clitoris.

She shot her hand out and gripped his hair as he increased his speed and pressure.

It was too much.

Jessica detonated.

A scream erupted from her lips. Her body arched off the bed, trembling from the orgasm taking over her. Her entire body was taken hostage by the sensations racing through her. Every inch of her body grew sensitive with the waves of her climax rolling from her head to her toes.

Finally, she fell back against the mattress. Her body was covered with a fine coating of sweat. Her breaths were still labored,

The bed shifted from Iker crawling to brace himself over her.

"Open your eyes," he ordered.

Her eyes flashed open to meet his feral gaze. His hair was standing up on end, and she could see the wetness on his face from her release. The blunt tip of his cock breached her opening.

"I want you to see who is fucking you."

"Iker," she breathed.

His eyes darkened at the sound of his name. The delicious stretch of her walls to accommodate his girth was a welcome sensation. There was no doubt in her mind who was possessing her body.

He sank completely into her.

Their simultaneous groans filled the air.

Iker held still. He lowered his head and claimed her lips. She wrapped her arms around him, allowing him to take control of the kiss. His tongue boldly stroked hers.

He withdrew from her body, only leaving the head of his cock in, then gave one hard thrust.

Jessica gasped, breaking the kiss from the force of his cock pushing into her.

He repeated the motions, unforgiving as he truly fucked her.

This wasn't sensual. It wasn't a cute round of sex.

No, it was downright fucking.

A claiming.

It was Iker reminding her that her pussy had only ever belonged to him.

Jessica held on to his arms, her head thrown back. She met him stroke for stroke. Her hips rose to meet his.

"Fuck," he rasped. He lowered himself to bury his face into the crook of her neck. Hot kisses were littered along her neck and shoulder. "Jess."

Her name was drawn out in a deep groan.

His hips quickened.

He lifted her leg, changing the angle, allowing his cock to rub her clit with each thrust.

Jessica couldn't handle it.

She crested again.

Iker joined her. He threw his head back and roared through his release. Thick coats of his seed jetted inside her.

He gently lowered himself to rest on her, his

arms keeping the bulk of his weight off her. Their breaths were labored.

He leaned down, resting his forehead on hers. Jessica opened her eyes and found his to be closed.

His semisoft cock was still buried inside her. She didn't want them to move. If she could, she would stay right here in this moment for the rest of her life.

IF THIS WAS what Heaven was like, then Iker never wanted to move. He glanced down and took in the sight of Jessica in his arms. He held her close while she slept.

Yesterday, after the bombing at the courthouse, he had sent her away so he could concentrate. He and his team had jumped in to help to get the injured out of the building. But he wouldn't have been able to focus if he'd known she was still there.

There was no way for him to tell if the area would have been safe, so he'd made her leave before they blocked all the roads ensuring she would have been stuck down there.

Zain had dropped him off. He remembered feeling exhausted.

Cruz hadn't been taken in the courtroom, so he

was not near the blast. Iker was fairly certain that bombing had everything to do with the fallen officer.

The Demon Lords was not going to stand for him testifying against Huff.

He had rung the doorbell and hadn't heard anything. After the second time, he had heard movement.

Iker didn't know what had come over him the moment she'd opened the door last night. The light had shined on her, revealing her sleepy face, her soft brown skin, and it hit him.

He had to have her.

It had taken everything he had to restrain himself to begin with. His initial instinct was to take her up against the wall in her foyer, but that wasn't how he wanted their first time to be after reconnecting.

Jessica was a classy woman who probably would have loved him fucking her against the wall.

But no.

He wanted to do it right.

He lifted a hand and trailed his fingers along her cheek. The sun was just rising, its rays floating in through the windows.

She was the most important thing in his life. His heart skipped a beat at her beauty. They had made love for hours. It was just like old times. They had utilized a few items from her nightstand drawer. He loved how they could just be free with each other during lovemaking.

Her dark eyelashes fluttered open, revealing her deep-brown eyes.

"Morning," she whispered.

"Mornin'," he replied. He lowered his head to her and captured her soft lips. They were still swollen from all of his kisses. This one was full of emotion. He wanted to convey what he felt for her.

They pulled away, breathing heavy.

His gaze landed on his wallet sitting on the nightstand. Seeing it was like getting a splash of cold water in his face.

"What's wrong?" Jess asked. Her hand petted his chest to get his attention.

"Um, Jess..." He exhaled and rubbed his face. Met her eyes. "It's probably late to mention this now, but I'm clean. I got tested about a month ago and haven't been with anyone for a long while."

"Oh." She sat up and rested her head in her hand. The blanket was dangerously low on her breasts. "Me, too."

He bit back a growl at the thought of other men tasting what she had, but he knew he had no right to say a thing. It didn't matter. They were back together.

Iker reached for her and tugged her back into his arms. She giggled and snuggled close to him.

"I've missed you, Jess," he murmured. He slowly rubbed her naked back.

"I've missed you, too, Iker." She kissed his chest. "Want me to cook breakfast?"

Jessica's cooking was to die for. She was a true Southern woman at heart, even though she wasn't born in the South. She could throw down in the kitchen with any notable Southerner.

"Sure." He pecked a kiss on her lips. "You're going to need it for what I have planned for today."

"Is that so?" She raised a perfectly sculpted eyebrow. Her finger slid down his chest as she watched him with her big brown eyes.

He slipped his hand beneath the covers and cupped her ample ass.

"We have a lot of time to make up, and I haven't even got to the good part yet." He squeezed her ass. His cock was stiffening just imagining what he wanted to do next.

"Well, then let me go get breakfast started so we return to our activities." Her grin spread across her face. She tossed him a wink and rolled out of bed.

Iker settled back against the pillows and watched her walk over to her closet.

It felt good to be back with his woman.

He had never stopped loving her and he was going to spend every day showing and proving it.

21

Jessica leaned against the counter in the kitchen. A silly grin was on her face, and she wasn't even going to try to remove it. She had put on a pair of cotton shorts and a tank to come down and cook them breakfast.

If Iker was promising a day in bed, then she was going to have to make something with hearty sustenance. There was no telling how long he'd keep her in the bedroom.

That man knew what he wanted, and she wasn't going to say no.

She had thrown together two-ingredient biscuits, not wanting to waste time with chilling butter. The sausage gravy was currently simmering on the stove.

She glanced down at her phone. There were a few messages she had missed.

One from Darby suggesting they go to lunch today.

Welp, she had plans now, so she sent a quick message to Darby that she couldn't and maybe another day.

The second one was from her elder brother, Irvin. She had forgotten he was to come over to her house to look at the sink by her washing machine. It kept backing up, and Irvin refused to allow her to call a plumber. Her brother was stubborn and determined that he would be able to fix it.

She sent a quick message to him asking what time he was stopping by. She slid her phone in the pocket of her shorts and returned to the stove. She stirred the sausage gravy, humming one of her favorite songs.

"Now this is what I've really missed." Iker's strong arms enclosed around her, pulling her back against him. He brushed a kiss on the crook of her neck.

"Really? So that's why you're here? My cooking?" she teased. From the feeling of his rock-hard member pressing on her bottom, food was the last thing on the man's mind.

"Partly." He spun her around and cupped her face with his large hands. He was dressed in sweats and nothing else.

Jessica's mouth watered at the sight of his perfectly sculpted chest and abs. He kissed her, leaving her weak in the knees.

"When did you get a change of clothes?" she asked when they finally came up for air.

"I ran out to my truck when you were sleeping," he said. He shrugged nonchalantly. "I always keep a bag in there just in case it's one of those crazy days at work."

She knew of those days. There would be times when SWAT would be gone out on calls for hours.

"I hope you brought your appetite." She wrapped her arms around his waist and leaned her head against him.

"You know I did. What do we have?"

"Oh, I just threw together sausage, biscuits, and gravy."

"That fast?" He scratched his head. He looked around. "Canned biscuits?"

"Hell, no." She moved away at the sound of the timer on the stove going off. She slid her oven mitts on and removed the pan of biscuits.

The doorbell sounded.

"Can you get the door? Irvin was supposed to be dropping by," she said, turning the stove off. She was glad she'd made enough food. She was sure her brother would want a plate as payment for fixing her sink. She grabbed the melted butter she had waiting on the counter and began bathing the biscuits with it.

"Sure. I haven't seen your brother in a minute." Iker chuckled, leaving the room.

Jessica grinned. Her brother was going to be in for a shock when Iker opened the door. She had yet to really share with her family she had broken it off with Bradley. They knew of him, but she hadn't brought him around them yet. She just hadn't been ready.

She grabbed three plates from the cabinet and paused.

Did Iker just curse?

He and Irvin had always got along fine. She didn't know who was more shaken about their breakup back in the day, her or Irvin.

Jessica turned the gravy heat off. Curious, she left the kitchen and wandered into the front of the house. Iker was leaning against the doorway, not speaking.

She glanced around him and gasped when she saw who was on the porch.

"Bradley?"

He and Iker were in the midst of a staring contest.

This was the wrong time for Bradley to stop by her home. The sight of Iker opening the door in nothing but sweatpants wasn't good.

She swallowed hard and moved in front of Iker.

"Jessica," Bradley greeted her with a slight smile that didn't reach his eyes. He was casually dressed in jeans and long-sleeved t-shirt. He flicked his gaze to Iker and motioned to him. "What is he doing here?"

"Why don't you ask me?" Iker's intense glare was directed at Bradley.

Oh shit.

This wasn't going to go over well. Not for Bradley at least.

"I got this, Iker. Just go back inside." She was practically begging him with her eyes. She would speak with Bradley.

Iker dropped his gaze to her. The muscle in his jaw twitched. He had his hands in his pockets as if it would make him appear casual.

It didn't.

He resembled a king cobra ready to strike.

"Because I was asking Jessica a question, not you." Bradley stated so matter-of-factly.

Jessica's head whipped around to stare at him.

Did he have a few screws loose?

Iker moved behind her, and she immediately turned back to him. She rested her hands on him, her heart all but leaping into her throat. If looks could kill, Bradley would be meeting his maker.

Iker's face twisted up with a scowl.

"Iker," she called his name softly. His muscles were tense beneath her touch. He was two seconds from beating Bradley to a pulp. She had to call his name again before his eyes swiveled to her. "I got it. Go back inside. Please."

He palmed his beard. He shot another glare in the direction of Bradley.

"Handle him, Jess," Iker's voice was a low rumble. He backed away, but not without one last parting shot. "Or I will."

Jessica turned back to Bradley and stepped out on the porch. She pulled the door shut behind her and leaned back against it.

"I'm sorry about that," she said. She tried to will her heart to slow down. Curiosity got the better of her. Bradley wasn't a spontaneous person, and for him to show up out of the blue was out of the ordinary. "What are you doing here?"

"Are you and him back together?" Bradley's dark gaze settled on her.

"It's complicated," she breathed. She didn't know any other way to admit what was going on between her and Iker.

"So after everything he's done to you, you're taking him back?" He folded his arms across his chest and leaned against the pillar at the top of the stairs.

"Like I said, it's complicated." She waved a hand in the air. She wasn't going to go into details about her and Iker with Bradley. She had shared her past with him, but that was where she would draw the line. "What are you doing here?" she repeated her question.

"I had stopped by to see if you had wanted to go to brunch."

"Bradley, I meant what I said. I don't think I'm the one—"

He held up a hand and walked over to her. He stood in front of her, not touching her. His eyes held a sadness in them.

"It would have just been brunch to talk. If you don't want to be with me, that's fine. But it doesn't mean we can't be friends. I still care about you, Jessica."

She softened on the inside and smiled. He was such a sweetheart.

"I'll be returning back to work on Monday. We can meet for lunch one day."

"I'll hold you to it." Bradley smiled and nodded. "I'll see you later."

He leaned forward, kissing her cheek, and spun around on his heel. He jogged down the stairs and got into his car. He waved one last time then backed out of the drive. He pulled off and drove down the street.

It was then Jessica exhaled.

Her phone vibrated in her pocket. She took it out and saw a response from her brother.

Something came up. I'll swing by tomorrow.

oͺO

IKER PACED the floor waiting for Jess to come back in the house. A stormy rage brewed in his chest.

What is he doing here?

A growl slipped from him. How dare that motherfucker ask a question like Iker wasn't even there.

Iker eyed the front door and saw them talking. He couldn't hear what they were saying. He had half a mind to go back out there and toss Bradley's ass off the porch.

Bradley moved to stand in front of Jess.

He was too fucking close to her. Iker snarled and walked back to the kitchen but then halted. He leaned back against the wall.

What the hell was his problem?

But then the image of Jess riding him last night came to mind.

She was his.

Had always been.

He would make it official to Bradley and the entire fucking world that Jessica Horton belonged to him.

The door opened, snagging his attention. Jessica came back into the house and shut the door. She locked it and turned back to face him.

Iker found his feet carrying him to her before he even knew it.

"What did he want?" Iker demanded.

Jessica's eyebrows rose high at his question.

He softened his voice and swallowed back a snarl. "What did he want?"

"He had stopped by to see if I wanted to grab something to eat." She walked over to him, stopping inches from him. She rested a hand on his chest and tilted her head back. "That's all."

"But I thought you ended it with him?" It was Iker's turn to raise an eyebrow.

"I did, but that doesn't mean he can't stop by to see how I'm doing." She sighed.

"That's not what he was doing," Iker bit out. He gathered Jess to him, unable to stand being near her and not touching her. Her audible gasp fueled the fire for her. He pressed his erection against her stomach. "He was coming around here because you are a beautiful woman, and he wants you."

He swooped down and covered her mouth, cutting off her objections.

He didn't want to hear her make excuses for the other man. Iker was a full-blooded male, and he knew what Jessica looked like. She was a beautiful person on the outside and inside. How could any male resist her?

He as sure fuck couldn't.

Iker tore his mouth from Jessica and didn't hesitate in bending down and tossing her over his shoulder.

"Iker!" she cried out.

He stalked to the stairs and took them with ease. He pushed the door open to her bedroom and stopped by the bed, tossing her onto it. She lay back, staring at him as if he had lost his mind.

Maybe he had.

Seeing another man so close to her did something to him. He wanted Jess all to himself.

"Take off your clothes," he bit out through clenched teeth.

Her eyes were wide, but she didn't argue with him. She must have seen something in his eyes that warned her against that.

He untied his sweats and pushed them down. He hadn't dressed in anything else. There hadn't been any point. After breakfast, he had planned to drag Jess back into her bedroom.

"We'll eat later?" she whispered, a small smile forming on her lips. Her shirt was tossed onto the floor, as were her shorts, leaving her deliciously naked. She scooted to the edge of the bed, her gaze locked on his cock.

It jerked under her perusal.

Jess reached out and gripped his shaft.

Iker wasn't going to say a word.

She ran her hand along the length of him. Wrapped her lips around the tip. He groaned, always loving when she sucked him off.

She swallowed more of him until he hit the back of her throat.

She moaned, her eyes fluttering closed as she moved up and down his cock. Her small hand skated along him in tandem with her mouth. She couldn't fit all of him, but her hand made up for it.

"Fuck," the word tumbled from him. Her hot mouth was working wonders on him. His body trembled from the sensation of her grazing him lightly with her teeth.

Iker reached up, his hand tangled with her short hair. He gripped the strands tight to keep from shouting. Jessica was trying to take his soul.

The sensation of her saliva coating him allowed her hand to slip up and down his length.

He dropped his hand and reached for her, settling his hand on her head as he thrust his hips forward.

He groaned, loving everything she was doing, but they were going to stop now. He planned to sink into her and stay there for a while.

Her mouth was about to bring all that to a halt.

"Jess," he rasped her name.

Her eyes flew open, and the sight of her looking up at him with those big brown orbs while her lips were wrapped around him almost did him in.

She blinked and released him from her mouth. Her hand remained, stroking him.

"What is it?" she asked. She tried to appear innocent, but she was anything but.

Hell, he had forgotten already what he was about to say. His mind was turning to mush all because of the hands and mouth of this woman.

"Umm..."

Fuck.

What the hell was he about to say?

He watched with bated breath as she wrapped those sexy lips around him again, taking most of him inside her mouth. His muscles clenched. He closed his eyes and immediately thought of taking his gun apart and the steps to cleaning it.

It was something he had done a million times. He owned a substantial collection of firearms and enjoyed collecting them.

But at the moment, he was struggling on the first step of dismantling a gun.

A tremor racked his body. He had to stop her now. He opened his eyes and pulled his cock from her.

"What are you doing?" The woman had the nerve to pout.

"Scoot back," he directed.

She slid back to the middle of the bed. He turned and opened her bottom drawer of her nightstand.

He had made her a promise earlier and he was intent on carrying it out. He had taken all night worshipping her, but he hadn't claimed her everywhere as he wanted.

She bit her lip, smiling as her gaze landed on what was in his hand. Without needing to be told, Jessica rolled over onto her stomach. She rested her head down on the bed, leaving her ass in the air. She wiggled it and glanced at him over her shoulder with a sensual look.

The wink she tossed him told him everything he needed to know.

22

Iker covered her back and trailed kisses long her spine. She smiled, loving how he always made sure she felt good all over. His calloused hands slid across her soft skin, sending a shiver through her.

She ached for him.

Jessica didn't know what it was about him when he got all alpha male. He might as well have banged on his chest before he tossed her over his shoulder.

Sucking him off was just a treat for her. She was sad that he didn't allow her to finish. She loved watching him fall apart with his dick in her mouth. She would have accepted everything he would have fed her. She licked her lips knowing that later, she'd do it again and there would be no stopping her.

Iker made it to the small of her back. He used his hand to lift her hips back up. This was one of her favorite positions. Most thought that this gave the man all of the control, but contrary to popular belief, it was the woman.

She gasped as he nipped her ass cheek with his teeth. Jessica's fingers dug into the mattress. His hand appeared at the slit of her pussy, and he dipped a finger inside. She was already primed and ready.

A rumble vibrated from him. She was slick, and her honey coated her thighs. He pumped two fingers inside her core while he scattered kisses on both of her rear cheeks.

Jessica moaned, widening her position. She knew she was about to be in for one hell of a ride. Her walls clenched around his fingers as he slowly fucked her with them. His fingers disappeared from her. She exhaled, her body trembling with anticipation. He spread her open, his tongue reaching her drenched clit.

"Iker," she breathed his name.

He dipped into her wet heat, traveling north to her dark rim. She tried to relax, but her muscles grew taut. He teased her, his tongue circling her dark hole. His large hands gripped her ass tight while he took his time.

"What is it, babe?" he asked, his voice low and husky. "Tell me what you want."

"You." She jerked from his teeth nipping her again. Her core clenched when he returned to his activity. "Inside me."

She tensed from the cool sensation of the lubricant being applied to her. She rested her head down on the bed, excitement filling her. Her breath caught in her throat as he pushed a single finger into her. Her rim at first protested, but soon relented, granting him entrance.

Jessica stretched her arms out, snagging the comforter, and balled it into her fist.

He slipped in a second one and stretched her. Biting her lip, she tried to keep still and not rock her hips against his hand.

"You still love being fucked here, huh?" He withdrew the fingers slightly, then pushed them into her.

She nodded to answer him, but he wasn't going to let her get away with that.

"I need to hear you, Jess. Answer me."

He removed them. More coolness met her skin.

"Yes," she breathed.

The blunt tip of his cock pressed against her hole. She relaxed her body as much as she could. The pressure was more this time. His wide cock demanded entrance into her. Her puckered hole relaxed, allowing him to enter her.

A cry escaped her.

The sensation of fullness was one she loved.

He sank completely inside her and held still.

"Jess." Her name fell from his lips in a long, drawn-out moan. His hands gripped her waist. His cock swelled, almost as if it were pulsating. "Don't move."

He rested a hand to the small of her back to hold her in place.

She whimpered when he pulled back slightly, only to thrust forward again.

"Iker," she ground out his name.

"You're so tight," he rasped.

She could feel he was trying to hold back and control himself.

"God, it's so good."

She no longer could hold still.

He had set a steady pace. She rocked back and met him stroke for stroke.

Their cries of passion filled the air.

His hand came to rest on her shoulder while his thrusts became harder and faster.

Jessica slipped her hand underneath her. She parted her labia and rubbed her clit. Her fingers were coated in her wetness that slid out of her. She cried out from the pleasure washing over her.

Iker growled, his hips slamming into her. His hand gripped her shoulder harder. She would probably have a bruise come tomorrow, but she didn't care.

She slid her fingers down to catch more of her juices and returned back to her clit. She increased her pressure, and the familiar signs of her orgasm raced to her. Her swollen clit was ultra-sensitive. She quickened, flicking her nub.

"Jessica," Iker growled her name.

His cock was going so deep, Jessica couldn't hold back any longer.

She cried out, her body trembling. Her muscles grew tight, a scream erupting from her as she fell into the abyss of her climax. Her entire body tensed, and she clamped down around Iker.

He shouted, pumping her full of his release.

She rested her head on the bed, her one arm no longer able to hold her weight. Her body was coated with a fine sheen of sweat. Her breaths were labored, making it hard for her to breathe. She slipped her arm from under her. There was no way she was going to be able to move without assistance.

Iker grew still, his cock lodged deep inside her. It was still slightly hard.

How had she forgotten about Iker's stamina? It had always matched hers.

Jessica grinned. If they kept this up, neither of them would be able to walk come tomorrow.

IKER WASHED the last plate and put it in the dish rack. He glanced over at Jess who sat on the counter watching him. He took her in and was captivated by the sight of her. She smiled at him.

"What are you grinning about?" He smirked.

They had finally come out of the bedroom hours after the visit from Bradley. Just thinking of the idiot had Iker growing angry, but then he remembered one thing. Jess was here with him. They'd made love for hours.

He had nothing to worry about. She'd made her choice.

He dried his hands on a towel and moved over to her. It was flabbergasting how he couldn't take his hands from her. He stopped in front of her and pulled her to the edge of the counter. This time, she'd only thrown on a long t-shirt. It was oversized and hung off one shoulder. It was pointless for her to dress completely.

He still hadn't gotten his fill of her.

"I always liked watching you wash dishes," she admitted.

He arched an eyebrow at that information.

"Really? Why?" He stole a kiss of her lips.

She brought her arms up and entwined her fingers at the base of his neck, trapping him to her. He hadn't planned to go anywhere. He slid his hands over her supple thighs.

"Well, first off you're currently shirtless, so I get to have some eye candy." She giggled, skimming a hand down his pecs to his abdomen.

He rolled his eyes at her silliness.

"Then there is just something about a big, tough man doing domestic things such as cleaning."

She fell into a fit of laughter. He loved seeing her this happy.

He vowed right then and there that he would do whatever he needed to keep her this way. She deserved the world, and he was going to do his damnedest to ensure she got it.

"So, am I not to be washing dishes?"

"Well, of course, but with the way you look, you could be a rugged lumberjack outside cutting down a tree." Tears streamed down her face as she laughed. She leaned forward, resting her forehead against his chest.

He barked a laugh at her.

Where did she come up with this stuff?

"A lumberjack?"

"All you're missing is a flannel shirt and an ax."

He tipped her chin up so he could stare into her eyes. He brushed away the tears and took her all in. He would do anything for this woman. There was no doubt about it.

Flashes of yesterday at the courthouse came to mind. The screams and destruction those two small bombs caused was still fresh in his memory. Had he not caught sight of her and ran to speak with her, he and his team would have been inside when that happened.

In the back of his mind, he knew they were meant for not only Diego, but the SWAT team as well. It would have been killing two birds with one stone.

He had to come up with a way to ensure she remained free of danger. He and his team were planning to turn up the heat on the Demon Lords.

But he wasn't going to make the same mistakes he'd made in the past.

"I have never stopped loving you, Jess," he murmured.

Her smile faded. She studied him with her brown eyes.

"Iker—"

He reached up and silenced her with his finger on her lips.

"Let me finish." He cleared his throat. He wanted to be honest with her and he was starting today. He didn't want to hide his feelings. Tomorrow was never promised, so he was going to take advantage of having today with her. "I'm in love with you. You are a beautiful person on the inside and outside. I'm thankful you are giving me a second chance and I promise I will do what I can to make up for everything."

"Oh, Iker," she sighed. Her eyes filled with unshed tears. She reached up and cupped his face. "I've never stopped loving you either. Even if we would have never reconnected, you would have always owned a part of my heart."

"I also wanted to warn you that me and the guys will be turning up the heat on the Demon Lords. I want you to start carrying your gun with you," he said.

"What?" she exclaimed. "What's going on?"

"Look, I can't tell you everything, but we all know that bomb was mean for us and Diego," he admitted. He hated seeing the fear in her eyes, but he promised he would be transparent with her.

"What does that mean? Why do I have to carry a gun?" Her voice ended on a shriek.

He slowly rubbed her thighs in an attempt to calm her down.

"It means that I want you to just be aware of your surroundings. How about we go to the gun range so you can practice." That would make him feel better. He wanted to make sure she would be able to handle herself should she get in a sticky situation. He wouldn't be able to be with her around the clock and just wanted to ensure she could protect herself.

"Okay. I don't know if I like the sound of this, but I guess I don't have a choice."

She bit her lip, and he held back a groan. Her plump lips were one of his weaknesses after her breasts, her ass, and pussy.

He lowered his head and captured her lips in a short, sweet kiss. He released her and watched her blink before focusing on him. He hadn't meant to scare her, but he needed her to understand what was going on in his work life.

"I promise, I will keep you safe."

"I know you will." She reached up and rested a hand on his chest. "Just promise me that you will be careful and watch your back."

"Always. I have six brothers and a sister in blue who always have my six." That was the truth. He never had to worry about his back when he was with his team.

His hand slowly went up higher on her thighs. She was bare underneath the t-shirt. His cock grew stiff at the thought. Heat flared in her eyes. His distraction from danger talk was working.

"Iker," she breathed. Her lips curled up in the corner with a small smile.

"What?" He made an attempt to appear innocent, but she saw right through him.

He abandoned the act and pulled her shirt over her head, dropping it to the floor. He untied his sweats and pushed them down to the floor. He kicked them away and grabbed her. He lifted her and positioned the head of his cock at her entrance. A shudder passed through him when it met her slick folds.

Shit, she was already wet.

Jessica wrapped her arms around his neck and

rested her knees on his waist. She rose then impaled herself on him in one easy downward thrust.

The sound of her whimper went straight to his dick. He captured her lips in a burning kiss and walked over to the wall to brace her against it.

He tore his lips from hers. He buried his face into the crook of her neck. He inhaled her intoxicating scent.

"Hold on, Jess. This might be a little rough."

"I'm always ready, Iker."

Jessica was back to work. Mr. Ablo had upped the security in the gallery. The gallery owner was taking what happened in his building very seriously. There were more guards patrolling, giving everyone a sense of being safe.

She had been back to work for two weeks now and hadn't missed a beat. Everyone was trying to get back to normal. The memories of the robbery haunted her every time she looked at that stairwell and elevator that went to the lower level.

Pushing that away, she turned back to her young client and her mother.

"Let me show you where we usually hold these events." Jessica motioned for them to follow her.

Today she was meeting with Mystelle and Odessa to go over paperwork and details of the sale. Before they signed anything, she always wanted to disclose how previous sales went, how many people attended, and what the gallery did to ensure they had a wonderful turnout.

The gallery wouldn't be taking a big profit from Mystelle. Mr. Ablo had been ecstatic that she had found such a young talented artist. He had a soft spot for children who loved the arts.

"We've actually been to the gallery quite a few times," Odessa stated.

"Really?

"Oh, yes. I try to come a few times a year. I just love seeing art from all around the world. It's like I get to travel and never even leave Columbia," Mystelle said. The teenager beamed, looking around.

"That is the point of art. You can even experience another time period also," Jessica noted.

They walked into the main room where the event was held. Jessica guided them around and described how Mystelle's work would be the center of attention.

"And being that you base a lot of your artwork off African culture, I have a few ideas that will go along with your theme." Jessica grinned. She spun on her heel and peered at the two of them. "What do you think?"

"I think this is amazing. I can't believe that you want to feature my work." Mystelle bounced around on her heels. Today her hair was pulled up in a huge afro puff. Her brown skin practically glowed while her eyes were full of amazement. "I keep pinching myself and expecting to wake up from a dream."

"I assure you, young lady, this is not a dream," Mr. Ablo's voice boomed behind them.

Jessica turned around to see her boss making his way to them. He was dressed in a perfectly tailored suit, as always. His smile was warm and welcoming.

"Mr. Ablo, if I may introduce you to Mystelle and Odessa Farmer." Jessica made quick introductions.

Mr. Ablo greeted them both with hearty handshakes.

"It's so nice to meet you, Mr. Ablo," Mystelle said. "I just can't believe you would want to feature me."

"You have to thank Jessica, my dear. She's the one who found you. This woman has an eye for great artwork. From what I've seen, she's made the right choice," Mr. Ablo said. He winked at Jessica. "I've never known her to be wrong."

"I just recognize beauty that should be shared with the world." Jessica shrugged.

"Well, I can tell you that your work will be selling off the shelves, young lady. I looked you up and found your social media. You are very talented, and your work definitely speaks for itself."

"I've been telling her that for ages, but teenagers never listen to their mothers," Odessa said dramatically.

They all shared a laugh. Mr. Ablo stayed to chat for a little longer before needing to go off to a meeting. Once he was gone, Odessa turned to her with a strange look, as if she wanted to ask something but was afraid.

"Any other questions?" Jessica asked.

"I do have one." Odessa raised her hand slightly. A bashful smile appeared on her face. "We heard about the robbery from a few weeks ago. May we ask what they were after?"

Jessica nodded. "Of course. I'm sure that would be a concern. I can assure you that Mr. Ablo has taken the necessary precautions to ensure we remain safe here."

"Oh, we are sure he has. I'm just nosey. What did they get?" Odessa's eyes grew wide.

"Come, I can show you what they were after," Jessica said. She motioned for them to follow her.

They walked together to one of the other large rooms where an Italian exhibit was displayed. They strolled over to a painting where a guard was stationed next to it.

"Here is what they tried to get from us. Thankfully, it was inside our high-tech vault."

"I've seen this before." Mystelle gasped. Her eyes grew wide, and she scanned the painting. "Bastiano La Civita's Women of Rome."

"You do know your artwork." Jessica laughed. She was truly impressed that a young sixteen-year-old would recognize such a masterpiece. "Bastiano La Civita painted this back in the early nineteen-twenties."

"And they wanted to steal this?" Odessa asked, eyeing the painting.

"Oh, yes. It's worth a fortune, and if it was sold on the black market, they would be able to pull probably double if not triple what it is already worth," Jessica said. She gave a nod to the guard standing by the painting. Every night, they were charged with putting the painting back in the vault. It was a timely ordeal, and that meant the painting could only be on display for certain hours to the public.

"We don't want to take up any more of your time. We do appreciate everything you are doing for Mystelle," Odessa said.

"It's no problem at all. Let me escort you out." Jessica smiled.

They walked to the entrance with the promise to speak soon. The show would be in two months, and that would give Mystelle time to get her stock together and for Jessica to plan a wonderful event.

Once the Farmers had left, Jessica went back to her office. Her ankle was aching a little. She had left the boot off and now she was rethinking it. She was tired of having it on but had brought it with her should she need it.

According to the doctor at her follow-up appointment last week, hairline fractures usually took their good ol' time healing.

"How did you find that little gal?" Tiff asked, catching Jessica as she sauntered into her office.

"A lead from a friend," Jessica said. She smiled and sat in her chair. "Isn't she cute as a button?"

"She is and she's about to blow up." Tiff laughed. She leaned against the doorjamb. "How are you feeling?"

"Okay. I'm glad to be back at work. I was going crazy at home." Jessica sat back, kicking off her flats.

At least she didn't try to put on heels today. She crossed her legs so she could reach her ankle. She gave it a slight rub and sighed. "How about you?"

"Not bad. Still a little antsy after the robbery."

Jessica understood. All of them were. But she was sure with time they would move past it and it would become a distant memory.

"Got anything interesting today?" Jessica asked.

"A few things." She glanced down at her watch. "Shoot. I forgot I have a conference call. I'll catch you later."

Tiff rushed away, cursing like a sailor. Thankfully, their offices were located away from patrons. Jessica closed her eyes for a second. She exhaled and tried to relax for a moment.

A knock sounded at her door. Her eyes flew open, and to her surprise, Bradley stood at the door.

"Bradley." He was the last person she expected to see standing there.

"Jessica, how are you? I hope you aren't busy." He smiled sheepishly and entered her office.

"Not at the moment." She stood just as he rounded the edge of her desk.

"You look beautiful," he murmured, giving her a one-armed hug and a kiss on her cheek.

"To what do I owe the surprise?" she asked.

"Well, I had said I wanted to take you to lunch. I'm actually free for the next couple hours and figured I'd stop by to see if today would be good for you."

He gave her an innocent look, and she couldn't help but laugh.

She glanced down at her calendar and saw that she didn't have any meetings for the rest of the day. Mystelle had been her last.

"I'm actually free." She laughed again. She had promised him lunch and she would go, but after today, she was going to have to distance herself from him. She didn't want to give him false hope about them getting back together.

He had suggested friends, but that wasn't going to work.

Iker's face, the day Bradley stopped by her house when he was there, flashed before her, and she knew he wasn't going for that. She had to keep her man from prison so he could arrest the bad guys who deserved to be there.

Yes, she was going to have to carefully let Bradley down.

Again.

"WHAT DO YOU THINK?" Bradley asked. He sat back in his chair and stared at her. For lunch he had brought her to a cozy Japanese bistro named Bento and Tea.

The lunch rush was thick, and he was able to snag them the last seats at the sushi bar. She sipped her drink and turned to him. There were a few others enjoying their meals along the counter.

A chef prepared their food before them. She was impressed by the restaurant's upscale yet casual atmosphere.

The miso soup was wonderful, as was the house salad. A pleasant Asian man was currently preparing their sushi.

"This place is nice. How'd you hear about it?" she asked.

"I've been here a few times. Sometimes for work, I'll bring clients." He shrugged and eyed her. A strange look passed on his face.

"What is it?" she asked. She would prefer to have him just ask her whatever he was thinking.

"Are you happy?" he asked.

She paused and thought about his question.

Was she?

The past two weeks with Iker had been wonderful. This time around, things were different. He was more affectionate and open with her.

The sex has even been enhanced and mind-blowing.

At the moment, she was in a good place.

"I am," she answered honestly. She met his gaze and smiled.

"That's good."

"Hot towels?" A waitress appeared next to them and offered a tray with small white rolled towels on it.

Jessica followed Bradley's example and cleaned her hands with the towel. She folded it and put on the empty tray. The waitress brandished another tray that held chopsticks on it.

"Thank you." Jessica nodded to her and picked up her set.

Bradley grabbed his and nodded. He showed her how to place them in the holder next to where her plate would be.

"Interesting," Jessica murmured.

Bradley chuckled at her amazement. Coming for lunch with him wasn't bad after all.

"Regular sushi lunch." The chef set Jessica's plate down in front of her and one before Bradley. "Sashimi lunch."

"Wow," Jessica gushed, glancing down at her plate. Everything looked perfect. She glanced at his plate, and the intricate presentation made it almost too pretty to eat. "Bradley, this place is amazing. Why are you just now bringing me here?"

"Not sure." He laughed and motioned to her food. "They have the best sushi in town."

Jessica took her first taste and groaned. The flavors exploded on her tongue. She dug in with a gusto, unable to stop eating.

"Here, taste this." Bradley offered her a piece of fish held between his chopsticks.

"What's that on it?" She studied it, tilting her head to the side. She normally wasn't a fan of raw fish.

"I dipped it in the soy sauce and then spread a small amount of wasabi on it."

"Isn't that super-hot?" she asked, taking a sip of her drink.

"The spiciness of it enhances the flavors." He motioned to it and grinned. "Try it. I'm sure you will like it."

"Okay, but I'm going to hold you responsible if my tongue falls off." She giggled and allowed him to place the sashimi in her mouth. The taste was one that was unique, and the wasabi wasn't too overpowering. She took another sip of her drink and smiled.

"And?" he asked, raising his eyebrow.

"Not bad. I wouldn't order it, but it's okay."

They continued to eat in silence, then Bradley spoke.

"Well, there is another reason why I brought you here," Bradley said. He reached for his napkin and wiped his mouth.

"What is it?" She turned a curious look his way.

"I've been offered a managerial position," he announced. A wide grin spread across his face.

"Oh my. That is wonderful." She put her sticks down and clapped for him. She truly was happy for him. "What does this mean?"

"If I accept, I'll have to transfer to Charleston." He went into details of the new position.

Hope blossomed in her chest. Maybe she wouldn't have to be cruel and cut all ties with him. If he moved, then that should do it. Him being in another town may increase the odds he'd meet someone else.

24

"It's a little early to be hitting the titty bar." Zain chuckled.

They were parked across the street from the Red Daisy Strip Club, watching the building.

"They got good food. I don't blame them." Iker's gaze was locked on the entrance.

They were currently waiting for their targets to come out of the building.

"Do you think they saw us?" Zain asked.

"I doubt it. They practically ran in there, like this was their first time going to a strip club." Iker massaged his beard. "They weren't thinking of nothing but seeing women getting naked."

Iker and Zain had tailed Floyd and John Boy

Rogers. He needed answers. The first one being, why his photo was in their father's house.

He'd looked into them, and they did live at the house. They weren't there when the bust happened, but both of them listed the meth house as their place of residence.

"Well, it's been a minute since I've seen a fine pair—"

"You thinking what I'm thinking?" Iker grinned.

"We have the best passes in the house to get in for free." Zain patted his badge hanging from the chain around his neck.

Iker and Zain were dressed in street clothes. They had both worked nights last night and had got off this morning.

Police work was never done.

Especially when it came to their own safety.

Iker needed to get to the bottom of this.

Why were the two of them following him?

He wouldn't be able to rest until he could ensure the Demon Lords weren't about to make a move on him.

"Well, let's go in, partner." Iker reached for the door and exited the vehicle.

They jogged across the street and headed to the door.

A bouncer stood on the inside of the door.

"Hello, gentlemen." The bouncer's deep baritone voice greeted them. He folded his arms in front of his chest. He resembled an NFL linebacker. He was tall and built like a house. "Welcome to the Red Daisy. Can I assist you?"

"You certainly can." Zain flashed his badge. "Two men just came in about ten minutes ago. Dark hair, jeans, t-shirts, look like they should be out in the country."

"Yeah, I seen them." The bouncer didn't appear to be fazed to have two cops standing in front of him.

Iker walked past Brickhouse.

"Where are you going?" the bouncer demanded.

Iker stopped near the edge of the wall that blocked the view inside the bar and leaned against the corner.

Iker scanned the front area of the establishment. Neon lights lit the room. There was a bar and tables where patrons could sit and eat. There was a nice lunch crowd, but it was half-naked waitresses walking around.

Some of the girls looked awfully young.

He turned back to Brickhouse and ambled over to him.

"What's your name?" Iker jerked his chin to him. He allowed a wide grin to spread across his face.

"They call me Bear."

"Hmm." Iker tilted his head and sized him up. "Very fitting."

Zain snorted.

"So, Bear. I'm sure your boss wouldn't want me and my boys to come running through this place." Iker's smile disappeared. He stopped in front of Bear and met his gaze with a hard one of his own. Bear had another inch or two on him, and about fifty pounds. "Or you can let us in so we can scoop up who we came for and we'll be out your hair in no time."

Bear stood, staring at Iker.

"Such a decision to make. One phone call, and the entire CPD can be down here tearing this place apart," Zain threatened.

"What will it be?" Iker lifted an eyebrow.

"Fine. Don't cause any trouble. Get who you came for and leave," Bear grumbled. He motioned for them to go inside. "They are in the main circle."

"Will do." Iker spun on his heels and headed into the club.

Zain arrived at his side and stalked down the

short hall. They turned the corner and made their way to the bar.

Iker casually leaned against the counter, allowing his eyes to adjust to the darkness. Zain parked next to him.

"Hello, gentlemen. Please tell me there is something I can do for you," a saucy voice spoke up behind him.

Zain turned around with a wide grin.

"Hey, doll. How are you?" Zain replied.

Iker rolled his eyes.

His friend could be corny at times, but it never kept the ladies from falling for his antics.

Iker glanced at the lady and found her to be a pretty woman with hot-pink hair cut into a pixie style.

"What are two delicious-looking cops doing here at the Red Daisy?" She lifted a glass to her lips and took a sip.

"Official police business," Zain said.

Iker rotated away from the two of them and scanned the area. They were there for a reason, and picking up women was not one of them.

Besides, Iker had a beautiful woman of his own who he was dying to get to after they were done.

"You should call me sometime," the barmaid murmured to Zain.

Iker's gaze landed on the duo they were trailing. He turned and slapped Zain on the shoulder.

"Make sure you tell her about that the VD you just got treated for," Iker announced.

Pink Pixie's eyebrows shot up high. She automatically leaned back away from Zain.

"What?" Zain sputtered. He flicked his gaze between the barmaid and Iker. "He's joking. Seriously. Tell her that's a lie."

Iker grinned and pulled Zain away from the bar. He wrapped an arm around Zain's shoulder and guided them toward the other side of the club.

"What the hell? Why are you cock-blocking?" Zain snapped, elbowing Iker. "Just because you are off the market, doesn't mean I have to be."

"I'm sure you'll thank me later." Iker pointed to the targets. "There's our boys."

"Yeah, whatever." Zain shrugged him off.

They stalked over to where the brothers were enjoying themselves. They were seated in a round velvet booth that allowed private parties to have their own personal entertainment.

The club smelled of cigarette smoke and weed. Iker grimaced, hating the scent. A few heads turned their way but soon averted their eyes once they saw the badges on Iker's and Zain's chest.

Floyd had shaggy red hair that appeared as if it hadn't been washed in weeks. John Boy had a buzz cut and was tossing singles at the women dancing on the poles before them.

Hillbillies coming into the city and dropping money like it was nothing?

Something was fishy.

"Well, look who it is," Iker shouted, slapping John Boy on the shoulder.

He swung around with a wide grin. It immediately faded the second his gaze fell onto Iker. His gaze dropped down to the badge hanging from Iker's chain. His eyes widened, and he fell back into his brother. Floyd froze in place before they both scrambled to leave out of the other side of the booth.

"Howdy, boys." Zain stood on the other opening.

They sat back and flicked their gazes between Iker and Zain.

The strippers bent down and gathered the money from the floor and took off, running away.

No longer having patience, Iker reached for John Boy.

"You two are coming with us."

THE BACK DOOR to the Red Daisy slammed open. Iker dragged John Boy out into the alley behind the building with Zain and Floyd following.

They pushed the two brothers up against the wall. The area was clear of anyone. There was a road for the garbage trucks to be able to drive and access the dumpsters. The air reeked of trash and urine. Iker didn't know which smelled worse, the alley or the inside of the club.

"What do you want?" Floyd hollered.

"We didn't do nothing," John Boy exclaimed, his wild eyes shifting back and forth between Iker and Zain. He held his hands up, palms facing out.

"Don't try to act innocent with me." Iker tightened his hold on the country boy's shirt.

Both of them had been following him and Jessica. What did they want? And who did they report their findings to?

"Oh shit. It's you." John Boy's eyes went round. His body trembled underneath Iker's hold.

"You recognize me?" Iker snarled. He glanced over at the brother who was focused on Zain.

"We need some information from you punks,"

Zain said. The ice coldness of his voice had Floyd's skin growing pale. "And you better answer them."

"Or what?" Floyd asked, his voice shaking.

"Or we'll run you in. I'm sure we can come up with some charges by the time we get to the precinct." Iker laughed. "We've already raided your father's home. I'm sure we can get really creative where you won't see the light of day for years."

The brothers shared a glance.

"What do you want to know?" John Boy turned his attention to Iker.

Iker released him and moved his jacket to the side, revealing his gun sheathed in its holster. He glared at the guy, daring him to run.

Zain wasn't too trusting. He kept a hand on Floyd's shoulder but stepped away slightly.

"Why was my picture in your house?" Iker said.

"What picture?" Floyd asked. He cried out from the punch Zain landed to his stomach.

Iker stared at Zain. He returned Iker's look with a shrug.

"Wait. I remember now," Floyd wheezed.

"Don't hurt my brother." John Boy made to move toward Zain, but Iker pushed him back against the brick wall.

"Don't try it. Answer the question and no one gets hurt," Zain snapped.

Iker didn't dare make any promises. Everything depended on why they were tailing him.

"Why was my picture in your house?" Iker hating repeating questions. He could sense they were stalling. He twisted John Boy's shirt into his fist. "Why?"

"You were a job!" John Boy hollered, red splotches appearing on his face. "Just a fucking job. We were told to follow you and report back what we saw."

"Who hired you?" Iker demanded to know.

Who the hell would hire these two numb nuts for anything?

"Don't tell him, Johnny," Floyd whined.

"I think I deserve to know who wants to be all up in my business," Iker retorted. He closed the gap between him and John Boy, his gaze narrowed on him. "You think you are afraid of whoever put you up to following me, you have no idea what I'm capable of."

John Boy's eyes widened, the color disappearing from his face. His shoulders slumped, and his gaze dropped to the ground.

"I don't know who actually gave us the job, but it was to show our loyalty to them," John Boy began.

"Johnny, no!" Floyd struggled with Zain but finally gave up. His breaths were labored as he focused on John Boy.

"A manilla envelope was put in our mailbox. It had your picture and instructions to report what we saw. We followed you for that entire day with that woman."

"Who is they?" Iker scowled, already knowing what the answer was going to be.

"Fuck. We're both going to get our asses handed to us," Floyd muttered. He rested his head back against the building. "We were gaining the trust of the Demon Lords."

Bingo.

Just as Iker thought.

They were coming for him.

He bit back a growl.

"What did you tell them?" Iker barked. His pulse raced at the thought that the gang was digging up intel on Jessica. The muscles in his jaw ached from him clenching it so tight.

"They wanted to know if you were with a woman, where y'all went, what you did. We had instructions to just watch and report. Nothing else," John Boy said.

"And you have no idea who wanted this information?" Iker stared at him, trying to distinguish if he was lying or speaking the truth. All he would need was a name. One single name and he could turn it over to Brodie who would be sure to uncover everything then.

"I don't know. They sent the envelope, we reported, then they paid us for it," John Boy said. He shook his head. "That was all. Easiest job we've ever pulled."

Iker stepped back. It didn't look like these two idiots knew anything. Zain eyed him and moved back away from Floyd.

"Let me warn you. Come near me or my woman again, and I can promise you, I'll be coming after you without my badge on," Iker warned. He turned on his heel and headed away from the two hillbillies.

"What's the plan?" Zain asked, walking along with him.

"Um, one more thing," Floyd called out.

Iker stopped and glanced at the brothers. They were whispering fiercely amongst each other before they broke apart.

"What is it?" Iker sighed. He dug a hand through

his hair; fatigue was starting to set in. It had been a long day, and it was only lunchtime.

"The woman that was with you," John Boy started.

Iker tensed, taking a step toward them. Zain's hand shot out and snagged his jacket.

"Is she all right? They were really interested in her. When I called to report, they knew her name."

Iker's blood ran cold.

Son of a bitch.

They were going after Jessica next.

Iker's gaze flickered to Zain's who must have read his mind.

"I'll drive," Zain offered.

They spun around and took off jogging toward the end of the building.

"You're not going to come after us, are you?" John Boy yelled out.

Iker ignored him. If anything happened to Jessica, there would be nothing stopping him from hunting them and every Demon Lord down.

25

"She's fine," Zain muttered. He pressed his foot on the gas, his car flying down the road.

Iker was quiet. He didn't want to think of something happening to Jessica.

This was what he had been afraid of.

Why he should have stayed away.

If she was hurt or harmed, he would never forgive himself.

His pulsed raced at the unknown. He'd called her cellphone, and she hadn't answered. It wasn't too uncommon for her to not answer if she was in a meeting or out in the gallery working.

"She may not have her phone on her."

Zain looked over at him. Iker hung up his phone and sat it on his lap just in case she returned his call.

Zain ran a red light and sped off.

They were getting closer to The Ablo Gallery.

Iker's hand closed into a fist. He would find out who had paid the Roger brothers to spy on him and Jessica.

Zain slowed down and took a left, pulling onto the gallery's street. He parked in front of the building. Iker didn't waste any time jumping out of the car once it rolled to a halt.

"I'll stay right here. Call me if she's okay," Zain shouted.

Iker nodded, turning to walk into the building. He entered and took note of a few security guards posted by the entrance. Iker nodded to them and strode up to the welcome station.

"Hello. Can I help you?" the woman asked. Her black glasses were oversized, taking up most of her face. Her gray hair was parted down the middle, stopping at her chin.

"Yes. Jessica Horton. Is she available?" he asked gruffly.

"Um, let me see if I can reach her by phone." The woman picked up the desk phone and dialed an extension.

Iker leaned against the desk and looked around. The two guards were eyeing him but remained quiet.

There was a nice amount of people walking through the establishment. All seemed normal. Nothing out of the ordinary.

Visions of the day he'd had to storm it with his team still haunted him. Seeing Jessica in the hands of the robbers had struck a chord with him.

Blowing out a deep breath, he focused his attention back on the woman behind the desk.

"She doesn't seem to be answering her phone. Is there something I or someone else can help you with?" Her gaze dropped down to his badge hanging around his neck. "Are you here about the robbery?"

"No, I'm her—" he stopped abruptly.

Fuck.

He didn't know if they were official or not.

The minute he saw her, that was getting clarified.

Quick.

"It's a personal visit. Is Tiffany working?" he asked.

"I can try her. I just saw her not too long ago. May I ask your name?" She picked up the receiver to the phone again.

"Iker Baldwin." He grew uneasy the longer he stood there waiting. He could have just run back to her office. He pushed off the desk. "I've been here plenty of times. I know where her office is. I'll just go back there."

"Are you sure?" the woman asked.

"Yup." He spun on his heel and marched down the main hall of the gallery. He went in the direction he had traveled before on the night of her art show.

He arrived at the back offices and walked to Jessica's door. He pushed it open and found her office dark.

"Iker?" Tiffany's voice appeared behind him.

"Hey, Tiffany. Do you know where Jessica is?" he asked. He tried to remain calm and walked in her direction.

"Oh, yeah. She said she wasn't feeling well." Tiffany gave a small laugh. "She did look a little green around the gills. She went home not too long ago."

Relief filled him, but something was still tugging in the back of his brain.

"Did she say what was wrong?" he asked.

"Probably some bad sushi." She shrugged and leaned against the doorjamb of her office. Her eyes slowly perused his body.

He shifted uncomfortably.

"Are you two back together?" she asked.

"I'm going to head out." That was his cue to

leave. He gave her a salute and stalked from the back offices, not giving her a chance to ask anything else.

It was none of her business. If Jessica hadn't told her anything, then he certainly wasn't.

Iker left the gallery and slid back into Zain's ride.

"She good?" Zain asked.

"Her coworker said she wasn't feeling well and went home." Iker coasted a hand over his beard. He didn't like the thought of her being sick and going home by herself. Why didn't she call?

"Do you want to swing by her house?" Zain asked, guiding the car into traffic.

"Yeah, I just want to make sure she's okay for myself." Iker settled back in his seat. He watched the scenery going by, only speaking to give Zain directions.

He took out his phone again. Maybe she wasn't answering because she was driving.

Or maybe she was throwing up and couldn't answer the phone. If she'd had bad sushi, then that would make anyone feel like shit.

He dialed her number, and it just rang before going to voicemail. He hung up and waited a second before hitting her number again.

As before, the call went to voicemail.

A sense of dread filled his stomach.

"I'm sure she's okay. She's probably asleep," Zain murmured.

Iker jerked his head in a nod, but he didn't believe it.

Something was wrong.

ZAIN PULLED into Jessica's driveway and parked behind her car. Iker exited the vehicle and walked past hers. He peeked inside and didn't see anything out of the ordinary.

The sound of another door slamming shut drew his attention. Zain stood beside his car and gave a nod.

"Go ahead in. I'll wait here." He yawned and glanced around the neighborhood.

Iker jogged up the front stairs, the sense of dread growing. He rang the doorbell, cursing that he no longer had a key to her house. He turned and scanned the yard.

Iker didn't hear anything moving in the house. No television. No music.

An eerie silence.

He spun back and rang the door again.

"Where are you, babe?" he muttered. Stepping

closer to the door, he peered inside, and his blood ran cold.

A body was lying on the floor of the foyer.

Jessica.

"Shit," he cursed. He grabbed the handle and jiggled it. Panic filled him. He prayed for the door to just magically open, but it didn't.

"What's wrong?" Zain asked.

"Call for an ambulance. She's on the floor," Iker snapped. He stepped back and banged his shoulder into the door, but it didn't give.

"This is Officer Roman, we need an ambulance," Zain began.

Iker drowned out his friend while he tried to force the door open. He threw himself against it again, but the damn thing was built solid.

"Here." Zain arrived next to him and knelt by the door.

Of course, Zain would have a lock pick kit.

Zain had the door open in seconds. Iker pushed past him and rushed inside. He knelt by Jess who was too still.

"Jessica?" His heartbeat pounded in his ears. He reached out and pressed two fingers to her carotid artery. There was a faint beat underneath his fingers.

"I'm going to leave the phone here with you on

speakerphone. I'm going to check out the house." Zain set his phone on the floor, then pulled his weapon out. He quietly disappeared into the house.

"Baby, can you hear me?" Iker asked. There were no signs of vomit or anything around her. He carefully rolled her over. Her body was limp and her breaths shallow." Come on, baby. Wake up."

"Sir, is she breathing?" the operator asked from Zain's phone.

"Faintly," Iker replied. He didn't see any injuries on her and scanned her body. "Get an ambulance here, now."

"They have been dispatched. Who am I speaking with?" she asked calmly.

"Officer Iker Baldwin. This is the home of my girlfriend, Jessica Horton."

"Are there any notable injuries?" she asked.

"Negative." He trailed a hand over her body and didn't see anything. There was no swelling of her face to signify she had an allergic reaction, or any goose eggs on her head from hitting it. His gaze landed on her chest, and his heart stopped.

Her chest was no longer rising and falling.

"Jessica!" he hollered, shaking her by her shoulders. Fear unlike anything he'd ever known crept through him.

"What's going on, sir?" the operator asked.

"She's not breathing," he snapped. He checked for a pulse again and felt a faint one. His basic life support training was kicking in. Iker had never thought he would have to perform CPR on someone he loved. Pushing down the anxiety and panic, he lifted her chin and covered her mouth with his. He blew, watching her chest rise.

"What's going—oh, shit!" Zain jogged back into the foyer. He paused before dashing and scooping up his phone. "How far away are they?"

Sirens sounded outside. Zain ran over to the door to wave them down.

Iker blew two slow breaths into Jessica then rested his fingers on the side of her neck again. His hands trembled. Her pulse was slow and thready.

The operator gave instructions while they waited for the EMTs to come inside.

Breathe for her.

One breath.

Two.

Repeat.

Check for a pulse.

Zain ran out to the porch and flagged the squad down.

Iker said every prayer he could think of. He

couldn't lose her now when he was only just getting her back. Her body was so still.

Tears formed in his eyes.

He bent down again, breathing for her. If he could, he'd swap places with her in a heartbeat.

"They're right here in the foyer," Zain said, waving the paramedics inside the house.

Two men walked in with a stretcher and utility bags.

"How long has she been down?" the older man with a baseball cap on asked.

He lowered the cart to the floor, while the other medic joined Iker on the floor near Jessica. He had an ambu bag in his hand. He immediately gave her more breaths while his partner unloaded their gear.

Iker moved out of the way as the medics began working on her. Zain came to stand by him, quietly watching them.

"She's breathing."

Iker sighed, standing to his feet. His pulse pounded in his ears. He couldn't take his eyes off Jessica as they performed life-saving measures for her.

Minutes passed slowly.

They got her on the stretcher and strapped her in.

"All right. We're going to head to General. Are you riding with us?" Baseball Cap asked.

"Yeah." Iker's voice was gruff.

"I'll lock up here and meet you there." Zain slapped him on the shoulder. He squeezed tight, meeting Iker's gaze. "She's going to make it."

Iker jerked his head in a nod and followed the EMTs outside. They loaded Jessica into the back of the ambulance. Iker climbed in with her and sat off to the side while the medics entered. They started IV fluids in her, connected her to a machine that monitored her heart rhythm.

"I think she's stable enough for us to go ahead," Baseball Cap said.

"Let's roll." The other medic left the truck and shut the door behind him. He got into the driver's seat, and they were off.

Iker eyes were gritty. His vision blurred from unshed tears as he stared at Jessica. All he wanted was to see her eyes open. Those pretty brown eyes were beautiful and captivating. He needed to see her smile, hear her laugh.

Iker didn't say a word as the medic monitored her. They radioed in ahead to the emergency department, giving them a report.

"Come on, Jess. You can't leave me," he

murmured. He reached out, taking her hand in his. It was cool to touch. He held on to her, trying to let her know he was there with her. He bent his head down, his eyes closed.

The medic cursed.

Iker lifted his head.

"What's wrong?" he asked.

"She's going into respiratory failure."

Iker's heart seemed to leap into his throat as he observed the medic work on the woman he loved. He was helpless, watching the medic do what he could to keep her alive.

Iker just prayed it was enough.

Iker sat in the waiting room of the hospital. He held his head in his hands as he stared at the floor. The images of Jessica in the back of the ambulance haunted him. She'd stopped breathing again, and the medics had to perform life-saving measures.

By the time they got her into the emergency room, she was breathing again. This time with a tube down her throat.

Once she was stabilized in the emergency room, they had moved Jessica to the Intensive Care Unit. He'd parked himself in the small waiting area for family members.

Soft crying filled the air. He clenched his fist and glanced up. His gaze landed on the Hortons. He had called them once they had arrived at the hospital. Her parents were needed since they were technically Jessica's next of kin. Once her parents were there, they had been in communication with the doctors who were taking care of Jessica. Since she'd been moved, Iker had yet to see her.

Cara Horton, Jessica's mother, was the spitting image of what Jessica would look like in twenty-five years. She used tissues to wipe the tears from her face. Her husband, Arnel, sat with his arm around her, comforting her.

Jessica's brother, Irvin, had been who Iker had called. He had been cool, and they had hung out a few times when Iker and Jessica were dating before. Iker hadn't been sure if Irvin's number was the same, but thankfully, it was.

Irvin came over and sat next to Iker.

"Thanks for finding her, man." Irvin's voice was low.

Iker ran his hand through his hair. He blew out a deep breath and glanced over at him.

"I just hope that she'll be okay," he said.

"My sister is a fighter. She'll pull through this." Irvin sat back. "Do we even know what happened?"

"No." Iker shook his head. "I had stopped to see her at the art gallery, and her coworker, Tiffany, had said that Jess left sick. Jess told her it might be bad sushi."

"My sister doesn't have a seafood allergy. That girl loves seafood." Irvin sighed.

"I know. Hopefully the doctors will figure it out."

Irvin stood and moved back over to his parents.

"I'm going to see if the physicians can give us an update." Arnel stood and walked out of the waiting room. Arnel was a tall, older gentleman with slightly graying hair. He and Irvin were of similar build and looks.

They all sat in silence waiting for Arnel to return. Irvin put an arm around his mother and held her close.

It pained Iker to see Jessica's family so torn. They were close, and this was obviously tearing them apart.

"Thank you for finding my baby, Iker," Cara said. She swiped her face again with the tissues.

"No need to thank me, ma'am. Finding her like that was not what I would have wanted." He had hoped that he would have found her asleep. Hell, he would have taken vomiting with her head in the toilet.

Anything but this.

The unknown was killing him.

What was going on?

"I can't imagine if you hadn't gone looking for her..." Her voice cracked. She dabbed her eyes with her tissues. She exhaled and sat in silence, then asked, "Are you two trying to work things out?"

"Yes, ma'am." Iker nodded.

"I don't understand you young people. Everything was fine between you two, then she comes and tells me that you broke up." She eyed him as if waiting for a reply.

"It's complicated, ma'am," he admitted.

"You young folks don't know the meaning of complicated."

Iker bit back a smile, remembering Jessica's mother was just as feisty as she was.

The door to the waiting area opened, and Arnel returned. Iker watched the older man walk over to his wife and take a seat next to her.

"What did they say, Arnel?" Cara asked.

"Well, the breathing tube is helping Jessica. They still don't know what is going on with her. They are still running a ton of testing to try to figure out what is causing this."

"Should we stay or go home?" Cara asked.

"Mom and Dad, there's nothing we can do right now. They have your number. It's getting late. Let me get you home, and we'll come back first thing in the morning," Irvin suggested.

Cara and Arnel shared a look, agreeing. Irvin helped his mother up from her chair.

Iker stood and walked over to them.

"I'm going to stay just a little longer," Iker said.

"We gave them permission to speak with you," Arnel said. "I'm sure there's a long, drawn-out reason why you're back in the picture. That daughter of mine has a strong head on her shoulders, so if you're back, then I'm sure it's because she wants you to be here."

"Yeah, mainly I was an idiot," Iker admitted.

"All men are at some point. We just have to come to the realization and know there is a person out there who will make us better men. When you find that person, you hold on to her." Arnel gave a soft smile and took his wife by the hand.

"I'll call you if something comes up," Iker said.

"Don't stay too long, Iker. You're no good for Jess if you don't take care of yourself." Cara patted him on the arm.

Irvin gave him a salute and followed his parents from the room, leaving Iker alone.

He blew out a deep breath and glanced around the empty room. He took a seat and leaned his head back against the wall. He closed his eyes and tried to will his body to relax.

But he couldn't.

He had to see her.

Iker left the waiting area and went down to the Intensive Care Unit's reception area.

"Can I help you?" The woman behind the desk let loose a yawn and covered her mouth.

Iker's gaze dropped to her badge.

"Yes, Patty. I was wondering if I may see Jessica Horton?" he asked.

"Visiting hours are—"

"Please, ma'am. I am the one who found her unconscious in her home. I just need to see her for myself." He ran a hand along his jawline, desperate to see her. "Please."

She stared at him for a moment, waving him to the door.

"She's in room five," Patty said.

"Thank you."

A low buzzer sounded. He jogged over to it and pulled the door open. The nursing unit was decorated in all white, giving off creepy sterile vibes. A few nurses were working at the nursing desk, ignoring him. He glanced up and saw that each room was numbered.

He followed the signs until he found her room.

A large glass window allowed him to observe Jessica lying in her bed.

His stomach clenched at the sight of her. His feet carried him into her room. There were so many cords and wires around her. The breathing tube coming from her mouth that connected her to the machine at the other side of the bed had Iker reliving those moments when he'd had to breathe for her.

His strong feisty Jessica looked tiny, fragile, and so still.

He walked over to her bed and sat in the chair next to her.

"Baby, I'm here." His throat constricted. He didn't like seeing her this way. It tore him up inside to think that she may not make it.

He gently reached out and took her hand in his. It was small and delicate. Her nails painted bright-coral brought a smile to his face. Jessica loved a good manicure and pedicure.

"I don't know if you can hear me, Jess, but I need you to fight. Come back to me," he pleaded.

The was no response. Not even a flicker of her eyes to confirm she could hear him.

It didn't matter.

He was here and would be for the long haul until she woke up.

Jessica was a fighter.

IKER LEFT the ICU in search of coffee. He'd officially been awake for twenty-four hours and was ready to crash.

But he couldn't leave the hospital.

What if Jess woke up?

He'd spent the last hour in the room with her just talking. He wanted her to know she wasn't alone in there. He spoke of the first time they had met. He had never been one to be tongue-tied over a woman until her.

He held a gym membership and had gone to work out. He and Zain had been lifting weights, and Iker was distracted by melodious laughter from nearby. He glanced up at the indoor track on the second level, and it was then he'd seen her.

Her and Darby had applied for the gym's trial membership and were walking along the track. Her smile alone had him tripping over dumbbells.

In order to get her attention, he'd decided to go running on the track. It took three days before he had worked up the courage to approach her. After their first date, they were inseparable.

So much time had been wasted due to his fuck-up.

Lost in his thoughts, he almost didn't hear his name being called.

"Iker."

He found Mac and Sarena standing in the doorway of the waiting area.

"What are y'all doing here?" He spun around and headed in their direction.

"Zain called us," Mac said. He waved Iker into the room. He went in with Sarena following behind him.

A lump formed in Iker's throat.

His entire team was there.

Declan and Aspen. Ashton and Deana. Myles and Roxxy. Brodie and Jordan stood off to the side having a quiet conversation.

Zain pushed off the wall and walked over to him. His friend met him with solemn eyes.

"How's she doing?" Zain asked.

All eyes turned to him.

"She's on the breathing machine. She hasn't woken up yet, and the physicians don't know what caused this." Iker sighed.

"It was luck that you found her," Ash said.

Deana stood by his side holding his hand.

Iker looked around the room. It was late, and there was no telling how long he would be there.

"You guys didn't have to come—"

"What are you talking about?" Myles said. "We're family and we're here to support you, brother."

Iker nodded, too choked up to speak.

"I'll go chat with the nurses and get the inside scoop. Sometimes there is more than the doctors want to tell," Sarena said.

"Thanks, babe." Mac kissed her forehead, then she disappeared out the door.

"Are they at least thinking foul play?" Brodie asked.

"We're not sure. The only thing I know is that she left work not feeling well and blamed it on bad sushi." Iker dropped into a chair and pushed a hand through his hair.

"You look like shit. I'll go get coffee since it seems as if it's going to be a long night," Jordan said.

"I'll come with you," Roxxy volunteered. She stood from her seat and glanced around. "Anyone else want coffee?"

All hands went up.

"I better come, too, and help carry," Aspen said. She stood and left the room with the girls.

"What do you really think happened?" Declan asked.

"I honestly don't know." Iker was dumbfounded that the doctors didn't know anything. They were running tons of tests, and so far, they still couldn't determine what was wrong with her. "It's not a stroke or her heart. There was no trauma noted to her. It's a fucking mystery."

"Have they done a toxicology screen?" Mac asked.

"Jessica doesn't do drugs," Iker snapped. He met his sergeant's gaze with a hard one of his own. How dare he suggest a thing? Jessica wasn't into that type of thing.

"I'm not saying she did. Maybe someone slipped her something," Mac replied.

"I'm sure they are checking all angles," Brodie said.

"They have to be. If they don't know what caused a young, healthy woman to collapse, they are not going to leave any stones unturned," Ash said.

They fell into a comfortable silence. It meant a lot to Iker that his squad was there. Myles was right.

They were family. There was no closer unit than theirs.

"Let us know if there is anything we can do," Myles murmured.

"Just y'all being here means a lot. If you pray, send one up for Jess," Iker said. He leaned back in his chair and rested his head on the wall. He was exhausted, but that wasn't going to keep him from the hospital.

"You want to head home? One of us can stay here and keep an ear out for you if you want," Ash offered.

"Nah, I'm good." Iker shook his head.

"You sure? You look like shit." Zain chuckled.

Iker held up his hand in Zain's direction and flipped his friend off.

"I'm good. As soon as the girls come back with coffee, I'll get my second wind." Iker sighed. He would not be able to get sleep. The sight of Jessica lying on the floor haunted him.

"Did you really have to perform mouth-to-mouth on her?" Ash asked.

Iker jerked his head in a nod.

There was no way he could answer that question at the moment. His chest grew tight with emotions.

That was something he hoped he would have to never live through again.

Just thinking if he and Zain hadn't gone to her house or had showed up ten or fifteen minutes later...

She wouldn't be here.

"Jesus," Ash breathed. "I'm sorry, man."

"We're here for you, brother." Declan leaned back in his chair, crossing his ankles.

Iker wasn't surprised that his team would camp out with him. It was pointless to suggest they leave. Each of them was just as stubborn as he was.

27

Three days.

At least Iker thought it had been three days. The time passed by in a blur. He had only left the hospital for short spans to go shower and change clothes. He'd taken catnaps here and there but didn't want to be away from Jess too long.

That morning, they were able to extubate her. Jessica was officially breathing on her own.

Now they just needed her to wake up.

Her parents were down in the room visiting her and speaking with the physicians.

Thanks to Sarena, they had been able to move her to a step-down unit that offered private rooms. It was right off of the ICU, so if they needed to take her back, it was close by.

Iker couldn't wait for the moment he could speak with her. He needed to hear her voice, hold her in his arms, and feel her pressed up against him.

Iker was never going let her go after this.

He'd come to a decision. He was thirty-four years old, and it was time for him to settle down. Jessica was it for him. He was going to roll the dice and take the chance on their future. He had a team who had his back and would be there to help protect him and his family.

Iker reached for his tall coffee cup and took a sip out of it. He had practically survived off of the dark liquid for the past few days. There wasn't enough caffeine in the world to fight his exhaustion. What little sleep he had got was riddled with nightmares. He shuddered thinking of them.

One particular one that bothered him was the one when he didn't make it in time. He dreamed he'd found her on the foyer floor and turned her over. She was already gone. It had been too late to save her.

He blinked and tried to clear the vision in his head.

He had made it in reality and saved her.

She was here.

Standing, he stretched. He headed toward the door. He needed to take a quick walk.

The door opened, and Cara and Arnel stood there. Smiles lined their faces.

"She woke up," Cara gushed. Tears streamed down her face.

"What?" Iker took a step back. His heart almost leaped in his throat. "She's awake?"

"Yes." Arnel wiped his face, wrapping an arm around Cara's shoulders. "We were speaking with the doctors and turned to look at her and found her staring at us."

Arnel brought Cara completely in his arms, hugging her to him.

Hope blossomed in Iker's chest. Everything was going to be okay.

"Iker, honey. She's asking for you." Cara leaned into Arnel with a smile gracing her lips. "Go to her. She's waiting for you."

Iker nodded and exited the room, leaving the Hortons to their private moment. He walked down the hall to the unit where Jessica was located.

He entered the unit and stopped in front of her door.

What would he say?

He eyed the wooden door. He pushed down his

nerves and opened it. His gaze landed on the bed. Nothing else existed.

Jessica laid in bed with her large brown eyes locked on him.

"Baby," he murmured, shutting the door behind him.

"Iker." Her voice was hoarse. Tears spilled down her face.

He strode across the room to her. He gently sat on the edge of the bed. She leaned into him, sobs racking her body. He enclosed her in his embrace and just held her.

There were no words needed between them.

Her small fingers gripped his shirt as she held him to her.

"It's okay, baby. I'm here," he whispered. He rubbed a hand over her back to comfort her. "I'm always going to be here for you."

She lifted her red eyes. Her face was slightly puffy, tears streaked down her face, but Iker didn't care. She was the most beautiful person he had ever seen.

He lowered his head and kissed her.

He hadn't thought he would ever do this again. Her lips parted, welcoming his tongue. Their kiss was soft and sensual.

They separated, breathing hard. Iker tipped her chin up so he could look in her eyes.

"I thought I had lost you," he began. His thumb caressed her cheek. He took her all in, wanting to memorize her features. He never wanted to be apart from her again. "When I found you, I thought—"

"I'm here because of you." Her hand came up to rest on his. She leaned into his palm, tears slipping from her eyelids. "My parents told me it was you who found me."

"I have never been so scared in my life." He rested his forehead against hers. It felt so damn good to have her in his arms again. He shuddered, recognizing what he could have lost.

His entire world.

"When you would come and talk to me, I could hear you," she whispered. "I wanted to find you. I was trying my best to get to you."

She pulled back slightly.

His hands trembled at the thought of her fighting for her life to get to him. He had spent countless hours talking with her. He had read somewhere that people in a coma could still hear what was going on around them. So, Iker Baldwin had sat and read to her. He'd picked up some magazines and just read the articles to her. When he ran out of things to read, he just talked.

The topics?

Anything he could think about.

"I don't ever want to be apart from you again," he admitted. He planted a chaste kiss on her lips, unable to get enough of the taste of her. "I'm keeping my hands and eyes on you at all times."

Her lips lifted into a tiny smile. "I'm going to hold you to it."

"I love you, Jessica."

"Oh, I love you, too, Iker."

JESSICA STARED AT IKER. Her parents had tried to catch her up on what happened. The last thing she remembered was walking into her house and tossing her keys in the bowl by the front door.

Then nothing.

Jessica drew back from Iker and drank in the sight of him. Her parents had shared with her that it was he who had found her. Performed CPR on her until the ambulance had arrived.

She wasn't sure when the last time he'd gotten a decent night's sleep. His beard was fuller, his eyes were bloodshot red, and his hair had a tousled look as if he'd been combing his fingers through it.

"Have you been taking care of yourself?" she asked. She trailed her fingers over his scruffy beard.

His lips tilted up in the corner at her question.

"Enough. I've been waiting for you to come back to me." He took her hand and kissed it.

Jessica could tell he was dying to ask her questions. The looks he stole said it all. Of course, he would want to know who did this to her so he could go after the person.

"The wheel in your brain is turning," she murmured.

"What are you talking about?" His eyebrows rose.

He could try to fake her out if he wanted to, but she could see he was dying to interrogate her.

She settled back against the pillows and folded her hands in her lap.

"Go ahead and ask me what you want," she said. It was the cop in him that would make him question her and make whoever did this pay.

"What do you remember?" he asked.

Her eyes fluttered open. She stared at the ceiling to try to remember. Everything was fuzzy at the moment.

"I barely remember the drive home. I'm not sure how I did that. I let myself in, sat my keys in the bowl, and that is it. Everything just went black." She cleared her throat slightly. It was still sore from the tube that had been in her throat.

Iker reached for the cup of water by her bedside and handed it to her.

Small sips.

The doctors had okayed her to be able to drink a little. The cool water felt great slipping down her throat. She couldn't wait for them to bring her food. Her stomach rumbled slightly.

"I had stopped by your job, and Tiffany had said you may have had some bad sushi. Where did you go for lunch?" Iker's curious gaze watched her.

She frowned slightly.

Where did she go?

Oh, yeah.

Lunch with Bradley.

"Bradley had stopped by, and I had promised him we would go out for lunch to talk." She was interrupted by Iker's low growl. She turned her gaze to him.

He ran a hand down his face.

"Bradley? Why would he want to take you out

for lunch? Does he need me to remind him that it's over between the two of you?" he snarled.

"Calm down." She rolled her eyes and handed him the cup.

He placed it back on the table.

"It was no different than when you and I went for lunch. It was to talk."

"I had an agenda to get you back. That's why we went out to eat." Iker snorted. "Do you honestly think he's just going to give you up without a fight?"

"Iker, it wasn't what you are imagining." She smiled softly at him. She reached out and took his hand in her hers. "He's moving away."

"What?"

Iker's eyes cut to her. They were filled with suspicion.

"We talked, and he shared with me that he had been up for a promotion and got it. He'll be moving soon." She petted his hand, trying to console him. "Don't worry, honey. I'm all yours."

"You better be," he replied gruffly. He brought her hand to his lips and kissed it. "I never was one to share."

"Anyway, I'll finish telling you what I remember," she said haughtily.

"Go on." He kept her hand in his.

It was comforting for her. She didn't want him to let her go. Her mind drifted off to the events of that day.

"We went to Bento and Tea, you know that sushi restaurant?" she asked.

Iker shook his head no. He wasn't much of a sushi man. His palate called for hearty meals such as steak and potatoes.

"It's a Japanese bistro, and they even make the sushi and sashimi in front of you."

The memories flooded her.

"What is it, babe?" Iker's voice broke into her thoughts. "Did you remember something?"

"I just remember by the time Bradley dropped me off, I wasn't feeling well." That was an understatement. Her arm had started to go numb, as had her cheeks and lips. She'd assumed she had a bad allergic reaction to something she'd eaten. The plan had been to go home, grab some Benadryl, and take a nap, but that never happened.

She turned her focus to Iker. Had he not come to check on her, she wouldn't be sitting in this hospital bed right now.

Tears filled her eyes. She wasn't ready to die yet. She was still young and had plenty of life left in her.

She blinked back the tears. She didn't need to

cry anymore. She had done so much of it when she'd first woken up and saw her parents standing at the bedside with the physicians.

"What were you coming to see me at the gallery for?" she asked.

Iker squeezed her hand.

"We believe the Demon Lords are going to make a move. I was coming to warn you and when I couldn't get a hold of you, I thought the worst."

He turned his tortured eyes to her, and her heart melted. He was coming to protect her.

As Iker always had done.

"I've never been so scared in my life," he admitted again. "I don't know what I would do without you."

He leaned forward and softly kissed her lips.

"I'm not going anywhere, Iker," she murmured. She cupped his face, holding him close to her a little longer.

He looked exhausted and half dead on his feet.

"When was the last time you ate?" she asked.

He thought before answering. "I'm not sure."

"Go get something to eat," she encouraged.

He moved as if he was about to protest, but she waved him toward the door.

"I will be fine. Go. Find something to eat."

He pushed up from the bed and leaned down, dropping another kiss onto her lips.

"I won't be gone long," he said.

"I'll be here."

He left the room, and she rested back against the pillows. Even though they said she'd been out of it for a few days, she still felt tired. A yawn escaped her. Maybe she would take a little power nap.

The second her eyes closed, her thoughts raced.

What had happened to her?

Could it have been an allergic reaction? She hoped not. She loved her seafood and would rather give up an arm than not be able to eat it.

Exhaling, she tried to relax.

She was sure with all of the testing the doctors were doing, they would find an answer for her soon.

28

The door opened again, and Jessica groaned. She had just got comfortable, and here was someone else coming into her room.

Ever since Iker had left, nurses had come and gone from her room. She had been poked and prodded so much she was beginning to think she was a pin cushion.

She sighed and opened her eyes to greet the newcomer.

"Bradley." She blinked, startled he was standing there inside the doorway.

He was dressed in a long-sleeved t-shirt, jeans, and boots. A beautiful bouquet of flowers was in his hand.

"How's my girl?" Bradley asked. A soft smile played on his lips. "May I come in?"

"Sure." She motioned for him to enter.

He closed the door behind him and strode across the room.

"These are for you." He sat the vase on the table by her bed. His eyes took her in. A strange look was in them, but it soon passed.

"They are so beautiful. You remembered how much I adore flowers." She smiled and sat up higher. She leaned over to get a whiff of the floral arrangement. It was breathtaking. She did like having fresh-cut flowers around. There were a few other arrangements on the windowsill. Her room was filled with their aroma, and she loved it. At least the scent of the flowers took away some of the antiseptic smell of the nursing unit.

"Of course, I remembered. There isn't much I don't remember about you," he murmured. He motioned to the edge of the bed. "May I?"

"Um, sure." She scooted over a little to allow him to perch on the edge of the bed. "How are you?"

"I should be asking you that question." He barked a laugh. He petted her hand. "I'm doing better, now that I see you are okay. When I heard you were in the hospital, I had to come see you."

Jessica wondered who had told him, but she left it alone. She was sure her entire job knew, and if he'd stopped by to see her at work, someone would have told him.

"Thank you for coming by, I appreciate it." She offered him a smile to comfort him.

He looked just as worried about her as Iker had been.

"What happened?" he asked.

She relayed him the same story she'd told Iker. There wasn't much to tell. Most of it she didn't remember since it happened when she was asleep.

"It was a good thing Iker was there," Bradley murmured.

"Yeah, if he hadn't come over to check on me, I wouldn't be here speaking with you." Her hands played with the edge of the comforter. It was a hard realization that she had been so close to death.

"They haven't come out and said what they've found?" he asked.

"No, but they are still looking into some things. I'm willing to bet it was the food from the Bento and Tea. Did you get ill after you dropped me off?" she asked.

"No." He shook his head. He glanced around the room before his gaze settled back on her. "Did you tell anyone about the restaurant? So they could investigate?"

"I think it was a bad case of food poisoning." That had to be it. She was sure something like this has had to have happened before when someone had eaten bad fish or sushi from a restaurant. She made a note to never go back to that place ever again. A shudder went through her at the thought of eating there. She was feeling physically sick just thinking of the place.

"No, that wasn't it," Bradley said quietly, shaking his head.

"What?" Her gaze flew to him.

He was staring at her with a weird glint in his eyes that she couldn't identify.

"Bradley, what are you talking about?"

"You lied to me, Jessica. I thought you were a stand-up woman, someone who would be honest with me." His voice was flat and void of any emotions.

"What are you talking about? I've never lied to you." Did he bump his head? Or maybe he had food poisoning and it was affecting him mentally.

"You never lied to me? The day you went out to eat with Iker, it didn't appear to be a talk to hash out what happened in the past. You two had been getting very close while on your little date," he sneered.

Jessica was taken aback. She'd never seen him like this.

"What—?"

"You were acting like a common whore. Did you sleep with him that day?"

"Were you following us?" Jessica cried out in disbelief.

"Me, follow you? No, but I had someone tailing you and him. I didn't appreciate him trying to come between me and what's mine," he snapped. He reached out and took her hand in his. "Tell me, sweet Jessica. Is it because I wouldn't sleep with you that you turned back to your ex-boyfriend?"

"I didn't sleep with Iker while I was dating you." She winced from the strength of his hold on her hand.

His dark eyes bored into her.

"You are hurting me," she said.

"How could you go back to him? You said that he broke you. That the breakup was hard, and it had taken you a long time to move past what was between him and you."

"I told you it was complicated." She tried to snatch her hand back from him, but he held on strong. The piercing pain shooting through her arm was worrying her. She tried to wiggle free, but he had a firm grip on her.

"You were mine. He ruined everything." Bradley's crazed eyes were wide and came to lock on her.

"He didn't ruin—"

"He did!" Bradley interjected. "Everything was just fine until he came back into your life."

"I'm sorry—"

"Shut up!" He barked, cutting her off.

Jessica jumped at the force of his words. She tried to pull away from him and move to the other side of the bed. Her body trembled in fear. She didn't know what had gotten into him, but she had to get away from him.

"Where are you going?" he thundered. He stood and dragged her back to the center of the bed. "Iker doesn't deserve you. If I can't have you, then no one will."

"Bradley, no—"

This time her words were cut off by his hands wrapping around her throat. Her fingers clawed at his hands to try to free herself from his clutches. He applied pressure, cutting her breathing and circulation off.

She tried to yell for help, but no sound left her lips.

Rage filled his face as he stood over her, pressing down on her neck. Tears blurred her vision. She blinked, but black specks came into sight. Her nails dug into his hands, but they weren't doing anything to him.

Spittle flew from his mouth.

"You should have been mine." His voice was hoarse.

Her hands stretched out, trying to feel for the call button, but it was out of reach.

Her lungs screamed for air.

The black spots swimming in her vision were growing larger.

Her life flashed before her. She closed her eyes, and sadness filled her.

Iker had saved her only to lose her.

She couldn't fight Bradley off. He was overpowering her. She was still weak from being in a coma for three days.

Her attempts to free herself were useless.

"You made me do this." Tears streamed down Bradley's face.

"What the hell?" Jordan's voice sounded in the room.

Bradley's hands fell away from Jessica's neck.

Jessica inhaled loudly, gulping in all of the air she could. There was a crash in the room.

Bradley's curses filled the air.

Jessica was unable to see what was happening, but there was a tussle going on. Her lungs had been on fire, and now that she was able to breathe, it settled the pain.

Her throat was raw and painful.

"We need help in here!" Jordan shouted.

Jessica laid on the bed, gasping for breath. Her head rolled to the side, and she caught sight of Jordan running out of the room while the hospital staff rushed in.

"Oh my God," the nurse cried out. She turned and ran to the door. "Call a code violet."

Jessica closed her eyes, tears streaming down her face. She was in disbelief that Bradley had tried to kill her.

What had happened to make him snap the way he had?

He had said no to her hypothesis of what happened the other day.

Was he behind that, too?

Her gut was screaming that he had something to do with it.

If so, this would be the second attempt on her life.

∞

"I'M HOPING their toxicology report will come back soon," Iker said. He took another sip of the coffee. He had run into Declan in the hospital lobby.

"I'm sure they will find something," Declan said.

The elevator finally opened. They stepped inside with Iker hitting the button for Jessica's floor.

"I just hate how long it takes. Why can't this be like in the movies?" Iker joked. It felt good to be able to smile and play around. His day was getting much better. Now that Jessica was awake, the doctors were thinking she would be making a speedy recovery and could be discharged home soon. If Iker had anything to do with it, she would stay with him.

His woman was tough, and she would be back to normal in no time.

"Jordan went on upstairs, and the others will be coming. They were parking," Declan said.

"Y'all didn't have to come and camp out here with me."

"Seriously?" Declan said. "You were there for me when shit hit the fan for Aspen. Plus, I don't mind.

You've been hogging Jessica all to yourself since y'all got back together."

Iker laughed. The guys had always loved Jessica. The elevator alerted them they were at their designated floor. The door opened, and Iker stepped out first. He paused at the sight of Jordan sprinting down the hallway.

He immediately tensed.

Declan came to stand beside him.

"What the hell is going on?" Iker snapped. The pit of his stomach gave way.

Something was definitely wrong.

He could feel it.

The nursing unit was going crazy. Security came rushing from the other elevator and headed in the direction Jordan had just come from.

"Code violet," the operator announced over the speakers of the hospital. She gave details of the unit and the room.

It was Jessica's.

"It was Bradley," Jordan yelled over her shoulder.

Iker tossed his cup into the trash near him and took off behind Jordan. She didn't have to say another word.

Declan was right behind him.

"He headed down that stairwell." Jordan pointed to where the stairs were located.

They arrived in front of it. Declan opened the door and went inside.

"The son of a bitch was choking Jessica when I went in to see her," Jordan said.

Iker didn't need to hear any more.

A red haze clouded his vision.

"Can you go check on Jess and make sure she's okay?" Iker asked Jordan.

"Will do." She nodded and backed up. "Kick that motherfucker's ass."

"That I can promise." Iker headed into the stairwell and brushed past Declan.

They began the descent. The sound of hard footsteps racing down the stairs echoed in the stairwell.

Iker's heart raced as he flew down the stairs. He could hear the heavy breathing and curses below. Iker leaned over the railing and saw the back of Bradley's head.

He pushed himself to go faster. Declan was right behind him.

They were gaining on Bradley. He wasn't in as good a shape as Iker and Declan.

"Bradley, stop!" Iker called out. This would be

his only warning to the man. When he caught up with him, he was going to beat the shit out of him.

This had been a long time coming.

Ever since he'd seen Bradley with Jessica, Iker had been wanting to do bodily harm to the fucker.

Bradley didn't answer and kept running.

The fucking coward.

Iker started skipping stairs and was catching up to Bradley. He was almost on top of him.

Bradley burst through the door at the bottom of the stairs with Iker right on his tail.

It led them out into the main lobby.

Iker tackled Bradley down to the floor.

"I said stop!" Iker tried to roll Bradley over, but he resisted.

"Get off me!" Bradley hollered.

He swung his fist, and it connected with Iker's chin. He bucked, trying to push Iker off him. They tussled on the floor, exchanging blows until Iker fell off Bradley, who took advantage and jumped to his feet.

Iker stood, eyeing Bradley who had pulled out a knife.

"Bradley, put the weapon down," Declan ordered. He stood by eyeing Bradley.

"Shut the fuck up," Bradley snarled, waving the knife around as a warning.

"You better know how to use that." Iker grinned. He wasn't afraid of the fucker. He wanted to fight down and dirty, then Iker would be all for it. "It's going to take more than a little knife to keep me from kicking your ass."

There was a crowd standing back watching everything. Security appeared and kept everyone back at a safe distance.

Iker didn't take his eyes off Bradley. He didn't trust him as far as he could throw him.

Iker rushed toward Bradley. He dodged the knife as Bradley's movements grew erratic. He blocked Bradley's uncoordinated punches. When he swung the knife again, it grazed Iker's arm, drawing a small amount of blood.

Iker was a dirty fighter, too, and wasn't going to give Bradley a chance to get his bearings. Iker landed a hit to the stomach and followed it up with one to the chin. The knife clattered to the floor.

Bradley took a step back. His lip was busted and bleeding, his eye swollen. He glared at Iker.

"You people always take everything from me," Bradley spat. He swayed on his feet while glaring at Iker.

Iker didn't know what the hell that meant. He hadn't taken shit from the crazed lunatic.

"I don't know what the fuck you are talking about," Iker snapped.

"Jessica was mine!"

Bradley let loose a roar and charged at Iker. He slammed his shoulder into Iker's abdomen.

That was his mistake.

Getting close to Iker was the wrong move.

And the son of a bitch was wrong.

Jessica was his.

Had always been his.

Iker brought down his elbow directly in the middle of Bradley's spine. He swiftly brought up his knee, slamming it into Bradley's face. His head snapped back, allowing Iker to send a mean hook to connect with this jaw.

Bradley flew back and fell down on the floor. Iker moved to follow but was jerked back by strong hands.

Declan.

"Freeze! CPD!" a hard voice commanded.

Iker turned and found Myles standing with his weapon trained on Bradley. Ash stood next to him with his gun pointed at him as well.

Bradley froze on the floor and stared at them.

"Turn over on your stomach," Ash said, inching closer. "Then put your hands on your head."

Bradley blew out a deep breath and flipped over, apparently giving up.

Iker stood to his full height. His knuckles were slightly bruised, but he would be fine. He shook Declan off him. He tried to push down the rage and the demand for vengeance.

Declan walked over with his handcuffs out. He had Bradley cuffed and off the floor in seconds.

"Do I even want to ask what is going on?" Myles secured his weapon into the sheath.

Ash moved over to Declan.

"He attacked Jessica," Iker growled. He moved to go toward Bradley. That rage was still festering inside him.

"It's over," Myles said and eyed Iker. "Calm down, you whipped his ass."

It wasn't enough.

All he needed was to be locked in a room with the man for an hour.

"There should be a squad car outside." Jordan came to stand beside Iker and pushed him back. "I called it in and had them send someone to take him in."

Declan nodded, leading Bradley outside with Ash tagging along. They passed Zain who was walking into the hospital. He had a curious look on his face.

Iker's frosty gaze was locked on Bradley until he could no longer see him anymore.

"What did I miss?" Zain strode over to them.

"Iker finally got to kick Jess's ex-boyfriend's ass," Myles said.

"Is she okay?" Iker asked. The adrenaline was starting to wear off. Fear of what had happened while he was out of the room overtook him.

Fuck.

He couldn't believe the asswipe had attacked Jessica. Bradley was one lucky man that it was Jordan who'd walked in on him and not him.

Had Iker been in the room, things certainly would have turned out differently.

"They want to do some scans on her neck. She's in pain, and he really did a number on her throat," Jordan said.

Iker ran a hand through his hair, a frustrated growl bursting from him. He should have stayed with her. He should never have listed to her and skipped lunch. If he had remained, none of this would have happened.

"Go to her. She needs you," Jordan encouraged. She rested a hand on his arm. "She's asking for you."

"We'll make sure he gets processed and taken in," Myles said.

Iker knew his teammates would take care of everything. If he went out there, he'd just beat Bradley's ass again and not give a shit that he was handcuffed.

Iker jerked his head into a nod and spun around on his heels.

Iker jogged back to the stairs. He didn't have time to wait on the elevator.

Swinging the door open, he took the stairs two at a time.

He had to see Jessica.

This time when he said he'd never let her go, he damn well meant it.

Iker stalked toward the nursing unit where Jess was housed. His muscles were strung tight. He ignored the burning sensation coming from his knuckles. He would have done worse had Declan not grabbed him.

Eyes of the hospital employees turned to him, but he ignored them. Up ahead, doctors, nurses, and security swarmed the area.

He needed to see Jessica. Had to put his eyes on her so he could see for himself that she was okay.

"Excuse me, sir. You can't come in here." A guard stood near the entrance of the unit. He moved toward Iker with caution. His eyes revealed slight fear while he held a hand up.

"The fuck I can't," Iker growled.

"We are on lockdown right now due to an attack." The guard swallowed hard.

"That's my fucking woman who was attacked," Iker yelled. "You're going to let me in there."

"We have policies that I must—"

"I don't give a shit about your policies," Iker snapped. He clenched his hands into fists, ready to fight his way into the nursing unit to get to Jessica. He narrowed his eyes on the man.

"Sir, please don't make me call the police."

"I am the fucking police," Iker hollered. His badge on his chain had flipped to behind him in his mad dash up the stairs. He was still slightly winded from the run to the floor. Iker reached around and brought it to the front so the idiot could see it.

"What's going on?" A nurse stood near the door. She glanced between Iker and the security guard.

Iker recognized her as one of the nurses taking care of Jessica earlier.

"Doing my job, ma'am. I was told no one could enter." The guard squinted at the woman.

"Please let him in. He's the significant other to the woman who was attacked." The nurse waved for him to enter.

Iker brushed past the guard without a second look and stalked down to Jessica's room.

He stopped outside it and took note of the staff inside. The physicians were assessing her and speaking medical lingo, and he had no idea what the hell they were talking about.

All he could see were Jessica's wide eyes.

He paused in the doorway.

"Miss Horton, we'll need to take some X-rays of your neck and throat," one of the doctors said. "He could have torn ligaments or something."

Jessica nodded. Her gaze landed on Iker. Her face scrunched up as the waterworks broke.

Iker dashed into the room and pushed the staff hovering over her out of the way. He sat on the bed and gathered her to him.

Sobs racked her body.

"I'm here," he murmured. His heart broke to see her this way. "I'm so sorry. I should have stayed."

"Sir, we need to get her down to radiology now," a doctor stated.

Iker's frosty gaze cut to the doctor speaking. The physician took a step back and swallowed hard.

"There's no way you can do an X-ray here? You see she's in no shape to go anywhere," Iker said. He was in protective mode. He didn't care who he'd have to go up against, he was going to make sure Jessica was safe. Iker looked at the man's badge and took in his name. "And at the moment, I don't trust her going anywhere in this hospital. She was fucking attacked lying in her bed while your staff was right outside the door."

"Um, yes. We can have radiology do a portable scan here." Dr. Armani motioned to one of the younger team members. "Put in a stat portable neck X-ray orders."

"I can call and have radiology up here immediately," the nurse announced from the door. She stepped from the room.

At least someone has some sense around this place.

"I'll return to go over the images once we have them," Dr. Armani said.

"Fine." Iker turned away, dismissing them all. He only had eyes for Jessica, who was still gripping his shirt.

Her cries had grown silent. Her body trembled. He tightened his hold on her to lend her his strength.

Iker tossed a cold glare over his shoulder. The rest of the people in the room got his message, really quick. They rushed from the room, leaving him and Jessica alone.

"Baby, I'm so sorry." He gently tipped Jessica's head back so he could meet her gaze. Her wince at the moment sent a rage through him. Iker moved her away so he could look at her neck.

The beginning phase of bruising marred her beautiful brown skin. They were ugly, red, and dark. It was going to get worse as time went on.

The wrath spreading through him snatched the air from his lungs.

"Don't look at it," Jessica whispered. Her red puffy eyes pleaded with him. "Don't go and do anything we would both regret."

"I'm going to kill him," he vowed. His fingers lightly touched the bruising that was forming in the shape of large hands.

"No. Please. It's over," she begged. Her fingers gripped his shirt tight. "I can't lose you."

"You won't." Iker tugged her back to him. Having her in his arms comforted him. He could have lost her now, twice. He pressed a kiss to her head. This woman meant everything to him. He wouldn't be able to go on if she were taken from him. Just imagining Bradley putting his hands on her had him dreaming up every way he could take him out.

"You're still thinking of going after him," Jessica mumbled against his chest. "Just stop, Iker. Please don't do anything. Do this for me."

Her body shuddered.

Iker blew out a deep breath. He would do as she'd asked. Justice would prevail, and Bradley would get what was coming to him. He would make it his life's mission to make sure Bradley paid his dues.

Jessica drew back. She stared at him, her gaze trailing over him.

"What happened to you?" she asked, her voice husky and strained. Jessica's small hand came to rest on his chin. "Who punched you?"

He didn't respond. He let her continue looking him over. Her gaze landed on his knuckles. Her eyes immediately flew back up to meet his.

"Who were you fighting?" she gasped.

"That fucker thought he was going to run," Iker began. He cupped her face and rested his forehead against hers. "When I came back up, Bradley had just run past. Jordan told me what happened, and I went after him."

"Oh my god," she whimpered. "Please tell me you didn't—"

"I should have," he continued, already knowing what she was about to ask. This woman didn't know how far he would be willing to go to ensure she lived and breathed.

He would sacrifice it all.

"Don't say that." She kissed his lips and pulled back.

How was it she was the one just attacked, but she was comforting him?

"I don't deserve you, Jess."

"Don't say that either. I'm coming to understand that everything was meant to be. What we went through made us who we are today, and now, it is our time to be together." She winced slightly and swallowed.

"Stop talking." He pressed a finger to her lips. "Just rest. I'm not leaving your side."

He helped her get comfortable in the bed. He was able to squeeze onto it with her, tucking her into his side.

She laid her head on his chest and sighed. Jessica's breathing evened out, signaling she had drifted off to sleep.

Iker leaned back against the pillow and stared at the ceiling.

Finally, he was able to relax.

The danger was gone.

"I'M NOT ARGUING with you. It's a done deal, and everyone agrees," Iker said.

Jessica tried not to roll her eyes. She hadn't even attempted to argue, but her stubborn man was insisting she was, and she hadn't even uttered a word yet.

"Okay." She smiled, sitting on the edge of the hospital bed.

It had been four days since the altercation with Bradley. Jessica was still in shock at how the quiet, sweet man had snapped on her. From what she was told, he'd been arrested that day and charged with attempted murder for his attack.

"Okay?" Iker echoed, pausing his organizing of her belongings that she'd be taking with her.

It was discharge day, and Jessica was ready to leave the hospital. The staff was wonderful, but she was ready to go.

"Yes, I'll stay at your place." She chuckled. Her throat was still healing, and thankfully, all of the testing revealed there wouldn't be any long-term damage.

She pushed off the bed and slowly padded into the bathroom of her private room. Her mother had brought her toiletries, for which Jessica was grateful.

She had washed her hair with her own shampoo and twisted her hair last night.

She didn't want to leave the hospital looking a mess. Her gaze fell to her neck. The bruising was definitely a fashion statement she didn't want to share with the world.

She began untwisting her hair while Iker packed up her belongings. She leaned in the doorway and looked at all of the flowers sitting on the windowsill. She had received bouquet after bouquet from tons of people when they had heard she was hospitalized.

"Why don't we leave the nurses the flowers at the nursing station?" she suggested. There were too many for her to take home. There was no room left by the window. "Or we can see if they want to put the flowers in other patients' rooms."

"I can ask." Iker zipped up her duffle bag.

Her mother had overdone it on what to bring to the hospital. She had packed enough things as if Jessica were going away on vacation. He walked over to her, his gaze dropping to her neck. His nostrils flared, and Jessica knew he wanted to go find Bradley and kill him.

Jessica had to prevent that.

She'd be damned if she had to visit him in prison for doing something stupid.

"I love you," she breathed, leaning into him.

That seemed to break him from whatever dark thoughts were running through his mind. His eyes softened. He bent down and captured her lips in a soft kiss. He had been acting as if she were a piece of china.

She was feeling fine. Her throat was still a little sore, but that was it.

Once they were at his home, he would need to stop handling her with kid gloves.

She loved his calloused hands, strong grips, and how rough he could be when taking her.

"I'll be right back," he murmured, his lips brushing hers.

She opened her eyes and inhaled. If she wasn't already leaning into him, she would have fallen to the floor due to her knees going weak with that one kiss.

"Hurry back." She smiled at him and watched him leave her room. She went back into the bathroom to finish taking her hair down. Once she was done styling it, she felt a little more human.

Going back to her room, she sat in the chair by the bed and slid on her sandals. She was only waiting for her official walking papers.

So far, they hadn't found anything in her system

to explain what had caused her to almost die. She shuddered at the memory of them explaining she had stopped breathing.

Had Iker and Zain not showed up when they had, her respiratory failure would have advanced to cardiac failure and she would have died.

She put her feet up on the bed, ready to relax until it was time for her to leave.

"Miss Horton?" a voice called her name from the door.

Jessica opened her eyes and saw Iker standing behind the detective who had spoken with her after the robbery. He had a badge hanging from a chain around his chest like Iker wore.

"Hi," she said. She couldn't remember his name.

He had a warm smile on his face as he walked into the room with Iker behind him. The other SWAT member, Brodie, filed in, too. He gave her a nod and wink. He leaned against the wall, and Jessica had the feeling they were coming to update her on things.

"Jess, this is Detective Clayton Best. You remember him?" Iker asked. He came around to the side of the bed where she was.

She put her feet down to allow him to sit on the bed close to her.

"I've known Best for a long time," Iker said. "He was one of the officers who trained me when I first joined the force."

"Nice to meet you again." She smiled. If he'd trained Iker, then that meant he must be someone Iker trusted.

"I was assigned to your case since I'm already familiar with you," Detective Best began. He held a folder.

"My case? We don't know what happened to me." Jessica looked at the men in the room. What was going on?

"Well, the physicians did what they could to save you," Brodie chimed in. "So in cases like these, we run special toxicology testing. We need to look for things that aren't normally checked on lab work."

"And Brodie has some friends in high places that can get results faster than we normally would." Best laughed.

Iker took her hand and kissed the back of it.

"Go ahead and tell her, Brodie." Iker nodded to his teammate.

"It would seem that you were poisoned. Hence why there is now a case opened to investigate," Brodie said.

"Poisoned? Wouldn't I have known that?" she cried out.

Iker squeezed her hand and shook his head.

"Not necessarily. If you knew, then the person wouldn't have been as successful," Iker said.

"What was I given?" Jessica's breath caught in her throat.

"What restaurant did you eat lunch at the day you collapsed?" Detective Best asked, pulling out a small notepad.

"Um, Bento and Tea," she replied wearily.

"There was a lethal amount of tetrodotoxin in your system," Brodie announced. He brandished his phone from his pocket and tapped out a few commands on the screen. He walked it over to her. "Symptoms are weakness, shortness of breath, nausea, vomiting, respiratory failure, cardiac arrest, and death if not caught earlier enough."

Nausea washed over her as she listened to the symptoms Brodie rattled off.

Jessica took it and read the reports that he had brought up. She didn't know what it meant, but there was tetrodotoxin noted with an amount that was documented in red.

"But where would this have come from?" she asked.

She watched the three of them share a look.

"Baby, you said you had sushi at the restaurant, right?" Iker asked.

She nodded, immediately sensing she wasn't going to like what he was about to say.

"We think it was in your food."

She stared at him and gave a slow blink.

She had trusted that son of a bitch.

"Bradley," she whispered. "When we were there, he had me try his sashimi. I ate one piece. He fed it to me from his plate."

Jessica felt cold inside. She had dated him, gotten to know him for months, and in the end, he'd tried to kill her because she had chosen another man over him.

Iker's gaze turned feral, and he glanced over at Detective Best. He gave him a nod.

"We figured this out and then went to the restaurant. I have some photos I want you to review and tell me if anyone looks familiar." Best gave Iker the folder and motioned for him to give them to her. "Just let me know if you recognize any of the people in the folder."

Jessica handed Brodie his phone. She was in disbelief at what Bradley had gone through to punish her.

"Okay." She blew out a shaky breath. She opened the folder and stared at the pages with photos lined on them. She recognized one immediately and tapped on the man's face. "He was the chef at the restaurant."

"Iker, hand her a pen so she can circle who she recognizes. Then after you do that, put your initials," Best instructed.

Iker grabbed a pen off her bedside table. She circled the Asian man's face and put her initials. She continued on and then paused.

She stared at the photo of another man she recognized.

"What is it, baby?" Iker murmured. He watched her with concern. "Is there someone else?"

She nodded and pointed to another man.

"This is Bradley's cousin, Jevonne." Memories from Bradley's cousin's wedding came rushing to her. The guy had given her the creeps and made her uncomfortable.

He's like a brother to us. We'd do anything for him.

Jevonne had warned her, she just hadn't listened.

But did it matter? If she didn't want to be with his cousin, then that was her right.

"Jevonne Cartright," Best said. "He's a known

member of the Demon Lords. Glad you identified him."

"Why?" she asked.

"He was the contact from the Demon Lords for Floyd and John Boy Rogers." Best met Iker's eyes.

Iker released a curse.

"What does this mean?" Jessica asked. She didn't like being in the dark about things when it came to her. She had been through so much that she needed to know what was going on.

"My theory, and now that you've just pointed out the players in the game, I guess I can tell you." Best shrugged.

Jessica nodded, appreciative of him sharing information with her.

"Bradley didn't take the breakup too well. I'm going to assume he didn't appreciate you leaving him for Iker. His cousin, Jevonne, is a known member of the Demon Lords. So, to put two and two together, Bradley tells his cousin that y'all broke up and he wanted revenge."

"When I went to their cousin's wedding, Jevonne sort of warned me about his cousin. I took it as a joke about breaking Bradley's heart. You know family intimidation when you first meet them?"

The three of them stared at her. She swallowed hard, realizing that it wasn't a joke.

Jevonne had meant what he'd said.

"Now what?" she asked.

"We've already sent patrol to pick up Jevonne. Uda Miyoko, the chef from the restaurant, is already in custody. Uda has already confessed that Bradley paid him to serve the blowfish that contained the poison," Best said.

Bradley had sunk so low as to have her poisoned instead of just leaving her to move on with her life.

"Don't worry, Jessica. The prosecutor has a solid case," Brodie said.

Jessica glanced at Iker, relief filling her.

"We're going to make sure the case is so solid that none of these men will be able to see freedom again," Iker murmured.

It was truly over.

A knock sounded at the door. A nurse stood with papers in her hand.

Looked like Jessica's walking papers were finally here.

Iker watched Jessica sleep. He was finally at peace. She was here in his home and in his bed. It had been a week since her discharge from the hospital. They had settled into a nice routine.

Her boss had given her all the time off she needed.

Iker had to admit it felt good to come home to her. No separate homes to travel between. Having her waiting for him was something he wanted to continue.

He knew what he was going to ask her in the morning.

It didn't make sense for them to continue living

apart. That was one mistake they had made before. They had kept their own residences.

After everything they had just been through, he wanted her to move in with him.

The bombing at the courthouse was still assumed to be directed at Cruz and the SWAT team. Each member of the SWAT team would keep their guard up. They would continue to protect their families and work together.

SWAT had been busy taking on the gang. They wouldn't let an attempt on their team stop their work.

Iker already knew he would give his life to protect Jessica.

He wrapped his arm around her and brought her flush against him. Her naked body was soft and warm. He brushed a hand down her spine and kissed the top of her head.

He made sure the blanket was tucked around her so she wouldn't be chilled by the central air.

"What time is it?" her muffled voice asked. She nuzzled her face into the crook of his neck.

"Not time to get up," he murmured. He eyed the clock on his nightstand and saw it was a little after four in the morning. He'd been working swing shifts to pick up overtime and had been sleeping like shit.

He had been content watching her sleep. "Go back to sleep, baby."

Her giggle went straight to his cock. It jerked against her stomach.

"How can I sleep with that thing between us?" She glanced up at him, resting her hand on his chest.

"Just ignore it," he joked.

"Like that has ever worked before," she replied haughtily. Her smile faded as she studied him. Her hand slowly caressed his chest. "What's on your mind?

"Move in with me," he blurted out. He had thought of a long and drawn-out speech to convince her that it would be best.

Jess studied him for a moment. Her smile returned, and she nodded.

"Okay."

"Okay? That's it?" He bent down and claimed her lips in a quick kiss. "I thought I was going to have to do more to convince you."

"Nope. You don't have to do anything else to convince me. I want to. I don't want to be apart from you, and it doesn't make sense for us go back and forth when we can have one place that we can call home."

"Baby, I'm so happy you agree. If you want, we can look for a new home to start over."

"I like the sound of that." She grinned. She reached up and wrapped her arms around his neck and brought him down, offering her mouth for him.

Iker slammed his lips onto hers. The kiss was one of deep passion. He poured all of his feeling into it. His hands skimmed her body, starting with her heavy mounds, then down to her waist. He rolled them over with him landing on his back.

Jessica straddled his waist. His cock was heavy with need, brushing against the swell of her ass.

She was the most beautiful woman he'd ever seen, and she was all his.

Pride filled him that she'd chosen him.

"Iker," she whispered. The markings on her neck had finally deepened, but now they were in the healing phase.

If he could, he would go kick Bradley's ass again.

But at the moment, Bradley was sitting in jail waiting for his trial.

"I want you to ride me, Jess," he muttered. His cock was fully engorged and ready to feel her hot sheath around him.

"With us living together, are you sure you will be able to keep up this stamina?" Her eyebrow rose. Her lips twisted into a sexy grin. She leisurely drew her nails down his chest. She teased his nipples.

"I'm going to damn well try."

She burst out laughing. She leaned down and kissed him. This woman was everything he could have ever hoped for.

He allowed her to control the kiss. Her tongue slipped inside his mouth, stroking his. He took advantage of the position and cupped her breasts. Those large mounds filled his hands perfectly. He massaged them, pinching her nipples, eliciting a moan from her.

She tore her lips away from his mouth, pressing kisses on his jawline then moving down to his chest.

"I hope so, because if I get to have this every night." She paused, reaching behind her to take his shaft in her hand. She slid along his length and gave it a squeeze. "Then I'll be one happy woman."

"Baby, you can have my dick as often as you like. All you have to do is say the word."

The smile disappeared from his face the second he watched her rise and nestle the tip of his cock at her entrance. She slid down slowly, impaling herself on him. It wasn't until she was seated completely on him that he exhaled.

The air was ripped from Iker's lungs. She was soaking wet, her warm cream coating his cock.

"You better remember that," Jessica whispered. She threw her head back and rocked her hips.

Iker rested his hands on her waist, waiting for her.

"Oh, I will." That was a promise he was willing to keep.

Jessica placed her hands on his chest then lifted, fell back down on him. He gritted his teeth at the sensation of her hot sheath surrounding him. Her muscles clinched around him, squeezing him tight.

She repeated her motion, taking her pleasure.

"Yes," she hissed.

Iker could no longer hold still. He thrust upward, sending his cock deeper. They fell into a steady rhythm. He held on to her, pumping his cock inside her.

Iker couldn't take his eyes off Jessica as she rode him. It was a beautiful sight to behold.

He growled, loving the sensations coursing through his body. Jessica's body was made for him. There would never be anyone else.

Jessica opened her eyes and met his. Their breaths grew faster as their movements became frantic. He would never get enough of this woman.

He pulled her down, covering her mouth with his. His hips continued on, sending him farther inside.

She tore her mouth from his when she crested. A cry spilled from her lips. Her pussy clamped down on him while she rode the waves of her orgasm. Iker could no longer hold his back and joined her. His hips pistoned while ropes of his seed bathed the walls of her womb.

Jessica collapsed on top of him, out of breath. She lay unmoving with her eyes closed.

Iker wrapped his arms around Jessica. His semi-soft cock was still buried inside her.

This was Heaven, and he never wanted to leave.

"That goes in the master bedroom," Jessica directed.

Myles and Ash walked past her carrying an antique dresser.

"Put it in the larger walk-in closet. It's mine."

It had been a month since she and Iker had made the decision to move in together. They had decided to start over and buy a home they would make into theirs. She had put her house up for sale, and it sold almost immediately, so she'd moved into Iker's home until they found one they agreed upon.

His SWAT team showed up to help to move them in, as did their families.

"Sis, where you want this?" Irvin carried in a large vase that she had purchased for their new home. "That goes in my office down the hall." She pointed in the direction for her brother.

"Having fun dishing out orders?" Iker's strong arms wrapped around her front and brought her back against him. He nuzzled her neck and breathed in her scent.

"Of course, I am. At least they listen to me," she joked. She stood in the foyer of their new home and glanced around. "Are you sure this isn't too big?"

"It's the perfect size." Iker lifted her left hand that showcased the very big diamond ring he had surprised her with.

She glanced down at it and smiled. There was no way she wouldn't accept this man's proposal. He was the love of her life. They may not have gotten it right the first time, but dammit, they would this time.

Jessica refused to make the same mistakes they had in the past. She was going to hold on to her man and keep him with her forever.

Bradley's trial was cancelled. He had accepted a plea deal to avoid facing life or the death penalty. His sentencing hearing was coming up next month, and Jessica planned to be there. Iker was against her going, but she wanted to see Bradley one last time.

She needed to look him in the eyes, and she was even expected to give a statement.

"It's just me and you. Why do we need a house this big?" she asked. She turned around in his arms.

He cradled her close as if she were the most precious thing in the world.

Their home had five bedrooms, five and a half bathrooms, and was close to four thousand square feet.

"If you didn't want that master bedroom you gushed over, or the two walk-in closets with the fancy en suite bathroom, we could have picked something else." Iker shrugged.

She had gushed over the house. It had everything she had ever wanted in a home. The kitchen was a chef's dream, and there was plenty of space. The yard was magnificent, and they were lucky to beat out the other potential buyers.

"You know I fell in love with this house." She rolled her eyes. She and Darby had gone crazy over it. Her friend was already upstairs helping to unpack some of the guest rooms.

Mac and Iker's brother, Dylan, walked in the front door carrying boxes.

"Hickory chips just helps enhance the flavor of the meat," Mac said, automatically walking toward the kitchen.

"But there is nothing better than mesquite and smoking a juicy brisket," Dylan said.

He and Iker were similar in build and looks. They could almost be mistaken for twins.

Of course, they were arguing about food. With the move and having everyone over, Iker and Jessica wanted to cook for them to thank them for helping.

"Are you sure we shouldn't have just ordered out?" Jessica asked.

"No, they both wanted to help, so we'll let them do their thing." Iker kissed her lips. "And this house is not too big. I'm planning to fill it with plenty of baby Baldwins."

Jessica's core clenched. Just imagining Iker as a father was enough to throw her hormones into overdrive.

Standing on her tiptoes, she pressed another kiss to Iker's lips.

"Let's finished getting everything in the house, feed our families, and then later, we can start practicing making those babies."

Iker growled, his hand gripping her ass. He planted another kiss on her lips, but this time, it was one of deep passion.

"Oh, will you two go get a room." Zain walked into the house.

They broke apart, but Iker kept his arm around Jessica, holding her close to him.

Zain carried a painting in, stopping by them. "Where does this go?"

"My office," Jessica replied.

Zain headed off in that direction, muttering something about back-breaking work while the owners made out.

"Ignore him, he's just jealous." Iker chuckled.

"Am not!" Zain yelled over his shoulder.

Jessica glanced up at Iker and felt her heart swell with all of the love she had for him.

Everything in her world was perfect.

⚬⚬

Sign up for Peyton's mailing list and get your free copy of Tempest: His Best Friend's Sister Romance! This book is not published anywhere! It's Peyton's gift to you!

Click here to get started: PEYTON'S GIFT

Dear reader,

I can't begin to say how much I love Iker and Jessica. This story wrote itself. I am just the messenger and I hope that you enjoyed this story as much as I did writing it.

Zain will be up next in Dirty Secrets, and I can't wait to dive into his story.

Thank you for reading Dirty Trust! Don't forget to leave a review. This is how I know you want more!

love,

Peyton Banks

Putting out fires was his life's work. This new flame, there's no way he's extinguishing it.

Click HERE to download this complete series today! Love audiobooks? Snag it HERE on Audible!

The Trust and Honor series is a steamy, contemporary BWWM romance. It is reserved for mature readers over 18 years of age.

ABOUT THE AUTHOR

Peyton Banks is the alter ego of a city girl who is a romantic at heart. Her mornings consist of coffee and daydreaming up the next steamy romance book ideas. She loves spinning romantic tales of hot alpha males and the women they love. Make sure you check her out!

Sign up for Peyton's Newsletter to find out the latest releases, giveaways and news! Click HERE to sign up or visit her website www.peytonbanks.com !

Want to know the latest about Peyton Banks? Follow her online:

ALSO BY PEYTON BANKS

Current Free Short Story

Summer Escape

Blazing Eagle Ranch Series

Back in the Saddle

Knockin' the Boots

Roping a Cowboy

Country at Heart

Cowboy, Take Me Away

Special Weapons & Tactics Series

Dirty Tactics (Special Weapons & Tactics 1)

Dirty Ballistics (Special Weapons & Tactics 2)

Dirty Operations (Special Weapons & Tactics 3)

Dirty Alliance (Special Weapons & Tactics 4)

Dirty Justice (Special Weapons & Tactics 5)

Dirty Trust (Special Weapons & Tactics 6)

Dirty Secrets (Special Weapons & Tactics 7)

Trust & Honor Series (BWWM)

Dallas

Dalton

Interracial Romances (BWWM)

Pieces of Me

Hard Love

Retain Me

Silent Deception

The Christmas Secret

African American Romance

Breaking The Rules

Mafia Romance Series

Unexpected Allies (The Tokhan Bratva 1)

Unexpected Chaos (The Tokhan Bratva 2) TBD

Unexpected Hero (The Tokhan Bratva 3) TBD

www.ingramcontent.com/pod-product-compliance
Lightning Source LLC
Chambersburg PA
CBHW061544190726
48289CB00004B/1160